FALSE DAWN

FALSE DAWN

CHELSEA QUINN YARBRO

DOUBLEDAY & COMPANY, INC.

GARDEN CITY, NEW YORK

1978

The first chapter of this book originally appeared as a short story entitled "False Dawn" in *Strange Bedfellows*, edited by Thomas N. Scortia, published by Random House in 1973.

Library of Congress Cataloging in Publication Data

Yarbro, Chelsea Quinn, 1947–
  False dawn.

  I. Title.
PZ4.Y25Fal [PS3575.A7]   813'.5'4

ISBN: 0-385-13144-5
Library of Congress Catalog Card Number 77-82777
Copyright © 1978 by Chelsea Quinn Yarbro
All Rights Reserved
Printed in the United States of America
First Edition

Quality Printing and Binding by:
THE MAPLE-VAIL BOOK MANUFACTURING GROUP
Pine Camp Drive
Binghamton, N.Y. 13902 U.S.A.

For

Bonnie Dalzell
Jane Robinson
and Diana Thatcher
who remember what happened to the dinosaur

Any reader so inclined can, with the use of U.S.G.S. topographic maps, follow the route that Thea and Evan take through the Sierra Nevada from the east side of Chico to the mountains below Kirkwood Lake.

*   *   *

CHAPTER 1

Most of the bodies were near the silos and storage tanks, where the defenders had retreated in the end. Caught between the Pirates and the Sacramento, they had been wiped out to a man. Mixed in with the few Pirate dead Thea saw an occasional C.D. uniform. The cops had gone over at last.

She moved through the stench of the tumbled, looted corpses, cautiously, carefully. She had not survived for her twenty-seven years being foolhardy.

Orland had been a shambles, heavy with the smell of burning and death. After dark she had made her way east into Chico—what was left of it. Here the Pirates had revenged themselves on the few remaining townspeople. There were men, terribly mutilated men, hanging by their heels from lampposts, turning as they swung. And there were women.

One of the women wasn't dead yet. Her ravaged body hung naked from a broken billboard. Her legs were splayed wide and anchored with ropes; legs and belly were bloody, there were heavy bruises on her face and breasts, and she had been branded with a large "M" for mutant.

When Thea came near her, she jerked in her bonds and shrieked laughter that ended in a shuddering wail. Don't let me get like that ever, Thea thought, watching the woman's spasmodic thrusts with her hips. Not like that.

There was a movement down the street and Thea froze. She could not run without being seen and she could not wait where she was if it were Pirates. She moved slowly, melding into the shadow of a gutted building, disappearing into the darkness as she kept watch.

The creatures that appeared then were dogs; lean, wretched things with red-rimmed eyes and raised hackles. Thea had seen enough of the wild dogs to know that these were hunting meat. In the woman they found it. The largest of the dogs approached her on his belly, whining a little. He made a quick dash and nipped at the leg nearest him. Aside from a long howl of laughter the woman did nothing: there was nothing she could do.

Emboldened, the dog came toward her, taking a more decisive bite from the leg. The response was a jerk and a scream followed by low laughter. The blood running over her foot excited the rest of the pack and the other dogs grew bolder. Each began to make quick, bounding attacks, taking token bits of flesh from her legs and feet, growing more confident when they met with no resistance.

Thea watched stonily from the shadows, fitting a quarrel to her makeshift crossbow. Then she braced her forearm and pulled the trigger.

The high sobbing laughter was cut off with a bubble and a sigh as the quarrel bit into the woman's neck. There was no sound then but the snarling of dogs, and tearing.

In the deep shadows of the alley Thea moved away from the pack. I'd forgot about that, she said to herself accusingly. There will be more dogs. And rats, she thought, after a moment.

As she walked she tightened her crossbow again and fitted another quarrel to it. She probably wasn't a mutant, she let herself think as she walked. The woman still filled her mind. Probably she was just healthy. Health was as suspicious now as obvious deformity. She did not want to consider what the Pirates would do to Thea herself, genetically altered as she was.

The sound of the dogs died behind her in the empty, littered streets. Here and there she saw piles of bodies, some dead from fighting, others from more sinister things. The "M" brand was on many of them. Twice she saw the unmistakable signs of New Leprosy on the blind faces, skin scaled over and turning the silver that allied it with the old disease. But unlike the first leprosy, the new variety *was* contagious. And the Pirates had carried it away with them.

She chafed her dark, hard skin, long since burned red-brown. So far she had been lucky and had resisted most of the new diseases; but she knew that the luck would eventually run out, even for her, even if she found the Gold Lake Settlement and they accepted her. Nothing could hold out against the contamination that flowed with the water and sailed in the air.

After more than an hour of walking she left Chico behind, striking eastward through ruined fields and swampland. The last crops had been forced from the ground and now stalks criss-crossed underfoot like great soggy snakes. A heavy phospho-rescence hung over the marshland, a light that did not illuminate or warm. Thea did not know the source of it, but she avoided the spot. Since the Sacramento Disaster four years ago the Valley had ceased to be safe land. Before the levees had crumbled it had been a haven from the pollution around it, a last stronghold of fertility in a sterile land. Now, with the Delta a reeking chemical quagmire, the upper river was slowly surrendering to the spreading desola-tion.

She stumbled and saw a dead cat at her feet. Animals had been at it: the chest gaped and the eye sockets were empty, but the fur was healthy. She shook her head at the waste of it. Bending closer she noticed with surprise that the front paws were the tawny or-ange of regenerating tissue. Maybe the cat had been virally mu-tated, as she had been. Or maybe the virus that caused the muta-tion was catching. A lot of other things sure were catching. Shaking her head again she dragged some rotting stalks over the little carcass, knowing this for the empty gesture it was even as she did it.

The ground grew soggier as she went, the old stalks becoming a vile goo, and sticky, clinging. She looked ahead for firmer ground and saw an oily stretch of water moving sluggishly under the wan moon. Beyond was the stunted fuzz of what had been cattails. Sliding the nictitating membranes over her eyes, she dropped to her knees and moved forward, her crossbow at the ready. The river was not a friendly place.

Once she heard a pig rooting along the bank and she stopped. Those pigs that were still alive were dangerous and hungry, and the big ones outmatched her in weight and ferocity. Eventually the pig crashed away up the bank and Thea began paddling again. One thing to say for the Disaster, she thought, as the stinking water surged around her. It killed a lot of insects.

Then she reached the cattails and slipped in among them for cover. There was a kind of protection that would last until first light, when she would have to find higher ground. She pulled her-self onto a hummock and curled up on it for a few hours' sleep.

The dawn brought more animals to the river, and a few foraging

Pirates, who swept by in the modified open vans that ran on methane. They had rifles and took three shots for two carcasses— the pig from the night before and an ancient horse with broken knees.

"Bring 'em in! Bring 'em in!" hollered the one in the lead van.

"Give me a hand, you snot-f——ing Mute!"

The first gave a shout. "Montague gave you hauling this week. Cox didn't change that. *I* didn't have maggots in my pack." He snorted mockingly as he revved the engine.

"You know what you have to do if you waste fuel, Mackley," the one doing the hauling said gleefully.

"Just you shove it!" shouted Mackley, panic in his voice. "I don't want to hear no threats from you. I could drop you right now."

"Then you'd have to do the hauling," reminded the second laconically, then added, "Cox says Montague's dead, anyway."

"Him and his guard," Mackley said, as if it were a curse. "They tried to stop Wilson and me when we got that Mute kid out of the cellar. Said to leave him alone. Said that we had to save the kid. A rotten Mute! Montague; he was crazy."

They were silent but for the whir of the engines and the sound of the dead animals being dragged through the mud.

Thea huddled in the cattails, hardly daring to breathe. She had seen Cloverdale after the Pirates had sacked it, the first of many cities that had fallen to them, in the days before Montague had organized them under that ironic rallying cry, "Survive!"

"That's one," said Mackley.

"Lick your c——."

Again there was silence until the one doing the hauling let out a scream.

"What's the matter?" demanded Mackley from the van.

"Water spiders!" the other shrieked in terror. "Dozens of 'em!" And he made a horrible sound in his throat.

From her protection in the cattails, Thea watched, crouching, fright in her eyes. Water spiders were nothing to mess with, even for her. She clung to the reeds around her and watched for the hard, shiny bodies with the long hooked mandibles filled with paralyzing venom. Three of them could kill you in less than ten minutes. Dozens, and you didn't have a chance at all.

The voice-rending shouts had stopped, and soon a body drifted aimlessly by, with the spiders climbing over the face toward the eyes. Thea looked away.

Up on the bank there was a cough and the motor whizzed as Mackley drove away too fast.

Thea waited until the body had slid out of sight around a bend in the river before she moved free from the cattails. Then she ran off through the brushy undergrowth, not pausing to look for Pirates or spiders. Her knees were uncertain as jelly and her fright made her lightheaded. She ran frantically until she was on higher ground; there she stopped and breathed.

She had come about half a mile from the river in those few minutes, and had left a wake like a timber run through the brush. There was nothing to concern her about that: it could easily have been made by an animal and would not be investigated. But the hunting party meant that the Pirates were still around, maybe camped for a time. If Montague was dead, as the men she had overheard had said, she knew that there would be many changes with the Pirates. Montague had been a stern, uncompromising man, but there had been those who said he was just. If what she had seen in Chico was any indication of what Cox would be like . . . She had to get away from them, or she would end up hanging from a billboard. She shuddered as she remembered.

She guessed that the Pirates would camp near the river, within walking distance of Chico, so she started away from that, off to the southeast, keeping to the cover of the trees. The scrub oak were gone, having succumbed early to the poisonous water, but the hardier fruit trees, long adapted to chemical growth, had run riot, spreading over the hills like weeds, their fruit made inedible by the stuff that had fed them.

Thea realized that if she had to she could climb up into the branches of the trees around her, and from there, pick off the Pirates one by one with her crossbow until they killed her. That would take time. And she needed time.

By midday she had put several miles between herself and the Pirates. The river lay below her, a greasy brown smudge. The east fork of the Sacramento was dying.

That was when she found the makeshift silo. Some farmer in the hills, perhaps one of the old communes, had built a silo to store grain, and there it stood: lopsided, rusty, but safe and dry. A haven for the night and a possible base for a couple of days, a place to come back to after scouting the hills for the best way into the Sierra and to Gold Lake.

She walked carefully around the silo, looking for the door and for the farmhouse it belonged to once. The farmhouse turned out to be a charred shell. The silo was the only thing left standing where once there had been a house, chicken coops, and a barn. She shook her head at the loss and touched the handle of the silo door. Bracing herself, she tugged it open.

In the next instant she was reeling back. "Stupid, stupid!" she said aloud. "Stupid!" For there was a man in the silo, waving something at her. She started to run, angry and frustrated.

"No! *No!*" The voice followed her. "Don't run away! Wait!" It got louder. "That's my arm!"

Thea stopped. His arm. "What?" she yelled back, ready to bolt.

"It's my arm. They cut it off." The words made a weird echo in the corrugated walls of the silo. "Last week. I think."

She started back toward the voice. "Who did?"

"The Pirates. In Orland, across the river from Chico. With a power saw." He was getting weaker and his words came irregularly. "I got this far."

She stood in the doorway looking down at him. "Why'd you keep it?"

He drew in a breath. "They were looking for a man with only one arm. So I pinned this into my jacket." He paused a moment, then finished, "I can't get any further without help."

She ignored this and cast a glance at the arm that lay on the floor of the silo. "Well, you better bury that."

His eyes met hers. "I can't."

Thea looked him over carefully. He was at least fifteen years older than she was with a stocky body made gaunt with hunger and pain. His wide, square face was deeply lined and the lines were grimy. He wore filthy clothes, but in spite of the dirt and rents, Thea saw that they had been well made.

"How long you been here?"

"I think two, or maybe three days."

"Oh." From the state of the arm she reckoned three days was right. She pointed to the stump just below his shoulder. "How does it feel? Infected? Can you feel anything?"

He frowned. "I don't think it's infected. Or not much. It itches."

She accepted this for the moment. "Where were you going? You got a place to go?"

"I was trying to get into the mountains."

Thea considered this, and her first impulse was to run, to leave this man to rot or live as it happened. But she hesitated, and saw disbelief and hope in his blue eyes. She thought about Gold Lake, so far away, and knew that getting there would be hard.

"I've got medicine," she said, making up her mind. "You can have some of it. Not all, 'cause I might need it. But you can have a little."

He looked at her, his rumpled face puzzled. "Thank you," he said, unused to the words.

"I got parapenicillin and a little sporomicin. Which one do you want?"

"The penicillin."

"I got some ascorbic tablets for later," she added, looking thoughtfully at the stump of his arm as she came into the silo. There had been an infection but it was clearing and she saw that the skin was the tawny orange color of regenerating tissue. "You left-handed?"

"Yes."

"You're lucky."

After releasing the crossbow's straps and storing her quarrels in a side pocket of her pack, she put the pack down, not too close to the man. He still had one good arm and had admitted that he was left-handed. "What's your name?" she asked as she dug into the pack.

"Seth Pearson," he answered with slight hesitation.

She looked at him sharply. "It says David Rossi on your neck tags. Which is it?"

"It doesn't matter. Whichever you like." He sounded tired now, and the color had gone from his face and his voice.

Thea looked away. "Okay. That's the way we'll do it, Rossi." She handed him a packet, worn but still intact. "That's the parapenicillin. You'll have to eat it; I don't have any needles." Then she added, "It tastes terrible. Here." She handed him a short, flat piece of jerky. "It's venison; tough. It'll take the taste away." She put her pack between them and sank to the floor. When the man had managed to choke down the white slime, she spoke again.

"Tomorrow I'm going east. You can come with me if you can keep up. There's one more bad river ahead, and you might have to swim it. It's fast though, and rocky. So you better make up your mind tonight."

She did not look for an answer. She took two more sticks of jerky out of her pack and ate them in guarded silence.

* * *

The north wind bit through them as they walked; the sun was bright but cold. Gradually the gentle slope grew steeper and they climbed more slowly, saying nothing and keeping wary eyes on the bushes that littered the hillside. By midafternoon they were walking over the crumbling trunks of large pine trees that had fallen, victims of smog. The dust from the dead trees blew in plumes around them, stinging their eyes and making them sneeze. Yet they climbed on.

The going got rougher and slower until they were forced to call a halt in the lee of a huge stump. Rossi braced his good shoulder and held out his tattered jacket to protect them both from the wind.

"Are you all right?" Thea asked him when she had caught her breath. "You're the wrong color."

"Just a little winded," he nodded. "I'm . . . still weak."

"Yeah," she said, looking covertly at his stump. The tawny shade was deepening. "You're getting better."

He started to make a flippant reply and his feet slid suddenly on the rolling dust. He grabbed out to her to keep from falling.

She stepped back. "Don't do that."

As he regained his footing, he looked at her in some surprise. "Why?" he asked gently.

"Don't you touch me." She grabbed at her crossbow defensively. Over his face she could see the hate that had been in Mackley's face at the river.

He frowned, his eyes troubled, then his brow cleared. "I won't." In those two words there was great understanding. He knew the world that Thea lived in, and the price it exacted from her.

With a look of defiance she tightened the crossbow's straps on her arm, never taking her eyes from the man. "I can shoot this real fast, Rossi. Remember that."

Whatever he might have said was lost. "Hold it right there," came the voice from behind them.

Aside from a quick exchange of frightened glances, they did not move.

"That's right." There was a puff of dust, and another, then a young man in a ruined C.D. uniform stood in front of them, a rifle cradled in his arms. "I knew I'd catch you," he said aloud to himself. "I been following you all morning."

Thea edged closer to Rossi.

"You people come out from Chico, right?" He bounced the weapon he carried.

"No."

"What about you?" he demanded of Thea.

"No."

He looked back toward Rossi, an unpleasant smile on his face. "What about you . . . Rossi, is it? Sure you didn't come through Chico? I heard a guy named Rossi was killed outside of Orland. One of Montague's men, Rossi."

"I don't know about that."

"They said he was trying to save Montague when Cox took over. You know anything about that? Rossi?"

"No."

The younger man laughed. "Hey, don't lie to me, Rossi. You lie to me and I'm gonna kill you."

In the shadow, Thea slowly put a quarrel to her crossbow, keeping as much out of sight as she could.

"You're going to kill us anyway, so what does it matter if we lie?" Rossi was asking.

"Listen," the C.D. man began. "What's that?" he interrupted himself, looking straight at Thea. "What are you doing?" And he reached out, grabbing her by the arm and jerking her off her feet. "You bitch-piece!" He kicked savagely into her shoulder as she fell, just once. Then Rossi put himself between them. "Move!"

"No. You want me to move, you'll have to kill me."

The young man wavered for a moment, his hands restlessly fingering the dark metal. His face twitched.

Without turning, Rossi said to Thea, "Did he hurt you?"

"Some," she admitted as she got to her knees. "I'll be okay."

"She your woman? Is she?"

Rossi turned slowly, forcing the man with the rifle to move back. "No. She's nobody's woman."

At that the other man giggled. "I bet she needs it. I bet she's real hungry for it."

Thea closed her eyes to hide the indignation and terror in her. If this was to be rape, being *used* . . . She opened her eyes when Rossi's hand touched her shoulder.

"You try any more dumb things like that, c——, and that's going to be the end. Understand?"

"Yes," she mumbled.

"And what will Cox say when he finds out what you're doing?" Rossi asked. He still kept himself between Thea and the other man.

"Cox won't say nothing!" the C.D. man spat.

"So you deserted." Rossi nodded measuredly at the guilt in the man's face. "That was stupid."

"You shut up!" He leaned toward them. "You are going to take me out of here, wherever you're going. If anybody spots us, or we get trapped, I am going to make both of you look like a butcher shop. You got that? . . . HUH?"

"You stink," said Thea.

For a moment there was anger in the young, hard eyes, then he grabbed her face with one hand. "Not yet, not yet." His grip tightened, the fingers bruising her jaw. "You want some of that, you're gonna have to beg for it, real hard. You're gonna have to suck it right out of me. Right?" He looked defiantly at Rossi. "Right?" he repeated.

"Let her go."

"You want her?"

"Leave her alone."

"All right," he said with a little nod. He stepped back from her. "Later, huh? When you've thought it over."

Rossi looked at the C.D. man. "I'll be close, Thea. Just call."

As the two men stared at each other, Thea wanted to run from them both, to the protection of the destroyed forest. But she could not escape on the open hillside. She rubbed her shoulder gingerly and went to Rossi's side.

"I'm a better choice," the C.D. man mocked her. "My name's Lastly. You can call me that, bitch-piece. Don't call me anything else."

She said nothing as she looked up the slope.

Rossi's voice was soft. "Don't try it now. There's cover up ahead and I'll get him into a fight."

In deep surprise she turned to him, seeing the sincerity in his eyes. She thought of the rifle in Lastly's hands and Rossi's one arm. "Truly? You'd do that?"

He would have said more but Lastly shoved them apart. "I don't want none of that. You don't whisper when I'm around, hear? You got anything to say, you speak up."

"I want to piss," said Rossi.

Lastly giggled again. "Oh no. You aren't gonna leave a trail. Not for a while, till we're in the trees. Hold it in; got that?"

With a shrug Rossi led the others as they began the long walk toward the rotting line of timber.

*   *   *

"What was that?" Lastly turned the barrel of his gun toward the sound that surged through the underbrush.

The ululation rose and fell through the trees, lonely and terrible.

"Dogs," said Rossi bluntly. "They're hunting."

In the deep shadows of dusk the scattered trees seemed to grow together surrounding the three people who moved through the gloom. The sound came again, closer and sharper.

"Where are they?"

Thea looked back at him. "They're a way off yet. You can't shoot them until they get close."

"We got to get out of here," Lastly said in fear. He swung his rifle uneasily. "Right? We got to find some place safe."

Rossi squinted up at the fading sky. "I'd say we have another hour yet. After that, we'd better climb trees."

"But they're rotten," Lastly protested.

"They're better than dogs," Rossi said gently.

But Lastly wasn't listening. "There used to be camps around here, didn't there? We got to find them. No dogs gonna come into camp."

"You fool." Rossi's voice was dispassionate, and whatever expression might show in his blue eyes was hidden by the waning light.

"No talking. I don't want to hear it." Lastly's gun wavered in front of Rossi.

"Then both of you stop it," Thea put in quietly. "The dogs can hear you."

All fell silent. In a moment Rossi murmured, "Thea's right. If we're quiet we might find one of your camps in time." There was doubt in the tone.

"You get moving then," Lastly said hurriedly. "Right now."

$$*\qquad*\qquad*$$

It had been a summer cabin once, when people still had summer cabins. The view below it had been of pine forests giving way to the fertile swath of the Valley. Now it stood in a clearing surrounded by rotting trees above the spreading contamination of the river. Oddly enough the windows were still intact.

"We can stay here," Rossi said after circling the cabin. "The back porch is screened and we can get the door off its hinges."

"We can break through a window," Lastly said eagerly.

"If the window is broken, the dogs can get in." When this had sunk in Rossi went on. "The back is secure. We'll be able to protect ourselves."

"You two get it done," Lastly ordered, pointing his rifle toward the rear porch. "Get it done fast."

As Thea and Rossi struggled with the door Lastly straddled the remains of the fence. "Say, Rossi, you see what Cox did to that Mute in Chico? Took the skin right off him, hey. Cox, he's gonna get rid of all the Mutes—just you wait."

"Yes," said Rossi as he pulled at a rusty hinge.

"Know what? Montague wanted to save 'em." He kicked viciously at the fence, splintering part of the brace so that it wobbled under him. "You hear that, Rossi? Montague wanted to save the Mutes. Why would someone want to do that? Huh? Why'd any real man save Mutes?"

Rossi didn't answer.

"I asked you something . . . Rossi. You tell me."

"Maybe he thought they were the only ones worth saving." He turned his back to Lastly, busying himself with the lower hinges.

"What about you, bitch-piece? You save a Mute?" He bounced on the fence as he stroked his rifle. The old wood groaned at this treatment.

With a look of raw disgust, Thea said, "Just me, Lastly. I'm saving me."

"What are you saving for me? I got something for you . . ."

"The door's off," Rossi interrupted, pulling it aside. "We can go in now."

Mice had got into the house, eating the dried fruits and flour that had been stored in the ample kitchen. There were boxes strewn on the floor that had held cereal and sugar. But cans were left, filled with food Thea could hardly remember. Pots and pans hung on the wall, most of them rusted, but a few were made of aluminum or enamelware and were ready for use. The stove that squatted by the far wall was a wood-burner.

"Look at it," Rossi said, his eyes lingering on the cupboards and their precious contents. "Enough to take some along later."

"Damn, it's perfect. I'm gonna have it right tonight. Hot food and a bath and all the ways I want it." He glanced slyly from Thea to Rossi.

"Smoke might bring the Pirates," Rossi said with a bitter smile. "Have you thought of that?"

"It's nighttime, Rossi. They ain't coming up here till morning."

Thea had wandered around the kitchen. "There's no wood. Not in here, anyway. That table is plastic."

They all stood for a moment, then Lastly announced, "You heard the lady, Rossi. There's no wood. You gonna get it for her, right? Right?"

"I'll go," Thea said quickly.

"Oh no." The rifle blocked her way.

"But he can't work with one arm."

"If he takes his time, bitch-piece. I'm gonna need time."

"What about you, Lastly?" Rossi asked evenly. "You're able and you've got the gun."

"And let you two lock me out with the dogs. I ain't dumb, Rossi." He moved around the table. "It's you, Rossi. You're it." He shoved a chair at him. "Sit down and catch your breath, 'cause you're going out there."

"Not without Thea."

Lastly made his too-familiar giggle. "Want it for yourself, huh? She ain't putting it out to you. She wants a man. A whole man, Rossi. Not you."

Thea gave Rossi a pleading look. "Let me lock myself in the side room. Then both of you can go out."

"Right!" said Lastly, unexpectedly. "That bitch-piece is right. We lock her up and we get the wood. Rossi?"

"If that's what you want, Thea."

She nodded. "Yes."

"I'll see you later?" he asked her, his deep eyes holding hers.

"I hope so," she answered, feeling very tired.

"Come on, bitch-piece. We're gonna lock you up." He took her by the arm, half-dragging her through the main room of the cabin to the side room. "There you are," he said, thrusting her inside. "Your own boudoir. You keep nice and warm while you wait. Think about what we're gonna do when I get back." And he slammed the door. There was a distinct click as Lastly pushed the bolt home.

She sat in the little bedroom, huddling on the bare mattress in the center of the room. The mattress smelled of damp mustiness and small animals. Tufts of wadding had been pulled from various small holes and made the mattress even lumpier than it had been originally. The low metal frame that held the mattress sagged at one corner and the interlaced wires that passed for springs whined in protest whenever she moved.

Thea listened for the sound of the men, knowing how much she wanted to run from them. But she was achingly tired now, and helpless. If she left the cabin, the dogs would find her, or the Pirates. Her shoulder was stiff where Lastly had kicked her and hunger was a hard fist inside her. As time passed insidious fatigue claimed her. She slumped, slid until she stretched on the low bed, asleep.

"You were supposed to get ready. I told you to get ready," said the harsh voice above her. "You knew I'd be back." She was pulled roughly onto her back and pinned there by a sudden weight across her body.

Barely awake, Thea pushed against the man, hands and feet seeking his vulnerable places as she battled her own fear and confusion.

"Shut UP!" Lastly growled, his hand slamming across her face. When Thea cried out he hit her again. "You listen, c——; you're for me. You think I'm letting a Mute-f——er like Montague get you? Huh?" He struck her arms back, catching her wrists in a length of rope. "We taught him and his pervs a lesson at Orland.

You hear?" He pulled the rope taut against the bed frame. "This time I'm getting mine. Right?"

With a sob of fury Thea launched herself at Lastly, teeth bared and legs twisting. The ropes sank deep into her flesh. Rage rose like bile in her throat.

"No, you don't," Lastly giggled. This time his fist caught her on the side of her head and she fell back, dizzy and sick. Her hands strained at the ropes, fingers like claws. "Don't give me a hard time, c——. It makes it worse for you."

Now rope looped her left ankle and then her right. Two tugs pulled her legs wide as Lastly secured the rope under the sagging mattress. Thea pulled vainly at her bonds, tension bowing her back.

"Don't," Lastly said, coming near her. "You do that any more and I'm going to hurt you. See this?" He put a small knife up close to her face. "I got it in the kitchen. It's real sharp. You give me any more trouble and I'm gonna carve you up some. Till you learn manners."

"No."

Ignoring this, Lastly began to cut off her jacket. When he had ripped that from her, he slit the seams on her leather pants. As he pulled these away she wrenched futilely at the ropes.

Immediately he was across her. "I told you." He put the knife to her, catching one nipple between the blade and his thumb. "I could peel this off, you know?" He pressed harder. The knife bit into her flesh. "No noise, c——. You be quiet or I take it all off."

In her sudden sharp pain the nictitating membranes closed over her eyes.

And Lastly saw. "Mute! Shit! *You lousy Mute!*" There was something like triumph in his voice. She cried out as he pulled the wrinkled bit of flesh from her. Blood spread over her breast.

With a shout Lastly wiggled his pants down to his knees and in one quick terrible movement pushed into her. Forcing himself deeper, laughing, he said, "Montague's Mute. I'm gonna ruin you!" Falling forward he fastened his teeth on her sound breast.

At that she screamed. He brought his head up. "You do that again, Mute, and this one comes off with my teeth." He hit her in the mouth as he came.

In the next moment he was off her, torn out of her and slammed against the wall.

"You filthy . . . !" Rossi, his hand in Lastly's hair, hit him into the wall again. There was an audible crack and Lastly slumped. Rossi stood over him as he fell.

Then he came back to the bed. "Oh, God, Thea," he said softly. "I never meant . . . I never intended . . . this." He knelt beside her, not touching her. "I'm sorry." It was as if he were apologizing for the world. Gently he untied her, speaking to her as he did. When he freed her she cringed, drawing herself into a ball, shaken with silent tears.

Finally she turned to him, shame in her eyes. "I wanted you. I wanted you," she said and turned away once more.

In wonder he rose. "I have only one arm and a price on my head."

"I wanted you," she said again, not daring to look at him.

"My name," he said very quietly, "is Evan Montague." And he waited, looking away from her through the broken door to the main room of the cabin where one candle burned.

Then he felt her hand on his. "I wanted you."

He turned to her then, holding her hand, afraid to touch her. She drew him down beside her, but pulled back from him. "He hurt me," she said numbly.

"Here I tried to save everybody, the whole world, and couldn't even save you," he whispered bitterly. He looked at her, at her bloody breasts and bruised face, at the deep scratches on her thighs. "Let me get your medicine."

"No." She grabbed at his hand, her eyes frantic. "Don't leave me."

His mouth twisted but failed to smile. He sat beside her, holding her hand while she shivered and the blood dried, until they heard the sound of engines, like a distant hive.

"They're looking for him. Or me," Montague said.

She nodded. "Do we have to leave?"

"Yes."

"If we stay?"

"They'll kill me. Cox wants to finish what he started. But not you. You're a woman, Thea . . . and you're a mutant, aren't you?"

She understood and shook spasmodically. "Don't let them. Kill me. Kill me. Burn the cabin. Please."

The terror in her face alarmed him. He pulled her fingers to his lips, kissing them. "I will. I promise you, Thea." Then he changed, pushing himself off the mattress, swaying when he got to his feet. "No. We're getting out of here. We're going to live as long as we can."

Sighing, Lastly collapsed, his head at a strange angle.

"Come on," Montague said, holding his hand out to her.

With an effort, Thea rose to her feet holding onto his arm until the sickness had passed. "I need clothes."

He looked about the room, to the dresser in the farthest corner. "There?" he asked, going to it and pulling open the drawers. The clothes were for children but Thea was small enough to wear some of them. Determined, she struggled into heavy canvas jeans, but balked at a sweater or jacket. "I can't," she whispered.

"Shush," he said. They heard the sound of the motors getting nearer.

"Tie these around your waist," he ordered, shoving two shirts and a jacket at her. "You're going to need them."

She looked at him doubtfully, but tied the clothes on. "What time is it?" she asked.

"Early. It's gray in the east."

"We've got to leave. My pack . . ."

"Leave it here," he said brusquely. "Neither you nor I can carry it."

"My crossbow . . ."

"In the kitchen. Put it on my arm. If you load it, I can fire." He started toward the kitchen but the engines were droning too loudly, too near. "Not that way. We'll have to leave the crossbow."

"We need weapons," she said, desperate.

Montague stopped to gather up the rope. "We have this. It'll have to do for now." The engines were closer, and over them rose an occasional shout. "I thought that was the way," he said ironically. "I was a fool." He went to the window and opened it, then slung the rope around his chest like a bandolier. "We go this way. And straight into the trees."

"Evan!" she cried as the cold morning air brushed the raw places on her breasts. "Evan!"

"Can you make it? You've got to," he said as he came to her side.

"Yes. But slowly."

"All right." He took her hand, feeling her fingers warm in the early chill. "We'll go slowly for a while."

As they climbed away into the dying forest and the dark, the sounds of the engines and voices grew loud behind them, shutting out the noise of their escape and sending the wild dogs howling away from them into the cold gray light before dawn.

CHAPTER 2

It was dusk before they stopped to rest. They were above the town of Paradise, in the wide cut that had once been the path of power lines. Now a few of the towers still stood, lonely as abandoned toys. The rest had fallen, their silver paint scaled and flaking.

"Here," Evan breathed, his voice an exhausted thread.

Thea turned to him, feeling her way around the tangled debris. "Where?" she asked, frowning.

"Look." He caught his breath, leaning heavily on the old struts. "We can pull some branches over this and stay inside it for the night." He pushed at the metal to show her how strong it was.

The broken tower creaked ominously and one of the braces bent.

"No," said Thea, backing away from the thing.

Alarmed, Evan stepped back as well. "Maybe you're right," he said. "But, Thea, I have to stop."

She looked at him, nodding. "What about another cabin?" she suggested tentatively.

"No, not up here. No one came up here but linemen." For a moment he puckered his brow. "Linemen," he repeated. "Linemen." He started away from the wrecked tower, going doggedly to the line of rust-colored trees. From the way he walked, Thea could see his hurt in the slow list of his steps, the hesitation as he moved; like herself, he had hidden his pain until now.

"Don't, Evan," she called after him, not able to say what she felt. Compassion exposed too much: she could not reveal her sympathy.

"Well?" he said, irritated. He stopped, leaning heavily into one hip, hooking his thumb into the coil of rope. "Thea, if there were linemen up there, they had to have a place to stay. That means a house or a cabin. If they had a cabin, it would be near a tower because that was where they did most of their work, on the towers. If we don't find something here, we'll go to the next tower." Then he waited for her answer, impatient.

"Maybe you're right about the branches. I guess we could make it safe." Her eyes were desperate again. Night was gathering in the east and the roseate pall that drifted over the Sacramento Valley was bright at their backs, sunset shining through it, lighting it like some exotic metal.

"A cabin would be safer." But even as he said it, he came down the slope toward her.

* * *

The branches pulled down easily, the rotten wood powdering where they broke the limbs of the trees. A resiny smell pervaded the place, cloying and sickly, mingling with the dust that made them sneeze and brought tears to their eyes. But the work went quickly and soon they had made a heap of boughs at the foot of the tower.

"Save the rope," Thea advised, and Evan nodded. He stirred the dirt with his foot. "There should be some of the cables left. They can't all have corroded away. The wire will be useful, if we can find it."

Thea dropped to her knees and began to push the dirt aside, fingers probing for the bite of wire. She moved blindly, putting all her senses into her hands. Cautiously she dug deeper and found a ridge of twisted cable. "Got it," she said grimly as she began to pull the cable from the earth. Much of the outer casing was pitted, but the inner wires of copper remained fairly intact.

They sat together at the tower peeling the wires from the cable, straightening them carefully as each section was freed. "It's copper, remember," Evan warned Thea as she worked one strand free. "The more you use it, the harder it gets."

"Too bad," she said. "I thought there'd be enough to string a crossbow. But I guess I can't use copper for that."

Evan held the branches in place while Thea lashed them to the metal legs of the tower. Work was difficult in the fading light; the copper wire proved hard to handle, and there were problems with the branches, which kept slipping and breaking if pulled too tightly against the legs of the tower. Their frustration mounted as night came on, and Evan snapped at Thea as she broke another wire while attempting to secure the branches.

"If you think you will do a better job . . ."

"I don't want to spend the whole night digging up more wire." He cursed as another branch snapped. "Why do we even try?" he asked of the air.

"If it's so hopeless, why do you bother?" She felt her words catch in her throat. In her fingers the copper wire seemed suddenly hot.

"Do you think it isn't hopeless? Do you know what the world was like just twenty years ago? Do you have any idea how much we've lost?" He flung two of the branches away from him and glared up at the sky, his body rigid in his distress.

For a moment Thea stood still, and finally, quite softly, she said, "But what do we do, Evan?"

He did not seem to hear her. Then, slowly the stress left his face and his shoulders drooped. He bent to pick up the branches. "Let's get the job done," he said, resigned.

"Are we going to have enough?" Thea wondered aloud later as she secured the last of the branches.

"Not for a roof," Evan said ruefully. "We're out of luck if it rains." He spoke as he crawled into the enclosure and began to pull off intruding twigs and limbs, which he threw into one corner to make a kind of bedding.

"It won't rain," Thea said, sniffing the air. "Not today, and not tomorrow."

"Good. This stuff couldn't keep the water out for a minute, even if we had a roof." He looked across the gloom as Thea joined him inside the crude walls. "You're tired," he said.

"A little."

"So am I," he said, hoping to see her face so that he could read her thoughts. She had withdrawn from him as they worked, and in some quiet, imperceptible way she had put more distance between them than the space they shared.

"You can get some rest. I don't mind."

"What about you?"

Thea shook her head wearily. "It doesn't matter." Now that she was safe her body was remembering. Once, many years ago she had been beaten by a farmer whose chicken coop she had robbed. There was still a knot in her collarbone where it had not healed properly. But at the end of the beating her body had still been her own, not like now, when her very self had been invaded, violated.

"I never understood that," she said quietly, more to herself than to Evan.

"Understood what?" He was making a last round, tightening the lashings as best he could with one hand. He had not been listening.

"About what happened. About violation," she said, finding that the word itself bothered her. Violation was too vulnerable, too personal. There had to be some other word, one that did not hurt so much. She turned her thoughts away and set her face in rigid calm. Only her eyes were troubled, and they shone with the glassy light of a frightened animal.

Evan had stopped his work as she spoke. He had felt a twisting in himself, as if some of her private anguish had slipped from her and touched him. He stood as near her as he dared, unmoving. As he watched, her face changed and he was grateful to turn their minds to other things. "There might be Untouchables up here. We'll have to stand watch tonight."

"Watch? Yes, I guess so." She said this slowly, and did not look at him.

"Do you want the first watch or the second?"

She shook her head. "I don't care," she said in a different tone. She had shut part of herself away.

"Why don't you take the first watch, then? Wake me about midnight, or sooner, if you get too tired."

"At midnight." Her placid face was remote.

"You can tell the time by the stars." It wasn't a question.

"Sure. Midnight."

He indicated a break in the branches. "This is about the best view you can get. The north is all trees and the south is too steep; nothing is going to come that way. This side"—he tapped the west wall of bound branches—"is where trouble will come from, if there is trouble." He moved aside so that she could get a look. "See, the way we came. The swath is clear enough and it's an easy climb. If the Pirates come after us . . ."

"Do you think they will?" The words came too quickly.

He shared her fear. "I don't think Cox is that kind of an idiot." It was true enough, but he remembered the men Cox had used when he had taken over, and there was no way to be sure of them. Gorren, Mackley, Spaulding, they were fanatics, and capable of things even Cox would abhor. "There is a chance they might try to come into the mountains, too, and that could mean they'll follow us. There's always that chance."

"I see," she said.

"Thea," he said firmly, "if you think something is wrong, anything at all, wake me."

She looked at him uneasily. "You *are* expecting trouble, then."

"I'm always expecting trouble." He scratched his short beard roughly. "It's a habit I got into."

"I know." After a moment she said softly, "There's too much trouble, isn't there?"

He nodded.

She moved a little farther from him. "Get some sleep, then. I'll wake you later." She looked up at the darkened sky. "Midnight."

He accepted her dismissal. "Thanks," he said as he sank onto the ground where he set about expertly with the loose branches, making a nest where he settled at last, pulling his jacket across him for a blanket.

Thea watched him, a slight frown clouding her features. She saw the harsh lines of his face soften with sleep, changing him from the severe man she had run with to the man who had released her from Lastly's ropes. She felt regret that he had been Montague who led the Pirates. There was too much destruction attached to that name.

She turned her attention to the outside. Her head felt stuffy from the rotten pine wood and dried sap she had breathed earlier; her body ached and she bit her lip to keep from crying out as her mind brought Lastly back to her once more. As the night grew colder she pulled on the jacket that was tied around her waist, but the rough denim rubbed the scab from her breast and her hot, sticky blood matted the raw hurt to the cloth.

Overhead the stars wheeled slowly, marking out the night. Thea watched them, wishing they could move faster. Fatigue pulled at her like grief as the hours went on. There was no movement on the mountain but the lorn wind that mourned in the dying trees.

Then, far down the mountain she heard a sound that rose with the wind, singing a weird harmony. Another voice joined, and another. The dogs were following their trail.

She listened intently now, straining to pick out each sound on the wind. For a little time she was sure she had imagined it, that the trees had made that keening sigh and not hunting dogs. But now the sound was louder and sharper, coming faster and more eagerly than the susurrus of the trees.

"Evan," she said, reaching out for him. "Evan; dogs."

He moved in his sleep, his face contorted. He did not waken.

"Evan!" She pulled at him, shaking him urgently.

With a shout he woke, his eyes wide. He flailed his one arm, striking out at her, pushing her away with bits of angry words.

"Dogs! Dogs!" she yelled at him.

He broke off. "Dogs?" Puzzled, he stared at her.

"They followed us, Evan. They're coming."

He rubbed his face as if to wipe his dream from it. Awkwardly he pulled on his jacket and stumbled to his feet. "Where?" he asked.

"Down there. They aren't in sight yet." She pointed away into the night as she motioned him to silence. The sound of the pack floated up to them.

"Moving fast," Evan said. He listened again.

"We'll have to get away," she said.

"Yes."

"They'll follow us," she said, certain of it.

"Maybe." He frowned deeply. "Do you have any matches?"

"No. Do you?"

He patted his pockets. "I did have . . ." At last he retrieved a greasy, battered scrap of cardboard with four tattered matches clinging to it. "They got wet, so I don't know."

"What are you going to do?" Thea was alarmed now.

"Start a fire," he said. "The wind is north-east; it'll blow the fire right down the hill at them. They can't follow through a fire."

"But what about us?"

His laughter was unpleasant. "I don't want to die for them," he admitted with a glance down the hill. "Fire will stop them."

"I don't want to burn, either," she said sharply.

"We won't. The wind will take care of that. Give me some help." He held the matches. "I can't do this with one hand."

She hesitated. "Where will we go?"

"We'll follow this cut into the mountains. Most of the danger will be on the roads. Up here, we stand a chance. We'll be harder to spot and we'll be able to move where the Pirates can't go."

"And food?"

He shrugged as he handed over the matches. "We'll worry about that later."

"I'm hungry now."

"So are those dogs."

She pulled one of the matches out of the book and scraped it over the worn abrasive strip. It left a red smear behind but nothing more.

"Try the other side."

Again the scrape and another track of red. "No good," she breathed.

Down the slope the sound was growing louder; the individual voices coming clearly through the night promised a large pack.

"There's about ten of them, maybe more," Thea said as she listened.

"Try the next match."

The wind whistled by them. "Be careful," Evan said, bringing his hand to shield the match.

"Get some branches. We have to have kindling."

He nodded and broke off a small branch, then held it close to the three remaining matches in her hands.

The second match sputtered, flared, then winked out.

"Damn."

"What if none of them light?" Thea asked as she tried the third match.

"Then we'll run for it." Evan held the branch nearer.

The third match lit, then died as the wind touched it.

"It's got to work," Thea muttered. "Put that branch closer."

He obeyed and held his breath.

The first scrape left only the same red track the others had, and Thea felt defeat and fear wash through her. "No."

"Try the other side," Evan said. "Quickly."

She nodded, her teeth clenched. Carefully she pulled the match over the trails of the others. It did not light.

"Again," Evan hissed.

Thea shrugged. She scraped it again and was rewarded with a tiny stain of blue as the match caught. Making a small cry she cupped her hands around it, sheltering the promise of fire. "Give it the branch," she whispered, almost afraid that sound would kill it.

"Here." Evan thrust the branch into her hands. The needles blackened and peeled back from the little flame.

"There's almost no match left," Thea said angrily.

"It'll catch," Evan insisted and held the branch steady. The needles continued to shrivel.

"Come on, come on," she muttered, all the time fearing that the rotten forest could not burn, that the branch would smolder and die.

Now the branch was charring, blackened for half its length, and it burned Evan's fingers. He slipped his fingers back.

"Well?" Thea asked uncertainly.

"I don't know. We'd better run for it."

She nodded, hearing the dogs coming nearer. The sounds had changed now, and in the howls there were yelps of anticipation.

Evan shoved the branch into the walls of their shelter. "Maybe it'll take," he said, then turned to Thea. "What do you think?"

"We're better off in the cut than in the woods. The woods will slow us down too much. Particularly if there *is* a fire."

He nodded his agreement. "Save your strength."

"Maybe we will find a cabin," she said, not believing it.

"Maybe." He said this as he pushed his way out of the shelter, the branches breaking before him, showering him with dust.

"How far away would you say they are?" she asked, looking anxiously down the slope.

"Half a mile. Or less." He listened. "They're tired. That's something."

Slowly at first, then more rapidly, they made their way up the mountain, away from the dogs. Their makeshift shelter faded into the dark behind them.

"What about the rope?" Thea asked as they went. "Is there time to make a trap?"

Evan tugged at the rope, considering. "No."

They went on in silence, trying not to listen to the sounds pressing nearer. Ahead of them loomed another tower, as dilapidated as the one they had left behind.

"Can we stop?" It was not really a question. Their strength was being sapped by hunger and fatigue. They could not continue much further. Evan did not bother to answer her as he stopped to unsling the rope from his chest.

Then a strange red flower blossomed in the night as their shelter burst into flame. The keening of the dogs changed to frightened barking as the fire broke out around them. One dog that ventured too near the shelter ran in panic, his coat singed, his ragged tail burning.

A fresh gust of wind fed the flames, and the fire sent out runners toward the trees. As if greedy for warmth the nearest boughs sucked up the fire, holding it like a treasure in the long needles.

Evan's eyes narrowed as the forest began to burn. "Cox might still be down there."

Thea watched the fire impassively. "He'll think we're dead."

"Maybe," Evan said. He turned away and half his face showed the warm glow of the fire. The other half was hidden in the night, making his expression unreadable. "Come on. It's late," he said to Thea. He turned abruptly, his heel grinding on the earth. He pointed up the hill. "We'll see if there's shelter at the crest."

*　　*　　*

It was morning before they found shelter in an old caboose where the rusted rail tracks crossed the power line cut. It sat in solitary grandeur, the color of old bricks where the paint had not flaked away. Its wheels had long since fused with the ribbons of steel it had ridden many years before. It listed badly and showed a break in the roof. Around it the brush grew as if trying to protect it from malicious and prying eyes.

"Is it safe?" Thea whispered to Evan as they crouched, watching, in the brush.

He shrugged, not taking his eyes from the hulk. "We can rush it now, and find out," he suggested, unwinding the rope from his body once again.

But Thea hesitated. "No. Not yet." Scooping a handful of gravel from the edge of the old railroad bed, she threw it at the caboose, letting the bits of rock spatter against the side of the old car. "Now, we'll see."

They waited together, but there was no sound, no rustlings inside the caboose, no fluttering alarms outside. Cautiously they moved closer.

"Who takes the door?" Evan asked as they came up beside the caboose.

"I do," she said, daring him to contradict her.

"Okay. Here. You might want this." He handed her several feet of rope with a knot in one end. It was heavy, solid. "Just swing that at anything that moves. It'll give a good clout. Remember."

She took the rope, swung it, testing it, then with a sprint she rushed for the door.

The wood crumbled under her hand, the rusted latch coming away as she grabbed at it. The air of the caboose that sighed out at her made her retch, and for a moment she swayed on the narrow metal platform that served as a porch. Holding her breath, she pressed resolutely into the car, her face protected by the flap of her jacket she held over her nose and mouth.

Whoever the three were, they had been dead for a long time. Their flesh had mummified, for the air was dry and hot. They lay sprawled as they had died, in desiccated pools of excrement, declaring even now the cause of their deaths. Amoebic dysentery had been common, ten years ago, and these bodies had been dead at least that long. Their clothes and blankets, once soaked with sweat and other things, had rotted, leaving a few threads clinging to the corpses, pitiful against the wrecked bodies. Watching them, Thea felt her body dry in sympathy.

"Any luck?" Evan called from outside. There was an edge in his voice, a not-quite-concealed fear.

She did not answer him. Instead she moved around the little room, looking at all the things left behind by the three unfortunates, wondering what use she could make of them. She and Evan needed so much; they could not afford to overlook anything.

"Thea!"

Carefully she backed out of the caboose.

"Well?" Evan masked his relief with anger.

"There are three bodies in there, real old. I guess dysentery got them. It sure looks like it. I don't think we should stay in the car. But we can stay under it. There's room under the caboose," she said beseechingly. "I saw some canvas in there. We could make a kind of tent. We could rig it around those braces . . ." She stopped talking abruptly.

"Is there anything else worth salvaging?"

"The canvas. I told you about that. There's no blankets we can use. There is a little rope, not as heavy as this"—she swung the rope he had given her—"but better for tying and carrying. There's three boxes of matches. And there's a few books."

"What about knives?" he demanded, staring at the caboose intently as if he wanted to decipher it, read its secrets. "Anything we can use as weapons? Sharp forks, anything."

She scowled. "The knives are rusted. We can't use them. But I saw a couple files. We could sharpen them."

Evan nodded, approval showing in his face. Absently he rubbed at the stump of his arm. "We'll make the tent, then. And we'll sharpen the files. And we'll pack up the matches. . . . And the books. . . ."

Seeing Evan touch his mutilated arm filled Thea with dread. "Does it hurt?"

"Itches." Embarrassed, he stopped. After a moment he asked, "Did you say there were books?"

"About a dozen," she nodded.

Dreamily he said, "A dozen. When I was a kid I collected books. I had hundreds of them. First editions only. All kinds of books." He shook his head as if just waking. "Maybe we'll have time to read a couple of them."

"I haven't read a book in a long time," Thea said, recalling the years at Camminsky Creek that had come to an end so abruptly eleven years before. "Jack Thompson made sure everyone did a lot of reading."

"What?" He was startled.

"Nothing. It's over." She looked apprehensively at the caboose. "I think we better take the stuff we can use and get away from here. This thing is awful conspicuous." Now that the sun was hitting the old rail car, the faded red paint that flaked from its sides grew brighter, a strong contrast to the pale-leaved brush surrounding it. Thea sensed its vulnerability, dislike growing out of her fear.

Evan felt it, too, for he said, "You're right, of course. We'd be a target if we stayed here."

Away in the brush a snake slithered, making the dry leaves crackle as it went. The sound was absurdly loud, making them jump.

"Come on," Thea said quickly. "We can take what we need and sleep under the caboose. But we can't stay here too long."

"No," he agreed, and followed her into the old rail car.

*   *   *

"But why did you take that book?" Thea asked him as Evan idly turned the pages. It was cool under the caboose and the canvas held them in its shadow, hidden from the world.

"I haven't seen one in a long time," he answered rather distantly. He was realizing how much he had forgotten.

"But we can't use a cookbook. We don't even have stuff to eat. How can you look at it?" She flung herself onto her side, away from him.

He paid no attention. "Look: veal and eggplant in Marsala. Sweetbreads Milanese. I had that once, in Parma." He riffled the pages, then set the book aside.

For some time Thea said nothing. "What's sweetbreads Milanese?"

Evan lay back, looking up at the rotting undercarriage of the caboose. "It's sweetbreads . . . that's organ meat. The membranes are removed and the meat is cooked in heavy cream with white wine, fine herbs, and mushrooms . . ." He broke off, his tone changing as he said, "It doesn't matter. It's in the past. No one eats like that any more." He turned heavily prone, his chin supported in the crook of his arm. "We'd better get some sleep."

Thea sat up, laced fingers and head on her knees. Slowly she reached out to touch the cookbook uneasily. After a while she opened it and began to read, trying to imagine what the strange dishes tasted like. Finally she said, "My mother used to put orange slices inside chickens when she roasted them, sometimes. She rubbed the outside with butter and honey." If Evan had said anything then, Thea would have wept.

But Evan was asleep.

* * *

The next day as they climbed, following the rusted towers, they saw a band of lepers making their way slowly along the crest of the mountain to the north of them.

"They're carrying the flag," Thea said, shading her eyes. In the distance she saw the yellow cross against the red. "There's about twenty of them."

"Must be a camp around here," Evan allowed, glad for the chance to shift the bundle tied to his back. With only one arm, he quickly lost balance as the load settled, and he was forced to stop frequently to adjust it.

"What about food? Do you think they know where food is?" Thea asked urgently as she tightened the cords of her own pack.

"If they do, we can't use it," he said grimly. There was too much danger from the lepers, both from their disease and the people themselves: he knew they dared not risk dealing with the terrible outcasts. "They can't share with us, Thea."

Around them the desolate peaks rose up. The forest had retreated farther into the mountains and now only rock and brush covered the steep slopes. Where the sun struck them the rocks glistened as if sweating from the heat; in the shadows dust touched them, moving restlessly whenever the wind blew.

"They might know about Gold Lake," Thea said wistfully, watching the line of figures growing smaller in the distant haze.

"You know better than that," Evan snapped. "If they knew about Gold Lake, if they'd been there, we certainly couldn't go there. Could we."

Slowly she shook her head. "Is that what it's going to be like? Are we all going to be lepers or Pirates before we die?" She turned to him, seeking an answer, but he had none for her.

"We've got to get moving." He turned away deliberately, refusing to look at the stragglers on the northern ridge.

"All right." Reluctantly, she hooked her thumbs in her belt, touching the sharpened file that swung there. The heat made a jacket unnecessary and she felt the sun bruise her darkening skin. Only the raw place where her nipple had been remained unchanged, defying the sun and her desire to forget.

"We'll use the tent if we have to tonight," Evan said, softening toward her. It was easy enough to stretch the canvas over the rope and a couple of poles. "But there might be a cabin up here: who knows?" He found it a pleasant fiction, not truly a lie.

"And if there isn't?"

"The tent will do."

"And what about food?" she asked, hunger making her angry.

"Maybe we'll find some. There's still some snakes up here. We can eat them. I saw a rabbit earlier today, I think. There might be more."

She shook her head resentfully. "And what if Cox comes along?"

Evan stopped walking. "What is it, Thea? What's wrong?"

His concern was anguish to her. "We could die out here," she said bluntly, terrified of the gentleness she read in his face. "Maybe we should go separately. Meet up again later, at Gold Lake, maybe."

"Are you saying you won't travel with me?" There was no accusation in this.

"No." But even as she said it she wondered if it was true.

He studied her, realizing that she was frightened of more than his body. "You can make it alone, if that's what you want," he said. "But I can't. Not with one arm. I can't even take off my pack without help. And without it, I'm lost. Stay with me, Thea. Please."

"I heard things are better in the mountains," she said noncommittally.

"Until the mountains, then. When we're back in the trees, we'll talk about it again." He touched her arm, intending companionship, and saw her flinch.

The wind moved the dust after them as they continued eastward.

*   *   *

There was water that night, where a creek tumbled down the rocks, and near it a lineman's cabin which the telephone company had built long ago. There were three neat rooms and, almost miraculously, kerosene lanterns with fuel still in them packed carefully in an insulated cupboard.

"Perfect," Evan said, smiling when he had finished inspecting the cabin. "Not even coons got in."

Thea dropped her pack on the kitchen table, ignoring the place. "Is there any food? Can we eat?"

Evan went to the shuttered shelves tucked into the pantry and pulled them open. "Nothing in here . . ." He tried to keep the disappointment out of his voice. "Wait." He reached deep into the dark and pulled out three small boxes. "Soup. We eat."

"Is it any good?" Thea asked, refusing to be enthusiastic about it.

"I hope so. We'll find out."

"If it isn't we'll die. So it doesn't matter." She slumped into the chair at the table. Her body was sore and there was an ache deep within her she could not salve. She turned disinterested eyes on Evan, who had busied himself locating cooking pots and investigating the wide-bellied stove. "Want me to get some water?" she asked when Evan had completed his search.

"I'll get it," he answered.

"You might hurt yourself."

"So might you."

She shrugged as he took the largest of the pots and strode out the door. While he was gone she thought about leaving, just getting up and walking off into the dusk, letting it all end. She clung to her elbows as if the tightness of her grip would give her strength to leave. But she would not be alone out in the mountains. If Cox or his men found her, she would not have a clean death. There would be the pain again, the invasion. . . . She thought of the woman hanging from the billboard in Chico and her face whitened.

"What's the matter?" Evan had come in, unnoticed, filling the doorway, growing more massive as he came across the room. "You're pale, Thea."

She shook her head, stumbled out of the chair, moving away from him. He was too big, too near.

He came after her, touching her shoulder. "You can tell me. What is it?" Although the words were gentle, his hand on her made her terror vivid.

Panic rose in her and she broke free of him and bolted for the door, running awkwardly, for her bones felt both brittle and liquid.

"Thea! *Thea!*" he shouted after her. "Don't!"

Without thinking she rushed to the creek, sinking down on her knees beside it, trembling uncontrollably now that the full force of her fright was on her. She heard him come up behind her and loathed herself for not having the strength or the will to move.

He stopped when he was close enough for her to hear him speak. His words were said clearly, calmly. "I'm not going to hurt you, Thea."

"Go away."

"Not until you tell me what's wrong." He squatted down behind her, out of reach. The position was uncomfortably out of balance, but he determined to keep it. "I am not a fool, Thea, and I'm not insensitive. When you saw me, you panicked."

"I know."

"Why?" The question frightened him much more than he had thought it would. His thighs ached and he welcomed the distraction.

She made no answer for some moments, then said, "Lastly . . ."

"I know what Lastly did." He had raised his voice and she

winced. He forced himself to speak cautiously. "I know what Lastly did. But, Thea, I'm not Lastly."

"I know."

"Then listen to me." How he wished he could see her face. Talking to her angular hunched back was worse than all his nightmarish childhood memories of the disembodied voice at confession. "You don't want to be touched. I shouldn't have tried. When I touched you all you thought of was Lastly."

"I was raped," she said, and the words were vile.

Again Evan waited as his muscles knotted. "I don't know what it was like. There is no way I can know. But I feel guilt because it happened at all."

"That doesn't change it," she whispered bitterly.

He ground his teeth, breathing deeply. "It's a bad thing to lose an arm, to watch while part of you is cut away. But when it is gone, it is gone. And in a way," he added, accepting the truth of his admission, "in a way, I wanted Cox to do it. I'm carrying too much evil around in me, and this was a compensation. So I can't pretend to know what you've endured."

"Yes," she said, angry now.

"I should have prevented it. That's what you think, isn't it?" He knew he should not say this to her, because it was what *he* thought, not she.

"No." She bit her lip. "You can't undo what's done, Evan, no matter how much you want to or what you say now. I can't change it, you can't change it. It's too late for that."

"Don't." He waited a moment, steadying himself. "Thea, listen to me. Out here alone, neither of us stands a chance, not with Cox coming into the mountains and lepers here. There are other gangs, too, and Untouchables. Summer is ending, Thea. They'll all be desperate."

The sound of Evan's voice blended with the running water. She let his words run with the creek, soothing and persuading.

"Winter comes early up here. That makes it worse. But together we might stand a chance, in spite of Cox and Untouchables and lepers and winter. It's a long way to Gold Lake, but we could make it, together. Will you come with me, Thea? Travel with me? That's all I ask of you, that we travel together."

"But why?" Much of her fright had faded, and now she felt foolish. Never in her years alone had she been so utterly frightened.

And never in her years alone had she felt the need for companionship as keenly as she did in that moment. She could not bear to be touched; she did not want to be alone.

So lost in her thoughts was Thea that she did not see the cold agony that came into Evan's face at her question. "I was wrong about the Pirates, about survival. I was wrong about so many things. I can't apologize for them; I can't atone. But I can do something worth while for once. Don't make me abandon you, Thea."

She said nothing as he spoke. The brook was shiny where the moonlight touched it. "Once there were crickets up here, and they chirped," she said idly, hardly realizing she had spoken aloud.

"Crickets?" he asked, stung that she had not heard him.

"There were crickets at Camminsky Creek. I remember them, sometimes. It was a long time ago. Mr. Thompson and his genetic engineering. He thought that was the answer; they all did. But they were playing, that's all. Playing. Most of them died of it."

"Camminsky Creek?" Evan was bewildered.

"It was in Mendocino County. Near Cloverdale."

Evan knew about Cloverdale—it was the first town completely destroyed by the Pirates, more than five years before he had taken them over. When he first joined the Pirates, their success at Cloverdale gave him the pattern for less bloody and more efficient raids. "I see."

"No. Not you. You didn't kill them. The C.D. did. It's more than ten years now." She shook her head as if clearing the past from it. Holding her breath she turned to face him, and found that her terror was gone. "I'll travel with you, Evan. Until we get to Gold Lake."

He dared to smile at her words. "Good. But let's stay here a couple of days. It's a long walk, and we'll have to go around, through Quincy."

She frowned, and the tickle of distrust was back. "Quincy? Why so far north?"

"To go around the lepers. We'll have to do that. They'll kill us if we get too close."

"Because we aren't lepers, you mean," she said, knowing the answer. "Quincy then. But fall is coming early. We'll have to travel quickly if we want to get to Gold Lake before the first snows."

Evan nodded, unable to express his relief. The tension which had held him so long left him and he toppled clumsily from his cramped position, twisting one of his ankles as he lurched forward.

Thea moved back fast, and in her hurry to escape him, slid into the creek. The cold water rushed around her, pulling her down.

By this time Evan had recovered his balance and he scuffled to the bank, holding out his hand. "Come on; I'll pull you out."

She hesitated, then reached up, putting her hand in his, her lean fingers gripping hard. Evan set his teeth, braced his legs, and pulled her from the creek. As she stood shivering beside him, he asked, "How wet are you?"

She touched her pants and loose shirt. "Wet enough." She wrung the tail of her shirt. "And you? Were you hurt?"

"I'm not wet," he said, which was no answer. He felt awkward still, all knees and elbow. "It wouldn't be a bad idea, come to think of it. It's been a while since I've had a bath. Maybe tomorrow."

"Soup," Thea reminded him and they went back to the cabin, walking close to each other, but not touching.

*   *   *

The next day Thea snared a rabbit, skinning it expertly with a paring knife found in the cabin. She kept the hide to cure it in urine.

"We won't starve, not if there are rabbits around," she said as Evan crumbled sage into the meager rabbit stew.

"No, we won't," he agreed, longing for carrots and onions, for chicken broth, mustard, and sour cream. Why not go all the way, he thought, and wish for a Pinot Chardonnay while I'm at it, and baba au rhum for dessert.

"That smells good," Thea said a little later while the stew simmered.

Evan sniffed the air critically, thinking that it smelled dreadful. "Thanks," he said, wondering what had become of his favorite smörgåsbord place in Stockholm. It was gone, very likely. Certainly there was no more smörgåsbord.

"I didn't know that weeds helped cooking."

"Not all weeds do," he said, trying to remember if he might find rosemary at this altitude. "Just some weeds. They're called herbs then, not weeds."

"Herbs," she said, startled. "My mother used herbs, sometimes. Oregano. Is that an herb?"

"Yes," Evan said, going to the stove to sample the flavorless stew and to shut out the memories that had flooded his senses.

For a little while Thea watched him, knowing that he had gone deep into his mind, shutting her out as he stirred the pot. She wanted to speak to him, to say that she knew he had his hurt, too. But the words did not come and her mind locked the insight away, keeping it hidden.

"We eat now," Evan announced somewhat later.

"Good. I'm hungry," she said honestly. "Anyway, we won't eat like this when we're traveling." She was angry, challenging him to argue.

"We probably won't," he said steadily as he heaped their cracked plates with the stew. "So enjoy this while you have the chance."

Thea gave the meat long enough to cool, then she took morsels in her fingers. She chewed eagerly at the tough rabbit, and found it strange that Evan did not consider the meal delicious.

*   *   *

The strips of rabbit hide held the small pack to his back in fair comfort. Thea inspected the knots before tying her own pack on. "You'll do," she said as she made a last minor adjustment. In the week they had rested she had made pack frames for them, and was pleased to see how well she had done.

Evan shifted his pack so that it did not impede his mutilated arm. He wished that the stump would stop itching.

"Don't do that," Thea said sharply as she caught him scratching the orange band of skin. "Give it a chance to heal. Let it grow."

CHAPTER 3

Evan's arm grew back as fall came on. It sprouted slowly as they left the contamination behind them, beginning as a tawny spatulate paddle below the angry cicatrix marking the path of the saw, and stretching out to bud fingers as flowers had once stretched toward the sun.

The cruel desolation above the Feather River canyon offered them scant shelter and less food, plaguing them with heat that made the rocks sing in the day, and insect-ridden nights—for here there were insects—that turned their sleep to torment. Occasionally they killed a rattlesnake, rationing its meat with desperate caution. There were no more rabbits. The granite soon made ruins of their shoes, so that the tracks that marked their passing were rusty with blood. Around them, clinging to the rising mountains, pines brooded, poking forlorn fingers at the sky, their needles shading to russet as they fought for life.

Gold Lake was a long way off.

Evan had made light of their danger at first, but as hunger etched lines into his face and Thea's eyes took on the haunted shadow of starvation, he admitted, at least to himself, that they had come a long way to die.

For Thea, hunger was a specter dogging her steps, but an unreal one. Far more real, more threatening, was the possibility of Pirates or lepers, who would make their dying long and messy. Anxiously she watched the rocks around them, and the dark shadows under the trees.

As the river rose in the floor of the steep canyon, they climbed high on the ridge above it, far from the thunder of the river and the danger of being trapped in the narrow gorge. Occasionally they caught a glimpse of buildings huddled against the canyon walls, some deserted, some carefully guarded. It was these buildings with their promise of food and shelter that made Evan feel the full weight of their distress, and in time he grew reckless. Knowing that he would make the attempt without her if she refused to help him, he outlined his plan to Thea as they crouched on the crest of the ridge above a small compound of houses and barns nestled inside wooden fortification.

"We'll have to wait a day," he said at the end. "We'll have to see how they schedule the patrol of the walls. It looks like they've got shotguns, and we can't go up against that kind of weapon."

Does he truly think he can succeed here? Thea wondered, saying aloud, "One more day won't matter." Her voice was listless. Evan went on quickly, "They'll be most vulnerable just before dawn. The animals won't be awake then and the guards will be sleepy. We've got a good chance, Thea," he added, as much to reassure himself as her.

"Why not?" she answered, her lean hands clinging to the frayed denim of her jacket, touching the fur tufts left on the rabbit skin thongs securing her pack. "If we fail the worst we'll be is dead."

"There is that crossroad," he pointed out, looking upstream to the bridge and the dusty tracks that met there. "It increases the chance of traffic, if there is any traffic now. It might be tricky getting away from here if that road is still used." It was his one note of prudence, so that she would know that he recognized the risks.

"If the road isn't overgrown, then it's used sometimes," she said. "Maybe they use it. Maybe someone else does. The Pirates don't come this far yet." She said the last with little conviction.

"Yes. But they will." He spoke with calm certainty. He had planned to increase the range of the Pirates years ago, and Cox was more ruthless than he had ever been. "I taught them, remember that. They're following my orders, even though Cox gives them."

Thea said nothing, looking at the farm below. The sounds from the barnyard, the cackle of chickens, tantalized her, making hunger twist in her like a trapped animal. Smoke rose, lamb-flavored, from the main house, and the armed men patrolling the wall turned toward the smell. Thea closed her eyes and breathed deeply.

"I know," Evan said, realizing that the tang in the air meant that the lamb was wine-basted. Each delicious entity of that smoke stirred memories in him. There had been lamb that night in Barcelona; he couldn't have been more than fifteen, and his father was accepting yet another honor. A Portuguese rosé was served with the lamb, and the man beside him was a somber Egyptian who smelled of sandalwood and something else . . .

"Evan!" Thea said sharply, and he was back on the ledge over-looking a walled farm in the canyon.

In a while a bell rang and the guards changed. Thea turned to Evan and shrugged. It was decided.

They awoke in the end of the night to the sound of shooting and the roar of engines. Scrambling to the edge of the ridge, they could see the fight below them. A gang of perhaps twenty men on motor-cycles was circling the high wall enclosing houses and barns. As Thea and Evan watched, the defenders blasted one rider from his cycle with a shotgun. The machine crashed into the wall, dragging its bleeding rider behind it. The reserve gas cans exploded as the cycle hit, sending fire greedily up the walls. The rider twitched once as he began to burn.

"Pirates?" Thea asked in a whisper.

Evan shook his head. "No one I know. They must be one of the independents. And sloppy ones at that."

The fire was spreading, tonguing the roof of the nearest barn and panicking the stock inside. Women ran from the main house to-ward the fire, the sounds of their voices carrying over the terrified cries of the animals.

Now one of the cyclists broke through the burning wall, trailing sparks as he roared by the defenders. His snub-nosed shotgun caught the nearest defender full in the chest. By the time the farmers killed him, he had run down two of the women and clubbed them with the butt of his shotgun.

"They're low on ammunition," Evan remarked critically.

Thea said nothing, thinking of all the burning towns she had seen, all the bodies festering in the open, unmourned. She closed her eyes, but this did not help, for though she shut out the horror below her, the other images were brighter in her mind.

Soon the fire had a full hold on one barn and was spreading down the wall to the next one. Two more of the men on cycles had breached the walls and were chasing after the farmers, yelling with the joy of slaughter. The fire colored their faces red, turning their features to devil masks.

One woman waited as she was ridden down, then calmly tossed a lighted oil lamp into the reserve gas cans as the cycle careened into her. She, her attacker, and his motorcycle erupted in flames.

"Come on," Evan said to Thea, pulling her toward him. As always, she drew back, but he kept his grip on her arm. "We're going down there. It's our only chance."

Thea nodded, taking hold of the sharpened file that was her only weapon. "The second barn," she told him, sliding in his wake down the steep wall of the canyon. They clutched the brush around them to slow their descent, watching the battle below with growing concern. If they were discovered, it would be impossible to escape . . . They would be easy targets for the people below them, and their vulnerability was increasing with the daylight that hung expectantly in the east, making ghosts of the granite rising upriver.

One of the houses was on fire now, sending heavy smoke rolling up the canyon toward the crossroad. Four horses had escaped from the larger of the barns and were lunging about, mad with fright, adding to the confusion that was already making the farmers' defense a farce.

More than half of the marauders on their motorcycles were inside the walls, running down the farmers, clubbing those who ran, capturing others. Two of them confidently dismounted from their machines and ran after a woman who had come out of a burning house. One of the men threw himself onto the farm woman, tearing at her clothes. She screamed, pushing against his chest and hammering at his face with a trowel.

High on the slope above them, Thea blanched, stifling a scream in sympathy as she jammed her knuckles into her mouth. She stopped moving, watching and hating to watch what was happening below.

"Thea," Evan breathed anxiously. "Come."

But Thea shook her head, her face rigid with fear.

"Thea." Evan looked down, seeing what she saw. Then he reached out again and deliberately pulled her off balance, wrenching her attention away from the compound below. "Don't look."

"She's . . ."

"I know. Come with me. There's very little time."

The woman's trowel connected at last and the man fell away from her, his head strangely askew, blood and other things staining his face.

In the flickering light of the spreading fire, Thea and Evan could count more than a dozen dead. Two of the farmers, trapped in the second barn as the fire consumed it, were screaming, but the sound was lost in the rest of the battle. More of the cyclists came through the wall, sure of their victory now and eager for the pillage. Seeing them, the women fled to the main house, but few of them made it to safety. Three of the cyclists fell upon one woman, two holding her down as the third pulled at her trousers.

One of the farmers attacked the three marauders, clubbing them with his empty rifle until the other cyclists saw what was happening and ran the farmer down, slashing him with long knives. Bleeding from the deep gash in his stomach, the farmer fell across the woman. She shrieked out, a sound that destroyed her voice. Then she was still as the farmer bled out his life on top of her.

Three of the buildings were afire when the first barn fell in, sending out cascades of sparks and the stench of burned flesh. The few remaining cyclists outside the wall put themselves between the houses and the river, knowing that if the farmers were to save their buildings now, they would have to come for water. The cyclists waited, certain of winning, needing only the last four defending men to have the rest of the holding and the women to themselves.

Sunlight was staining the tops of the mountains, throwing long shadows down the canyon to take the place of night. More farmers fell, one with a baling hook in his neck, another crushed by a burning beam dropping from the second barn. The few farmers left bolted for the central house, calling to the women to bring rifles from the other houses. As soon as they were secure in the central building, some of the cyclists brought flaming boards from the outer compound wall and laid them against the house, laughing as they saw the fire take hold of the wood.

Thea and Evan were nearing the second barn, coming as close to the wall as the flames would let them, keeping as much to the leaping shadows as they could. So long as the confusion held, they might be able to raid the barn and get away with precious meat before they were suspected or discovered.

The marauding cyclists let out a cheer to the sound of splintering wood, and this was followed by the crinkling of chain.

"That's the door going," Evan said quietly. "We'll have to be fast. This will be over soon."

Thea nodded numbly, shading her face against the glare of the fire. "I know," she said after a moment. Already she could hear the sounds of the men in the house as the cyclists sought them out. Mercifully the fire and the barn blocked out the sight.

Evan pulled her around the corner of the wall and beyond the fire. There were paddocks and a couple of pigpens on this side. The paddocks were empty, but for a few hysterical chickens and a dog with a maimed leg. In the largest pigpen one angry sow guarded her litter.

"Piglets. We can get a couple of piglets," Thea suggested, watching the sow warily. "We might have to kill *her*, though." Already the sound and knowledge of the slaughter behind them were fading as she thought of having food again.

"There's a pitchfork on the wall," Evan said as he ran his eyes expertly over the outbuildings. "We can hold her off with that and grab a couple of the piglets. And maybe a couple of chickens," he added, looking over his shoulder to the hens squawking in the paddock.

Thea had already taken the pitchfork off its hook and was climbing cautiously over the wall of the pen. The sow made a rumbling noise and started forward. She was a large white Dorchester with close to three hundred pounds behind her threat. Thea knew enough about pigs to respect their strength, their intelligence, and their cunning. Holding her pitchfork at the ready, she called out, "You'll have to be fast, Evan. She's not going to be fooled for very long."

Without taking time to answer, Evan vaulted over the gate into the pen, moving carefully to the squirming pile of piglets that lay near the empty water trough. He flexed his half-formed fingers carefully, feeling them still weak with newness.

At their backs the fire ate steadily down the wall like invincible locusts, masking the stillness that fell suddenly inside the compound. A last wail of agony rose into the morning and then only the fire crackled and chuckled evilly.

Evan had grabbed two of the piglets by their hind legs, then swung them expertly into the wall to stun them. But the sound caught the attention of the sow, and she wheeled about with surprising speed, rushing at Evan in full maternal rage. Thea cried out, throwing the pitchfork at the sow. She had the satisfaction of seeing the tines sink deep into the sow's rump, but aside from making the animal even angrier, the wounds did little to halt her rush at Evan.

Quickly Evan grabbed the edge of the trough and with all his strength he pulled one end of it free of the mud and heaved it at the charging sow. He caught her full across the front and she staggered before collapsing under its weight, making a grunt like metal on metal.

From the burning wall there came a shout, and Thea looked up to see three of the cyclists pointing at them from the stock gate.

"Evan!" she shouted, frightened.

"I see them," he called back, motioning to her. "This way, Thea," he ordered, waving toward the brush that lined the farm track leading to the crossroad beyond. Looping a rabbit-hide thong around the piglets, he scrambled over the fence and set out at a run.

As she raced toward the brush, Thea sensed Evan's nearness. He still had the piglets and held the thong tight, running with the force of panic. Wordlessly he guided her toward the first bushes, nudging her to bend low. The gravel of the road tore at their feet as they went, making her stumble, lurching his body against her.

"Steady," he panted. "You can, Thea, you can." When she faltered, he dragged her to her feet. The answer she gave was a sob, but his words were strength to her, for she dived into the scrub with him, making new rents in her jeans as the stiff thornlike branches pulled at her. They blundered through the brush until they were sure they had not been followed, and then they sank onto the ground sucking air into their lungs in long, shuddering gulps.

"What now?" she asked when she could speak again.

"We wait. They might not come after us with all that loot down there. I wouldn't let the Pirates waste their time on scavengers like us."

Thea nodded, recalling three times when the Pirates had left her alone in exchange for pillaging a few old houses, or seizing valuable food stores. It was one of the reasons she had traveled alone until now.

"So long as we're out of sight and quiet, they'll leave us alone. Unless they want to come after us on foot, and that takes time they don't have to spare. They haven't enough ammunition to waste by shooting at random."

"Unless they find more ammunition in the houses. Then it might be good sport, hunting us."

He nodded acknowledgment, but said nothing. Some minutes later he rolled onto his side. "At least we can start on these," he said as he took the paring knife from his belt, drawing it with difficulty across the piglets' throats. As soon as the bleeding started, he efficiently gutted the two carcasses and tied their hind legs together to let them hang as they bled. The rabbit fur on the thongs was matted with blood, and sticky, but it held the piglets firmly.

"Smoke them?" Thea asked as Evan finished his work.

"Probably the best way," he agreed. "As soon as we can get out of here . . ."

There was a roar from three of the cycles that interrupted them and made Thea jump. "They're coming. I guess they found that ammunition."

"But they aren't going to catch us," Evan promised. He slung the piglets on his belt and pointed up the hill. "We can cross the road up there and make our way back to the ridge. We'll go quietly, and they won't be able to find us."

"You do think they have more ammunition, don't you?" she asked as they started the grueling crawl up the slope.

For an answer, buckshot sprayed into the brush behind them. "I guess so," Evan said dryly. "We'll have to zigzag to keep them confused."

It was slow going, and the advancing light made it worse. The tight branches and flat leaves offered good protection, but once in full sunlight they would not match the shadows and it would be an easy matter for the cyclists to pick them off as they emerged from the brush.

Another round of buckshot crashed through the brush, but not as close as the first had been. Thea glanced over her shoulder. "I think they've found the guts," she whispered.

"They're welcome to them," Evan laughed softly. Tugging at her sleeve he pulled her farther away from the path of the buckshot.

"There are more of them," Thea said, pausing long enough to peer down at the track. "They've got help. There's five or six of them now."

"Damn!" Evan's fingers sank into her arm. "Look there."

Ahead of them, where the dirt road crossed the old highway, dust was rising. The sound of wagons coming, drawn possibly by oxen or other heavy, slow animals, grew steadily louder, seeming to increase with the sun.

Dismayed, Thea looked at Evan. "Now what?" she asked, looking from the coiling dust over the road to the armed cyclists on the gravel track.

But Evan motioned her to be silent, squinting impatiently at the road ahead. "I wonder who's coming?" he murmured aloud, rubbing at his unkempt beard.

The noise on the road grew loud enough for the cyclists to hear it, and there were shouts as the men changed direction, their engines whining as the thick wheels tore into the gravel. With shouts of malicious joy the cyclists rode forward to meet the strangers on the road.

But their delight was short-lived, for as they rounded the bend, Thea and Evan heard a cry of horror go up from the marauders and the words, "Untouchables! Monsters! *Monsters!*"

Gingerly Evan crawled through the brush, motioning Thea to stay where she was so she could keep an eye on the cyclists. She nodded her quick understanding and positioned herself between Evan and the burning buildings, lying flat on the ground with her sharpened file clutched firmly in her hand.

The cyclists careened back to the burning farm, shouting to one another. In their moment of panic, they had dropped one of their shotguns at the crossroad, but none came to retrieve it.

Slowly the caravan that had frightened the cyclists drew into view; a pathetic band of men and women traveling in rough carts drawn by emaciated cattle. That they could use such livestock and go unmolested by the starving and desperate people who roamed the mountains attested more eloquently than any other thing about them to the horror they carried in their wagons.

Evan beckoned Thea to come nearer, and she made her way in cautious silence through the underbrush to his side.

"Poor bastards," Evan muttered as he moved closer to the road. His eyes dwelled for a moment on the cart with the children, then he turned away. Even in the years when he had led the Pirates, he had not got used to the terrible deformities that were appearing more and more in the diminishing number of live births of the few surviving men and women. These children in the carts were no exception: only one looked close to normal, all the other seven had defects ranging from a few extra fingers on each hand to hideously stunted bodies, to limbless trunks, to hornlike growths on lead-colored skin. Evan saw that two of the women were pregnant, and wondered, as he had often done before, what could drive them to bear children, with the hopeless testimony of the children riding in the cart.

Thea seemed to sense his thoughts. "What choice is there?" she said to him. "At least they're fertile. They have that value." She felt bitterness burn in her. The worth of a female was determined by her fecundity. She had seen women bought and paid for on the merit of a successful pregnancy. Never mind that less than half the children survived, or that many of the women died in childbirth.

Behind them the cyclists were loading their loot onto their machines as fast as they could, leaving behind the burning buildings and the women they had fought so determinedly to possess. Ash from the burned-out barns drifted lazily on the air above them as they rushed to escape, and one lonely cock crowed for morning.

"They're fools. They can't catch it," Thea said softly. "They've already got it inside of them. We all do."

Just short of the crossroads the carts stopped and three of the men gathered at the head of the pathetic little band and talked. One of them indicated the smoke overhead with an impatient wave of his hand, and the oldest of the three looked about uneasily, gesturing nervously. Eventually one of the younger men was sent ahead to the crossroad to act as scout. He came back quickly enough and after a few moments of consultation, the carts moved forward again, turning at the crossroad onto the gravel track, toward the burning farm.

Thea and Evan watched in silence, keeping very still as the group of wagons rattled by them, the wheels crunching loudly as they rolled onto the gravel.

When the road was empty once more, Thea asked, "Do you think the fires will spread into the brush?" She did not want to talk about the Untouchables who had gone by. She knew herself the unreasoning fear that mutations engendered in those who felt themselves normal.

"Not if they give the women some help, if the women are still alive," Evan replied, carefully avoiding the mention of Untouchables as well. He listened intently for a moment, then crawled toward the road. Nothing, no one was in sight. He got to his feet and started toward the crossroad, the piglets tied to his belt flapping against his leg as he ran, smearing his pants with blood.

"Evan," Thea called after him, alarmed. But her concern turned to surprise as she watched him search the bushes and the crossing and emerge with the shotgun one of the cyclists had dropped. She climbed out of the brush eagerly and was standing waiting for him as he came back with it. "Is it loaded?"

"Both barrels. It won't take us very far, but we might find some cartridges for it somewhere. Maybe farther upstream."

She shook her head. "Don't count on it. But, Evan, we *can* make a crossbow," she said with more enthusiasm than she had shown for weeks. "And we can make quarrels from the barrels."

"Is that how you made the other one?" he asked, starting the long climb back to the ridge. "Come on. We've got to smoke these things before the meat turns bad." He jiggled the rabbit skin thong and the piglets twitched like puppets.

She fell in beside him, her greedy eyes on the piglets and the shotgun. At their backs the smoke diminished, mixing with steam as the Untouchables carried water to the farm compound, working alongside the few women who were alive after the raid. The echo of motorcycles had faded from the canyon, leaving the soft sound of voices and the lowing of cattle to fill the narrow gorge.

*   *   *

Higher up the canyon they crossed the river on the remnants of a railroad bridge and climbed at last to the far rim to a burned-over plateau which hung over the river like a double chin. Knowing that they had food gave them a reserve strength they had not tapped until then, and when they found a sheltered outcropping of rock, Thea surprised them both by locating a small, cold spring that dribbled a thin, pure trickle from the rocks.

Against the boulders they made a small lean-to for smoking one of the piglets. The manzanita that covered the old scars from the burning gave them enough dry wood for a fire; while one of the piglets hung in the lean-to in the slow pungent smoke, the other was roasted in the coals of the fire. Evan had found some wild garlic and had smeared the roasting piglet with it, and the steam that rose from the crackling skin put a sharp edge on their hunger.

As they waited for their food to cook, Thea toyed with the shotgun. "It would be more practical to make a crossbow," she said to

Evan when she had been silent for some minutes. "We can't be sure of finding shot for this, but we can always make quarrels out of scrap metal. There's all kinds of things that can make good quarrels. Nails. Bits of cars. All kinds of things."

Looking across the banked fire, he remembered his first sight of her in the deserted silo above Chico. She had had her crossbow strapped to her wrist then, and had hated to leave it behind when Cox and the Pirates got too close. "You'd rather have the crossbow, wouldn't you?"

"Of course. It's a good weapon. It doesn't make a lot of noise and it packs a lot of power. You can put a quarrel through almost anything if the tension is tight enough in the bow." Her chin had gone up defiantly, showing the clean angles of her face, and lighting her dark, intelligent eyes. She hated being challenged like this, and her cheeks grew bright.

"And can you make this into a crossbow? Quickly?" He hefted the shotgun, balancing it in his hand for a moment, as if weighing its potentials.

Her eyes lit with excitement. "I could. Truly, Evan. I could." She reached out for it, her hand almost trembling. "I'll show you."

He put the shotgun down. "If we found another, could you make one for me as well?"

She nodded happily. Evan handed her the gun, watching as she touched it. "But save the shells for me. We can still use them. Buckshot is a good weapon, too." He laughed at her absent reply before reaching to pull the roasted piglet from the ashes.

The warm smell spread itself between them like water. Thea tore herself away from the beautiful, deadly shine of the gun barrels, looking feverishly at the piglet. The skin was shiny and crisp, cracked in places with juices running out.

They ate little bits, and slowly, being too hungry to hold much at first. The flesh was sweet; swallowing it almost hurt. The taste only made their hunger sharper, reminding them how long it had been since they had eaten a sound meal. The dandelion greens which Evan had used for stuffing were bitter in contrast to the pork, and welcome. Finally Evan stopped both of them, wrapping the remainder of the piglet in part of his shirt to keep it for the morning.

"Never mind, Thea. We can eat again, tomorrow. We can eat for a week on what we have here," he said softly, seeing fright return to her face, and hearing the one quick gasp she made as she reached convulsively for the meat. "We'll be sick if we eat too much at first."

"I know. I know. It's just that . . ." She let her words trail off as she watched Evan put the wrapped piglet in the smoking lean-to with the other. Sighing, she sank down by the rocks, close to the fire. It was getting cold and the circle of warmth was precious.

Evan lay down near her, sensing his own regret that Thea held off from him. He knew that her hurt was still in her, raw as ever, and that watching the raiding party at the farm had brought back all the pain, the invasion. She slept away from him, curled around herself, separate, shutting him out. He wondered as he watched the stars slide over the sky how long he could go on not touching her. Their desolate world ate the heart from him, pulling him away from the dreadful thing his life had become. Thea had the courage to live on in the ruins, to shore herself up against the terrible future. Maybe at Gold Lake, with others, they could hold off the bleak years ahead. He took hope from that thought, though he had little faith in it. As they were now, if this was all they would ever know, he feared what would become of them. He looked toward her huddled form. It would have been a solace, to lose himself in her body. But Thea did not want him. She cringed at his touch. There would be no comfort in her, not even a momentary satisfaction. There would be only more desolation, greater guilt. So he lay silently, and breathed in the smell of the piglets in the lean-to.

Late in the night Thea murmured, saying, "Evan?"

"I'm here."

"Good." Then she was asleep again, and Evan was not sure that she had ever been awake.

* * *

With the morning they decided to cut across the mountains, leaving the river to wind slowly out of its canyon. The passage would be hard, but they faced no danger from men on motorcycles or stray Pirates. There had been no sign of lepers for almost a week. There was a certain risk, of course, but that risk was there no matter which route they took, and this way they would cut down the time to Quincy by nearly three days.

Away from the river second growth pines rose in spindly protest from the brush, their needles brick red. They had once been ponderosa, but had been forced to change. Botany no longer had a name for them; they were on their own.

Striking east across the mountain ridge, Thea and Evan came on the old Pineleaf Mine Road winding up out of the gully where the mine had been. It was overgrown and rutted, showing ancient potholes through the weeds, but it marked a path through the mountains, skirting Smith and Snake lakes. Here there were more trees, some of them still standing green, a testament to the pure water left in these high lakes. But it was a futile gesture, for poison moved in the air and fell with the rain. It would not be long before the trees succumbed.

Pineleaf Mine Road merged with the Snake Lake Road, though neither of those pitiful trails deserved to be called a road. It led them over the last shoulder of the high country. Below them and to the east lay Quincy, protected by mountains, in the warm pocket of the American Valley. From their vantage point, Thea and Evan watched the small cluster of houses, remembering that they had less than a quarter of a piglet left, and knowing that in houses there were meals.

"It looks peaceful," Evan said doubtfully. "Not even armed gates."

"Then there's something wrong," said Thea. "They're on a highway; they must have had trouble before now."

Evan weighed the paring knife in his hand, thinking it a travesty of a weapon. "A trap, do you think?" He was thinking aloud. "We're taking a chance, going down there."

A horse-drawn buggy moved down the main road of the town, unremarked and unhampered. "They aren't starving, that's certain. They still have horses," Thea observed. She cradled her crossbow with a grimace. "That means they must have food for themselves and feed for their animals. Why?"

Frowning, Evan watched the town. Food and horses meant they were prosperous. It made even less sense for them to be unguarded and open to attack. No leper flag hung red and yellow over the roofs, no pesthouses huddled outside the town, their doors telltale black. There was no sign of contamination in the color of the trees.

Idly Evan tossed a pebble down the slope watching it bounce through the brush. Startled by the disturbance a large deer with a heavy bisonlike hump on its shoulders lumbered from its hiding place, thickened antlers pulling on bits of scrub as he went. Part of his flank was the tawny color of regenerating tissue.

"Maybe that's what's wrong," Thea said. "If they're mutants, we can try for Gold Lake from here. It's a way to go, but we'll manage. We can find other food. We don't have to go down there."

"Mutants? Because of that deer?"

"Maybe they're Untouchables. That would protect them." She glanced questioningly at Evan. "Gold Lake will take us in, I know it."

Rubbing ruefully at his new arm, he responded, "They might take us in here, too. If they're mutants, we certainly qualify."

"You don't know that." She pulled her tattered jacket, holding her elbows tightly. "Winter will come soon," she said, thinking that they would have to travel quickly to reach Gold Lake before the snows came. They did not have time to stop in Quincy. With food scarce as it was, she did not want to be alone in the mountains after winter set in.

"Yes. There is winter."

She studied Evan's face, but read no answers there. Under his sandy beard, matted now and white-flecked, his face was carefully devoid of expression.

* * *

In the afternoon they began the hike down, keeping to the old road, moving cautiously toward the town. They took their time, watching for sentries or other outlying, hidden guards that might be concealed along the trail, ready to snipe the unwary traveler. But there were no guards and by nightfall they were less than two miles from the edge of Quincy, camping in a bend of a creek.

"What now?" Evan asked, looking toward the pale lights glowing yellow in the distance. "Do we go in? Do we wait?"

"We wait until morning. It doesn't seem like it, but we could still be walking into a trap. A bad trap."

"All right," Evan agreed, and began to loosen his pack from his back. His new fingers ached, but he knew they were growing stronger.

* * *

It was two hours later that the men came to their fire. Thea grabbed for her crossbow, but found a boot on her hand and a large man, surprisingly clean-shaven, staring down at her. "Don't do that, missy. We didn't come out here to make trouble. Don't you make any."

Very carefully Evan stood up, keeping his hands in plain sight of the men who stood just out of range in the shadows beyond the fire. He was terribly aware of the color of his right hand, of the clumsy newness of it. "We don't mean you any harm," he said slowly. "We saw the town and thought maybe we could get some food. That," he pointed to the last bits of pork on the spit over the fire, "is all we have left." When the men made no answer he went on. "We're healthy. We're willing to work." And, he thought, if these men were slavers, they would work.

One of the men in the dark laughed, a sound not of menace but of sorrow. "Don't be too sure of that," said the voice that went with the laugh.

"Y'see," explained the man with his foot on Thea's hand, "we're Untouchables here. Hasn't been a normal birth in over two years. We got a dozen kids who're pretty bad off. Some deformities, some mental trouble. Now, I don't mean the kids are useless or *vegetables* or any of those things. They aren't . . ." He scuffed at the ashes by the fire. "They look kind of strange and some of them don't talk so good. But they're our kids," and looking up fiercely, he glared at Evan, daring him to contradict this.

"Yes," Evan said, reaching down for Thea to help her to her feet.

"Oh," said the large man and moved his foot. "Sorry. I saw you go for that crossbow. Didn't mean anything, you know." Flushed with embarrassment he moved back. Thea stumbled away from him toward Evan, her eyes blind-looking.

"That's all right, Thea," Evan spoke softly and let go of her hand.

"Thea," said the large man making amends. "Now, that's a pretty name. Always had a liking for Thea. One of my aunts was named Thea. She was a fine woman. Pretty, too. Lived in San Francisco right up until the evacuation. Had a place on Russian Hill. Said it was the best view in the city."

"It's Althea," she said coldly, angry now that the worst of her fright was gone.

"That's nice, too," the man said clumsily. "Mine is Hobart. They call me Honey 'cause I raise bees." He said the last all but squirming with discomfort. Then he waited for the same courtesy from Evan.

"I'm Evan Montague," he replied, returning Hobart's steady look.

One of the men in the shadows asked sharply, "The Pirates' Montague? You're *that* Evan Montague?" It was a question Evan dreaded, but he answered it promptly. "Yes. I was."

"Was?" asked the voice, not needing to be seen to sneer.

"At Chico this summer," Evan said with resignation, not expecting to be believed by these suddenly stern men. "We had taken Orland and were crossing the river to Chico. It was a bloody hell. In the middle of it all, Cox took over. He trapped me and two of my men." He closed his eyes. "They killed Pearson and Rossi, first. With a saw. They were going to do the same to me, but . . . but they started too late. All they got was my arm." He held out his right arm with the strange new growth below the jagged scar. Making an effort to smile he went on. "I was lucky. They didn't get a chance to finish me. And they forgot I'm left-handed. When Cox left me, I got away."

"You're Montague," another one of the faceless voices declared, and it was an accusation. "You're the Pirate."

"No more. There's a price on my head. If they catch up with me, Cox or his butcher-boy Mackley will be happy to do the job right. It will be worse now, because Cox is out to destroy Mutes. Obviously, I'm one." He held his hand out to Thea, wishing she would take it. But she didn't and he went on, "Thea is, too."

"Don't believe him," said the first voice in the shadows. "He's scouting for the Pirates. They've found us, and they want our land and stock."

"Shut up, Simon," Hobart said lazily. "Is she your wife?"

"No," Evan said more bitterly than he knew. "She's traveling with me, that's all. We met up after Chico. She's the reason I'm alive."

"Chico," repeated Hobart. "I heard about Chico. I remember hearing things about Cox. Maybe you're telling the truth."

The fire snapped as a branch collapsed in the flames under the piglet. "Our food is burning," Thea said, glaring at Hobart. "This is the last of it. We can't waste it. And I'm hungry." She knelt to rescue the charred remains of their meal, ignoring the men around them.

It was as if a spring had snapped. Three men came out of the shadows, one with hands that started where his shoulders ended. "Don't worry about your supper," said the one Hobart had called Simon. "We got food to spare at home."

The man with no arms bent with supple grace to rescue the meat on the spit. "The lady's right: no sense wasting this." He smiled kindly at Thea. "My wife can make something for the dogs with it. They like a little pig now and again."

"Do you have dogs?" Thea asked, still startled at the obvious prosperity. She remembered seeing men fight over the emaciated carcasses of dogs and cats. To have pets was a luxury.

"They're our guards," he said, as if to excuse a weakness. "Most of us have dogs, and there's cats around. They get rid of vermin. We've still got trouble with rats, sometimes." He offered his hand to help her to her feet.

Sensing that she must not refuse this offer, yet dreading to be touched, Thea looked to Evan and saw encouragement in his face. She felt her body grow sticky cold, recalling Lastly's hands on her, and his knife as it cut into her breast. Teeth clenched, she took the man's hand and rose quickly to her feet. "Thank you," she mumbled, and looked away.

"I'm Lockhart," said the armless man. "That's Simon. And the one with the face scars is Zimmermann."

"Zimmermann," Evan said. "Carpenter."

With remnants of a German accent, he said, "Yah. Carpenter to you. But to me, Zimmermann."

* * *

Zimmermann and his family fed them dinner. While Thea and Evan ate rewarmed beef stew with dumplings, their host regaled them with his memories of the city that had been his home forty years ago.

"It was Hamburg, you know," he said with a ponderous sigh. "A beautiful, beautiful city once. As a child, as a boy, before the trouble, I loved it. . . . The Elbe was so magnificent then. A splendid river, one that poets could write about and be proud. . . . It became so . . . ugly . . . after the accident. Who would have thought that the power plant at Dömitz would not be shielded enough. They ran tests, and everyone said it was safe, that there was not one chance in ten thousand that anything could go wrong. But one in ten thousand does not always mean the ten thousandth time. It might mean the second, or twelfth, or nine hundredth." Even with the distance of miles and years, his eyes were bright for his city. "So, so lovely a city, Hamburg. My father," he went on briskly, afraid to think too much of his vanished home, "considered carefully. He decided that these mountains would be his stronghold. He did not know that he had brought his own contagion with him."

Thea watched him nervously over her steaming bowl. She had seen her fill of cities, and did not know how anyone could love them. Filthy, rat-ridden places they were, and dangerous. "I've been to Sacramento," she said uncertainly. "It was awful." Once more she could see the huge buildings, their slablike walls pitted and their windows broken, showing holes like missing teeth. The streets had been a battleground for the few people left and the river stank with chemical mire.

Katherine, Rudy Zimmermann's young wife, put an affectionate plump arm around her husband's shoulders, chiding him gently. "They know what has become of the country, Rudy. The death of a thing is always sad for those who will miss it. Don't let's dwell on it."

But Evan stopped her. "I was in Hamburg once." He saw interest in Rudy Zimmermann's eyes. "I was very young at the time. My father was there to conduct the symphony."

Rudy Zimmermann leaped up, a tragic smile on his ruddy face. "Was he that Montague?" he demanded, almost desperate. "The one who loved Mozart so? The one who did the great *Requiem* of Verdi's in the cathedral? Was he your father?"

"Yes." Evan's face was also alight, brightened by a smile he must have worn as a boy. "Did you hear him? In the cathedral?"

"Yah. I heard the Verdi. Did he also conduct the opera there? I think I recall a *Nozze?*" Zimmermann was near tears. "I haven't heard Mozart for so many years, not as it should be. Not with the instruments and the lights, and the people all around me."

Thea looked uncertainly at Evan. "Mozart? He wrote music once, didn't he? I can't remember any, but I think that Iris Thompson used to play some of his things on the piano." She had never seen Evan so perilously happy, and it alarmed her as much as it pleased her. For that moment he was beyond her, and she knew that she could not reach where he had gone.

"He died in 1791. More than two hundred years ago. His music's been around a long time." He looked warmly at Zimmermann, finding the days of his childhood growing brighter in his mind. "Thank you. I had almost forgotten the *Nozze*. He did a *Giovanni* in London that year, too. I couldn't have been more than eight."

The old German began to sing in a quavering baritone, *"Dove sono i bei momenti, Di dolcezza e di piacer?"* His voice broke. "I will not go on," he said roughly.

Evan laughed and echoed Zimmermann with a voice that might have been beautiful at another time, in another place. *"Se vuol ballare, signor contino, se vuol ballare, signor contino, Il chittarino le suonerò . . ."*

"Il chittarino le suonerò, sì, le suonerò, sì, le suonerò!" they finished together, Figaro's comic promise of vengeance giving them amusement precariously close to tears.

*   *   *

"What did it mean?" Thea asked Evan later that evening when they climbed into the almost forgotten comfort of blanket-covered cots. Their room was small, scarcely more than a large closet, and the soft glow from the stove in the adjoining kitchen cast just enough light for them to see the shape of one another on opposite sides of the room. "What were you singing about?"

Evan thought for a moment, going over the words slowly in his mind. "The first one said, 'Where have they gone, those sweet moments of pleasure?'" Evan rubbed his eyes with his hands, then looked across the darkness to Thea.

"And the other?" she prompted.

"'If you want to dance, Count, I'll play the tune.'" He said this more quickly, thinking about all the elaborate plotting that came from those few words.

"What does that mean?" She did not dare ask why it had pleased him so much at first to sing those words, and why it now distressed him.

"That we all pay the piper, I guess." He settled back onto his pillow, humming a little. Then he stopped and angry pain clouded his face. "It should have worked. Damn it, it should have worked. It shouldn't have gone wrong. Cox and his fear of mutants—it's paranoid. It's *useless*. Who does he think can survive this? And the rest believed him. They want to kill mutants."

"Maybe they just want to kill," Thea said, surprisingly gently.

"And you think that makes it better?" He propped himself on his elbow. "Thea, I was born in 1967. We didn't even *have* mutants then. Oh, we had a few mistakes, thalidomide babies, that kind of thing. But not like today. Women were fertile then, almost all of them. Almost no one had mutant children. There were no Untouchables. It's taken less than fifty years to come to this. Christ!" He flung himself on his side, his back to her.

"Evan?" She waited, but there was no response. "Evan, Cox would have been that way, no matter what. There are people like that."

At that Evan winced. "More of them each year. It doesn't make it any easier." He was silent for a while. "Cox'll make it worse now. There's no one to stop him. He'll make war on mutants, and mutants are our only chance. God, oh God, I should have realized what he is. I should have stopped him."

"But you didn't know."

"I didn't care. I didn't think it was important. I reckoned that when the time came, the men would be on the side of survival. What an arrogant son of a bitch I was." He gave a crack of jeering laughter and then was silent.

Thea lay awake long after Evan's regular breathing told her he was asleep. Alone, softly, to herself, she sang over and over again, those few fragments of music, trying to understand them, to learn what Evan had known when he heard those notes, where his pain had come from.

*   *   *

The days with the families in Quincy faded into weeks. The air grew chill and the last of the crops were brought in and stored against the coming of winter. It was a pleasant life, warm, industrious, friendly, which made its Spartan simplicity easy to bear.

The children, what few there were, wore their deformities without shame and their parents took pride in them and were pleased by their accomplishments. Evan found a strange comfort in this, for it proved him right, if only to himself.

"This is what I should have done," Evan remarked to Rudy Zimmermann as they walked back from the old community college building where they had been trying to tune the old pianos.

"What do you mean?" The air was still wet from recently fallen rain and their breath made ghosts as they walked briskly toward Rudy's house.

"I mean that here you've got what I was trying to build with the Pirates. You have homes, families; you've got . . . hope." He looked away, feeling awkward. "It's too bad about the big Baldwin. I wish there were more strings for it. We could make real music, if we had better strings."

Rudy accepted this turn of conversation. "There's still the Chickering. We haven't tried that one yet. I liked the idea of trying the *Mother Goose Suite* next."

"I'm too rusty for that." Evan blew on his hands. "It's colder."

"There will be snow soon."

Evan nodded absently, his mind elsewhere. Then he stopped, motioning Rudy to do the same.

"What is . . . ?"

"Shush!" He held up his hand for silence, his face intent while he listened. Above the whisper of the trees there was another, buzzing noise. Evan's face set in hard lines. "Methane-powered vans," he said softly.

"I don't hear . . ."

"Listen!" His blue eyes were ice cold. "Six, maybe seven of them. We've got to hurry!" He slapped Rudy on the arm and began to run, not waiting for the German to follow.

"But what is it?"

"It's Pirates, Rudy! They've found you!"

* * *

Only four of the townspeople had been hurt, and now they were being tended expertly in the little infirmary on the north side of town.

"It could have been worse." Honey Hobart was cleaning his shotgun in the middle of the town hall.

"Tell me how?" Evan asked. He was sitting at one of the broad tables, sketches around him and a map spread out for the other men to see.

"They didn't kill any of us, and we wiped out four of them." He put his shotgun down and picked up a rifle.

"Yes, and eight got away. One of them was Joel Mackley, Cox's pet killer. He'll tell Cox what he's found, and they'll be back." He pointed to the map. "Look, Honey, even if that canyon road is in bad shape, there's the railroad bed, and you said yourself that it's being used by Untouchables all the time. If they can follow it, so can Cox's Pirates. And they will. They want your town and they want Thea and me."

Simon shook his head. "All we have to do is lie low, they'll leave us alone. They've stayed in the Valley all these years . . ."

Evan cut him short. "I know these men, Simon. I led them. If you have what they want, they'll take it. You've got to build fortifications, right now. Not today, not tomorrow, now. Start tonight. Get every firearm in town, put it in working order, mount a guard, build watchtowers. You don't have much time."

Honey Hobart stopped his work and held out the oiled rag in his hand. "You said that one of them recognized you. You sure that it's not just your own skin you're protecting?" He paused. "You don't got the right to ask us to ruin our town for you, Montague."

"I'm not asking you to, Honey." Evan had risen, his face desperate. "I'm trying to help you save yourselves. If you won't arm yourselves, protect yourselves, you'll be wiped out."

"Is that a threat, Montague?"

The room was suddenly very still. Evan met Honey Hobart's steady eyes, and when he spoke, there was despair in his voice. "What do I have to do, Hobart? Bleed? Martyr myself? Tell me."

Hobart turned away. "We'll have to vote on it."

*   *   *

It was Simon who told Evan of the decision in the Quincy Council. "We don't really want to, Evan, not even Honey. But you understand," he pleaded, spreading out his hands to demonstrate his helplessness. "You'll have to leave. And Thea, too; they must know she's with you. It's for your own good as much as ours. You've got to understand. It's too dangerous for you here."

Evan watched Simon and saw the dull hurt in the man's eyes. "I hear you," he said, acknowledging the trouble. "And it isn't just us they want, no matter what Hobart thinks. You realize that, don't you? They won't leave you alone now that they know you're here. You have things they want. You have livestock, you have shelter, you have food reserves, all the things the Pirates look for. But it's not only your food and your livestock which attracts them—Cox is fighting a Holy War against Mutes. And it was Mackley who led the scouts. He hates Mutes, too. He's fanatical. He'll bring Cox for the mutants alone."

Simon looked miserable as he drank some of Katherine Zimmermann's herb tea. "We realize that, of course. That's why we're going to send the kids away. Just for the time being. We know a couple of places they'll be welcome, not too far from here. I think maybe we can negotiate about the food. We can explain things to him. We'll work out terms."

"If you pay the Danegeld, you'll never be rid of the Dane," Evan reminded him without rancor.

"But we'll explain all that. We'll arrange to grow more next year, and if they'll co-operate with us, then we'll be able to share. Cox should understand that. You understand it."

"I'm not Cox," Evan said. He knew that Simon was trying to convince himself, but he could not contain himself. "You think Cox is sure to be reasonable? Understand your point of view? Cox only understands the things that enrich him. The things that bring him power and notoriety."

At that Simon flared up. "We have to try it, Evan. Otherwise we might as well lie down and die right here and now." He got to his feet, upsetting the mug, watching unhappily as the green stain spread over Katherine's linen tablecloth. "Damn it, Evan, we're not cruel. We're not going to send you away naked. We'll give you and Thea clothes and supplies. And tools. We'll make sure you have two pair of strong shoes. We aren't monsters, Evan. We know what winter is like. We'll do everything we can to make sure you get through it."

"Except let us stay here."

"Except let you stay here."

Rudy Zimmermann had come to stand in the door, watching.

"Is this what you want, Rudy?" Evan asked, wondering where Thea was, and if she knew what was about to happen to them.

"It is not what I want. You have become my friend, and together we remember the good things which are lost. But this is my home. I must defend it, protect it, no matter what. I have run as far as I'm going to. If you had lived with us, one, two years, perhaps it would be different." He did not meet Evan's eyes, and did not see the compassion there.

Slowly Evan stood up, looking toward the kitchen where Katherine was making supper. He thought idly that he wanted to stay

with these people in this little pocket where there was still a sem-
blance of civilization and life could be pleasant. But he knew that
there was no chance to save Quincy now that the Pirates had seen
it and wanted it. Quincy was doomed, no matter what he did.

"I'll talk it over with Thea. I promise I will go. I cannot speak
for her." He rose and left the dining room, going to the room off
the kitchen where he and Thea had slept together and apart, for
the nine weeks they had been in Quincy. He looked over the small
pile of belongings they had and thought wistfully of the joy of
houses where it was possible to have more than what you could
carry on your back. Kneeling, he touched the shoes Rudy Zimmermann had made for him. Those shoes would have to take him a
long, long way, he thought.

"Evan?" Thea had come into the room behind him, silently.

"They've asked us to leave. They say we make it too dangerous
for them, now that the Pirates are coming."

"But there are Mutes here . . ."

He cut her off. "I know. And who knows? Perhaps they know."
Turning to her, he saw her dark eyes grow distant under her
straight dark brows. "What is it, Thea?"

"Nothing. I thought this might happen. We can go to Gold
Lake now."

"I'd forgotten Gold Lake," he said sadly. He did not want to
pin his hopes on so little.

But Thea did not hear him. "Here. It's yours, like I promised
you." With those jumbled words she thrust a crossbow into his
hands, then turned abruptly and went into the kitchen.

Evan was still, turning the crossbow over in his hands. It was
made from a rifle stock, with the crank from an old coffee mill
scavenged from the abandoned houses on the south side of town.
The trigger release was better made than the one on Thea's own
crossbow. He touched the metal groove; it had been painstakingly
fashioned from the barrel of a 30-gauge shotgun. The wood that
held it was polished and carved in clumsy designs of leaves and
animals.

He came and stood in the kitchen, wondering what to say to
her.

Without facing him, she said, "I'm going with you."

CHAPTER 4

Hobart advised them to stay away from the roads and to seek the high country. "I know it's tough going up there, what with the rocks and snow and all, but the water is pretty pure and no one goes up there, except maybe to hunt. The Pirates won't follow you. They'll stick to the river and follow the highways. You'll be okay up there."

"And you?" Evan asked, adjusting the pack Zimmermann had given him. It was a large affair, holding several pounds of supplies and attached to a sturdy frame that fastened, harness style, to his back.

"I've got a job here still."

"After that, Honey? What if the Pirates come? They will come, you know."

"You're probably right," he allowed, rubbing at his nose.

"You can go into the high country. Join us at Gold Lake."

"Well, I might. If we can't hold out here. Winter's almost on us, and it looks to be a long one. There's lots of berries where the berries still grow." He stepped back from Thea and Evan. "Take care of yourselves. And you can come back in the spring, if you like, when things are better," he said rather foolishly. "Well, good-by." And he turned to walk back into his town.

Evan buckled his jacket tighter as he looked toward the rising mountains south and west of them. "It's a climb," he said.

"I'm ready." Saying that she came as close as she ever did to smiling.

*   *   *

So they backtracked westward into the Sierra Nevada, to the spine of the range, to its rocky summit and safety. They followed the old Buck's Lake Road, bypassing the two burned-out towns they found on the way. The road was steep, and in some places, entirely washed out. They went slowly upward, fighting the mountains and the gathering cold. Soon they would strike south, they told themselves, along the crest to Gold Lake and the community where they would be welcome, where they could help. The Gold Lake community was famous for taking in people with special knowledge, who wanted to rebuild the world without making the old mistakes. It would be good to be at Gold Lake. It would be worth the long, agonizing trek.

The third day out they knew they would not reach Gold Lake before the snows came, for the first light snow had already fallen, and the skies promised another fall in a little while.

There had been strip mining at Buck's Pass. Great slices of mountain had been washed away leaving raw scars against the precarious line of pines. Many of the trees had fallen, their roots exposed and dead where the sluicing had robbed them of their precious topsoil.

To avoid the muddy wreckage of the mining, Thea and Evan took to the trees, but found even this was uncertain. The ground shifted underfoot and they got too near the exposed earth too often. Many of the trees around them, though standing, were dead, habit alone keeping them vertical. As the new snow weighted their branches, they would fall as the others had fallen, widening the swath of destruction across the front of the ancient mountains.

When they reached the crest of the range the air was biting, taking life from their faces and finger tips. Thea pulled her hood closer about her face and wished for heavier mittens. Evan tugged their tarpaulin from his pack and with branches rigged a kind of umbrella against the snow.

It was sunset when they came at last to Buck's Lake. They could see the ice gleaming in the slanting cold rays of the dying day, lighting the lake with an eerie greenness. On the south side of the lake stood the remains of an old resort, and beyond that, a stamp mill from an old mine. In the fading light the buildings looked like headstones, dark shapes without dimension standing as markers to a ruined world.

"Where?" Thea asked breathlessly. The wind was cutting through them, touching them to the bone and slowing their pace.

"The stamp mill. It's more recent. And I bet it hasn't been touched." Evan was rubbing his hands together, the new fingers taking a paler color now, though whether from growth or cold, he could not tell. He tested it and found the joints were stiff. "Another thing," he said after a moment, "if we have heavy snows this winter, the stamp mill is higher. We'll dig out easier, if we have to."

"There could be animals," Thea warned. In her years of traveling alone she had come to fear animals, and knew what hunger could do to them.

"I have a crossbow," he said with a smile. "It's an excellent crossbow."

Thea glared at him. "I don't make bad crossbows. And even if I did, I wouldn't give one to you." She tugged her own crossbow loose from its straps, fixing her dark eyes on the lake. "We might get fish there, but others will be wanting fish, too. This is going to be a bad winter. The ground is getting hard early. There was too little rain, and there'll be too much snow. A lot of plants will die. And a lot of us will die."

As he pulled at his beard, Evan pondered what he had said wrong. There was a set iciness in Thea's face that threatened anger. "Thea, I didn't mean to insult you." He started to move toward her, then changed his mind. "I don't know how I did, but I'm sorry I offended you."

"I hate being patronized," she said, then brusquely changed the subject. "We must get to the stamp mill." Then, as they started down the last decline to the lake, she stopped him, her face drawn and serious. "No, Evan. That isn't what I meant, entirely. I'm cold and frightened. Other times I might not be angry—not very angry. But when I'm frightened, I lash out."

"Frightened? Of what? Of me?"

"I don't know," she said, not entirely honestly. She took her lower lip in her teeth, turning toward the lake to resume her descent. Catching herself on the brittle scrub, she had an excuse to ignore his call that followed her down the mountain.

"Thea!" The word was urgent, but she did not turn. In a while he came down the mountain in her wake, a fine line of worry growing between his brows.

* * *

The old resort had been ransacked some time before, perhaps when the owners left it years ago. Animals had been in since, and there was the unmistakable smell of skunk and a pile of raccoon dung. An old sofa in what had been the lobby yielded tufts of cotton batting and a strong odor of mildew. Most of the linens in the maintenance room were rotting, but two or three blankets were acrylic and were salvageable, if somewhat stiff.

In the kitchen they found four large pots. Evan seized them happily, seeing his tasks as cook becoming easier.

"It's almost dark," Thea called to him from the dining room where she had found utensils for them. "We must get to the stamp mill or be caught here tonight. I don't want to spend the night here." She shifted uneasily. "It's too open."

Grabbing at their bounty, they set out through the dusk to the stamp mill, arriving in the shelter of its steeply slanted roof as the last of the light left the sky. Carefully they made their way up the stairs, testing each riser before they put weight on it. Once the wood gave way, and both cried out as Thea's foot fell through the new hole, splinters flying around it. But at last they came to the office and infirmary, high against the side of the mill, above the workings of the stamps. They had to smash the lock to get in, and once inside, they searched for a chair to jam under the knob to hold the door shut.

In the darkness Evan felt in his pack. "I can't find them," he said after a moment. "I should have candles . . ."

She groped her way to his side. "Hold still," she told him and pulled the pack from his shoulders. "This won't take long. It's easier this way." With a last effort she pulled the flap back, then rummaged around in the pocket. "Wait a minute." At last there was the scrape of a match and a light flickered in the dark.

They looked around in silence. The candle wavered, then shone steadily, giving hints of the room. On one side sat a pot-bellied stove, cold now, and growing rusty. Beside it a rack with books and magazines stood, their shiny covers dull and the photographs faded. Beyond the rack were three chairs, then a door. On the far wall were two more chairs and the door to the infirmary, its label still readable. In the wan light of the candle the walls of the room were mud-colored.

"Home sweet home," Evan said as they stood in the little halo of light. The unused smell was strong, but it would disappear quickly. Already the wax scent of the candle was submerging it.

Thea handed him another candle and lit it from hers. "I'm going exploring," she said, and disappeared into the inner office. In a few minutes she gave a crow of delight and reappeared smiling. "Evan, there's a toilet in there, and a sink. And everything."

"Is the plumbing still good?" he asked, skeptical. It had been a long time since the stamp mill had been occupied, and with freezing winters, the pipes might have long since burst.

"I'll check it," she said eagerly, stepping back into the adjoining room. A few clangs and then a gurgle and the distant sound of splashing. Some more strange sounds followed this, and Thea called, "It empties outside, but it will flush. I think there's a water tank for it on the roof. When it freezes, we can keep a can of water in here, and it'll work okay."

"Well," said Evan to the walls, "that's one less thing to worry about."

"The sink runs off of that tank, too. There isn't any hot water, but that doesn't matter. And once the snows come, there won't be any trouble with getting water." She was genuinely excited as she returned to the outer office, her face showing more color than it had in some time. "What about the infirmary? Have you been in there yet?"

"I leave it to you," he said.

The report from there was good as well. There were five beds and although the mattresses were musty, the room had remained closed, and so there was no real damage done. Once the stove was set to burning, the mattresses could be hauled in to dry. An electric heater in the infirmary was totally useless. They decided to cannibalize it, taking the wire coils and other parts that could be of value. In one of the tall cupboards Thea found more blankets, and luckily these were in good shape aside from needing an airing.

"Oh, Evan, it isn't going to be so bad after all. Not like being outside or in the Valley. We can live here for a while."

"If we're careful," he agreed, kneeling by his pack and pulling out his bedding. "But tonight, even with the blankets, we're going to be cold. Listen to the wind."

The rising wail made the stamp mill thrum as new gusts pressed over the mountains. Thea gave it a moment's attention, then went back to the blankets. "I've been cold before," she said, thinking back to the ten years she had spent by herself, when she had been grateful for a dry spot under a bridge or a barn with enough hay to wrap up in.

"That's no reason to keep on being cold," he said. "We've got to make plans. I think we'd better confine ourselves to one room. Otherwise we waste heat trying to keep everything warm. We'll waste candles, too." As he spoke he dragged the chairs into the center of the room, arranging them so that he could drape a few of the blankets over them, making a kind of tent to insulate them against the freezing night. "We're on the windward side of the range. There's a big chill factor. We'll need to do something about drafts."

"We'll need more than that," she said, and left him for a moment to return lugging a mattress from the infirmary. She flopped it near the chairs. "It doesn't smell very good, but we can put a couple down for sleeping on, and pile a few around the chairs. It ought to help some."

By the light of their two candles they made up their sleeping place, and when it was finished, crawled, fully dressed, into it. "Thea," Evan said in the dark, very softly, "Thea." He felt her shrink from him. "Don't, Thea. I won't touch you if you don't want me to. But it's cold, Thea. We can lie on our sides, back to back. It will help keep us warm. Thea."

"I know." She spoke in a still, small voice. "I don't . . ." She sought his face in the dark, wishing to see what was in his eyes. "It's not you, Evan, not *you*. It's *me*. I just can't. I can't." He reached out his hand to her as she spoke and she grasped it for a moment in hers. Then she pulled away once more. "Let's just sleep. If we get cold, we'll move closer anyway."

* * *

The morning brought new snow. It fell gently from the scudding gray clouds, turning the mountains white and masking the ground so that brush, rocks, and road alike hid under its smooth, treacherous beauty. The trees were bearded in white, but as the wind rose they cast off the snow, postponing the inevitable.

Thea went out early to gather wood, knowing that it would be more and more difficult to find as the winter deepened. She had an ax in her pack now, but it was not designed to bring down full-grown trees. At best she could use it for lopping branches and chopping logs. So she searched with care, returning three hours later, heavily laden with boughs and with the news that she had seen bear tracks on the north side of Buck's Lake. "They'll hibernate soon. But it's not going to be easy with them around.

They're hungry and grouchy." She dumped the wood in the office and set out for more, taking some extra quarrels with her for her crossbow.

Evan re-enforced the door with a drop bolt of heavy planking taken from the mouth of the stamp mill. He found a good supply of candles in three large boxes in the infirmary and five kerosene lamps, all gone dry. He felt relieved to have the candles although the lamps would have been better.

Soon he had the stove fired up, filling the rooms with the dusty stench of disuse until the heat at last burned it off. The mattresses were dragged in near the stove and were aired along with the blankets. Then Evan found another, even larger stove in the shed where ore had been sluiced, and with a great deal of effort and a makeshift block and tackle, he got it to the office and set it up where the desk had been. With Thea's help he attached the chimney of the second stove to that of the first. He felt a first inkling of hope, and said to Thea, "We aren't off to a bad start. We might make it."

"Maybe," she agreed. "We'll be warm when we starve; that's something."

*　　*　　*

Thea caught no fish that first day, nor the second. She was patient, persistent, but she warned Evan that they would have to find food soon. The cans the Zimmermanns had given them would not last much longer, even if they rationed the food more strictly than they were doing already.

"There are more of those strange deer around," she said when they had been at Buck's Lake for several days. The snow was almost a foot deep now, piling up in deceptive drifts. Evan found bark strips and improvised snowshoes for them.

"Strange deer?" he asked as he finished wrapping wire around the heel of the last shoe. It was not a very expert job, but the things worked, and he was not that concerned now about the cosmetic effect.

"You know, like the one we saw outside of Quincy."

Their living quarters were cozily warm, having come to a kind of truce between utility and neatness. Twine stretched between coat hooks had become their clothesline; it held two gently steaming shirts at the moment.

"What was strange about it?"

"It had that hump, remember? Something like cattle, but heavier. Well, there are more like that around here. I saw a couple of them on the north side of the lake. They were feeding on scrub. Maybe I can trap them. I couldn't get close enough for a good shot at them. They'd give a lot of meat, Evan."

Evan nodded. "We might look for traps in the resort. I already checked the stamp mill. Nothing there. But the resort might have had traps around the kitchen, to keep the animals away from the food and maybe pick up a little money on the side from the pelts." He held out two finished snowshoes to Thea. "There. I think it will hold now."

She came closer, bending over his work with him. "They look heavy enough. I guess they'll do. They better." It was getting dark, the twilight coming early as the snow-laden clouds crowded the sky. "Can we see about the traps tomorrow? The snow is getting deep and we'd better put them out soon."

"If that's what you want. Any fish?" He was gathering up his supplies, prepared to store them in the infirmary.

"Not today. There were cat tracks on the ice. We've got competition for the fish."

"A cat? What kind? Puma?"

"No," she shook her head, frowning a little as she visualized the paw prints she had found in the snow. "Not big enough for a puma. It looks more like a bobcat. There's probably some of them left around here."

"A bobcat'll raid traps," he reminded her, feeling cautious.

"Not before I do."

*   *   *

They found the traps they needed, old rusty metal devices with cruel teeth. A good scrubbing put them back in operation, and they set them out near the edge of the lake and around the resort. Each morning they made the rounds of the line, taking their crossbows with them. But it was a lean winter already, and their take was disappointingly small: only one raccoon the first week, and a maimed fox. There were no more signs of the deer.

The catch from the lake was not much better. There were fish in Buck's Lake, that was certain. But they were wary and wise. They avoided holes in the ice, keeping to the deep water.

One snowy afternoon Thea found a bobcat, near starvation,

scrambling at the nearest ice hole after a fish. As she watched, the bobcat overbalanced and fell thrashing into the freezing water. It yowled, making the sound more hideous in its terror. Knowing that she could do nothing, Thea watched as the bobcat lost its strength, growing feeble in its battle, until it slipped under the ice, keening until his head disappeared. She felt an unfamiliar regret in the death of the bobcat, and fell silent then, her thoughts far away. For eleven rootless years she had been on the move, keeping ahead of the Pirates when she could, sliding through the wake of their destruction when they passed her. And it all led to this. She stared at the hole in the ice for a long time.

She remembered the small, protected community outside Cloverdale, tucked into the folds of the hills; it was warm there, and pleasant, and they were prosperous enough. The men who led the group had known from their teaching days at Davis that it would take more than determination to survive what was wrong with the world. They had decided to adapt. They adapted their children. Viral modification, they had called it, when it worked. When it didn't work, it was because of environmental factors. She slid the nictitating membranes over her eyes, her most obvious and most successful modification. In those slow years at Camminsky Creek they had waited, smug in the belief that they would ride the horror out, and in a generation or two emerge as the guiding force of the new world.

Then the C.D. had come, and though they were not Pirates and Montague did not lead them, it was the end of the small, protected community, and the beginning of her wandering. She was wandering still.

The next time she went to the ice hole she thought she saw the bobcat die again. She sat on the ice and wept.

*   *   *

When they finally found one of the deer, it was by accident. They had been without food for two days. The deer, wallowing trapped in a snowdrift on the leeward side of the mountain crest, was much larger and heavier than they had anticipated. At last Evan rigged a sling and between them they dispatched the animal and dragged it out of the drift. They left the guts there for the raccoons to fight over, and by making a rude harness, they hauled the deer back to the stamp mill.

They hung the carcass in the stamp room, hacking up the joints on the big wooden supports that had once held the rockers. With an improvised counterweight, they hung the meat from the ceiling in the freezing air, out of the reach of hungry animals that stalked the mountains. They were all too desperate to do otherwise.

Evan took the upper ribs and with fishing twine rolled a standing roast, reflecting ironically that when he was a child, a standing rib roast of venison was a luxury, available only to the very rich and the privileged. Now it was the best he could find, because most cattle had been slaughtered long ago.

In the wreckage of the resort kitchen he had found bottled herbs, and used them now to make the gamy meat more palatable. "I wish we had some greens, anything green," he complained as he stuffed the meat with the last of the juniper berries. Greens were long under the snow, and he had hurt his new hand digging for them.

"It's this or fish," Thea said, feeling the lack of vegetables as much as he did. "If you like, I'll try digging tomorrow."

He thought it over. "If you have the time, we could use it. There's sure to be dandelions up here somewhere."

"Sure," she agreed quickly, and kept her real opinion to herself.

*   *   *

Sometime toward the end of December the worst blizzard of the winter rolled in out of the north, an angry torrent of snow and ice that buried the world in its wrath, howling down the mountains in demented fury. For three days it clawed at the mountains, wounding them and bandaging them at the same time.

"We're awfully low on wood." Thea frowned at the last remaining stack in the corner by the door. "If this keeps on much longer we'll be like everything else out there—waiting to thaw."

"We can break up the chairs," Evan said shortly as he worked with his file on new quarrels. His regenerated hand ached abominably and his muscles were taut against the hurt.

"And then?" she demanded, waiting for an answer. "We break up the chairs . . ." When the silence grew heavy she slammed down the whetstone she was using on their hunting knife. *"And then!"*

His eyes were clouded as he looked at her. "Then we freeze."

She was about to make a sharp retort, but kept it to herself, returning her attention to honing the knife. They both worked in silence; only the muffled howl of the wind whispered to the fire that crackled in the larger of the two stoves. Only the occasional *whick* of their tools ventured against the sound of the storm.

As the early darkness closed in, Thea moved closer to Evan, who had the only candle—and that was sputtering now, nearly used up, guttered—and jealously guarded the little light.

"Maybe we could save the wax," she said, seeing the puddle at the bottom of the dying candle.

"Do you want me to get another candle?" he asked as the one they had winked out.

"How many do we have left?"

"Eight or nine," he said after touching the box. In the muted light from the fire in the stove, he counted out the remaining candles and reluctantly set up another for burning. "It will take us through tonight, and part of tomorrow night. If we're careful, maybe we can get a whole week out of what we have left." He sounded almost confident, but it went no further than the force he gave his voice.

"Maybe we can make up torches. There's enough of the old kind of pines around. We'd have to tap them for sap," Thea said, her eyes fixed on the piles of cut wood which had shrunk quickly during the blizzard. "We have to get more fuel, anyway. We might as well get enough to make torches."

"Sure," he agreed, believing none of it. The very thought of torches in a wooden building brought back memories of towns in flames, always the aftermath of a Pirate battle. Burning towns had a special smell, a smell he had come to hate. "It isn't a good idea to use torches in here, though. Too easy to catch fire, and then where would we be?" Very deliberately he kept his tone flat, emotionless.

Reluctantly she accepted that, her hands going white at the knuckles to show the strain she felt. They worked silently once more, each shutting out the other as they battled private worry. The night deepened, spreading cold like a deadly frosting over the mountains, sending a numbing chill into the little office of the stamp mill, a subtle cold that defied the fire Evan kept burning in the big-bellied stove.

Thea put her scissors down, the last of the items she had set out for sharpening. Her hands moved stiffly now, and when she tried

False Dawn

to speak she found that her face ached. "Does your arm hurt?" she asked Evan in order to ask him something.

"Some."

"I'm sorry." She moved slowly to her mattress on the far side of the stove and there she sank tentatively to her knees, shivering. She fingered the blankets, lost in thought. Then, quite suddenly, she said, "Oh, Evan, let's get out of here. We'll die if we don't; I know we will."

"In the dead of winter?" It was an automatic response.

"It's better than sitting here waiting."

Startled by the urgency in her words, Evan looked up, his irritation forgotten.

"We can start for Gold Lake as soon as the blizzard is over. It's southeast of here, and we've got a compass. Hobart told us the trails we should take. We can find them, if we look. Evan, please, *please,* I don't want to die here, trapped. I can't."

"Thea," he began as calmly as he could. "If we start before the thaw comes, it will be worse out there than it is in here. Believe me. You think it over."

"It's not worse!" she shouted with venom as she tore at the old blankets. "Anything is better than this. My hands are swollen. My teeth hurt. I bruise all the time. And when the thaw comes it will be worse. We've just about fished the lake out now. We've scavenged everything we can reach that's halfway edible. What do you think it will be like when the bear come out of hibernation? There aren't going to be enough rabbits to go around. There aren't going to be enough *mice.* Are you up to fighting a bear, Evan? Right now? It'll be worse then. We won't have any strength. Could you fight a hungry puma? Or coyote?"

"They don't attack people," Evan said reasonably.

"Would you like to make a bet? They've had a lot of lean years, these animals. I don't imagine they're too particular about the meat they get, as long as it doesn't have too many maggots." She had hugged the blankets to her and now was rocking back and forth. "Puma, bears, foxes, there's a lot of them with teeth that are hungry. When the thaw comes, it'll be lots of them. They'll be hungry, hungry."

"Stop it, Thea," he said, putting his work aside.

"Bones and bones and bones," she murmured, ignoring him. "Blood first, for fertilizer, and then the bones. They'll grow a bumper crop. Bones, all over bones. Bones grow in poison where nothing else grows. And there's enough poison to go around, everywhere . . ." Her crooning was cut short. Evan dragged her to her feet, shaking her with a fear that made him rough.

"Stop it!" His shout brought no response to her glazed, unseeing eyes. *"Thea! STOP IT!"*

Recognition came back into her face. "Evan? Evan . . . I didn't . . . I never meant . . ." She began to tremble, the strength gone out of her now. Shamed, she knelt on the mattress, her face white. At last the trembling passed, and she said in a still voice, "I've never had to wait like this. There was always something I could *do* before. It's killing me, this waiting. When I sleep, all I dream about is getting away. I wake up, and there's no way out. I can't escape. But I've got to do something, Evan. I can't wait any longer: I'm going crazy."

Standing beside her, Evan longed to comfort her, but knew that he didn't have the words for it. Gently he touched her shoulder, and for once she did not draw back from him.

"You don't have to leave with me," she said reasonably. "There's no reason you should. But I've got to get out of here as soon as the blizzard stops. Really. I must." She plucked aimlessly at the blanket, unable to look at him. "I used to think that it was only those people who couldn't deal with the world the way it is who went crazy. But that's not so, is it?"

"We're all vulnerable, Thea." For a moment memories of the Pirates were vivid in his mind. How had he ever consented to such barbarity? What had made him think that he could salvage civilization through rapine? "And there's more than one way to be crazy. I know. *I know.*"

* * *

The next day the blizzard began to abate, but the snow still fell and the winds pawed at the stamp mill, like some wild creature hunting food. Where the winds had sculpted crests and hollows the snow now came there, smoothing away the roughness, wrapping safety and danger alike in white swaddling.

In the stamp mill, Thea and Evan at first made feeble jokes about their last candle, but when it had burned down and winked out, they did not speak to each other. Shortly after that they ran out of cut wood for their stove, and ended by breaking up the heavy desk in the inner office, feeding it bit by carefully rationed bit into the dying fire. Eventually that, too, was gone and they were left to the dark and the cold.

Then, through the stillness there came light. It touched the snow and made rainbows there. The brightness seeped into the stamp mill, making it glow softly as if the rooms were under water. And although the cold was no less intense than it had been through the night, the morning made it more bearable.

"There's a shovel in the infirmary." Thea made this announcement through stiff, chapped lips. "I think we can dig out if we try."

Evan pulled himself uncertainly to his feet. "The door will be snowed in," he said, thinking of the lower level door, which by now was under six feet of snow.

"There's that porch off the infirmary. We can go out that way." To say those words, words that meant her release from this frozen prison, lightened Thea's mood, giving her a burst of new strength. She started gathering up her few belongings to arrange them in her pack. "I'll be ready to go in a bit," she said as she worked.

"Do you want to do that now or later?" Evan asked, growing impatient with himself. "It's going to take time to dig out. We can do that today, get some wood, do our packing tonight, and be underway just after sunup."

"So long? I thought . . ." She realized then that she hadn't thought, and she considered his suggestion. "Maybe you're right. Maybe we'll get something to eat. Then we won't have to walk hungry." She nodded at her own resolution. Now that she knew her stay in the stamp mill was almost over, she was not frightened by it. "We'll dig out now, to hunt. You can get the wood. You're right about leaving, we can't do it today. Tomorrow morning, then. Early."

*   *   *

Even with her enthusiasm it took them over three hours to clear a trough through the snow into the day. After the dark of the cramped office in the stamp mill the sun off the snow dazzled them and made the expanses around them disorienting. It was as if they had stepped into an entirely different world from the one they had left, so changed were the mountains after a mere four days.

Shading his eyes, Evan blinked back the glare. The prospect of traveling in this shattering brightness did not please him. Everywhere lay the flawless, treacherous snow. "When I was a kid," he said as he tested the surface, "we'd go skiing. All the skiers talked about powder and packed base and slush." He felt the white stuff turn to water in his hand, running through his fingers leaving only cold behind. He wondered what those long-ago skiers would have made of this waste. Snow then had been a recreation, an escape from the organized tedium of winter cities. Skiing snow was not at all like the snow that clogged traffic and turned city streets to slippery, hazardous trials. This snow was of another sort—vast and dangerous, like the sea, beautiful, like the sea, deadly, waiting for that one mistake to wrap them in its frigid embrace forever.

"It's awfully bright," Thea said, thinking of the long days' walks they would make through the mountains. This light would be like shards of glass in their eyes. She knew enough about snow blindness to fear it.

Evan sensed her worry and shared it. "Yes. It's going to be difficult."

"I don't see any tracks, do you?" There was an anxious note in her voice.

"No. We'd better get our snowshoes."

Several hours later they found a couple of frozen rabbits, and when he cleaned and gutted them, trimming away the worst of the flesh, precious little was left to go into the stewpot. While Evan worked on this unpromising meal, Thea gathered up the boughs which the weight of snow had pulled off the trees. This took her longer than she had anticipated and it was almost dusk when she returned to the stamp mill.

"I was getting worried," Evan said lightly as Thea lugged two large branches in through the infirmary.

"So was I." She swung the branches into the room. "I've got another three of these. That should take care of tonight."

He looked at the boughs. "I'll use the hatchet on these. Do you need help with the rest?"

She rubbed her hands briskly. "No. But I could use a fire. We've got a couple boxes of matches left, haven't we?"

"More or less." He had taken the hatchet from its place on the wall, and now, going onto one knee, he began to chop the boughs into manageable sections. "One last night," he said when she came back with the other branches. "Tomorrow, off to Gold Lake."

Thea finished securing the doors as he said this, and coming back into the room, she said, "It'll be better there, Evan. You'll see. It won't be like this."

Out of his doubts, Evan asked, "What *will* it be like, Thea?"

She thought this over before answering him. "It will be different."

*   *   *

Packing was painful, for they had to leave some of their things behind: food and eating utensils, a pot or two, one box of matches, a few small knives, part of their dwindling supply of first aid equipment, all were sorted and sifted, then packed carefully in order of need.

"Too bad we can't take one of the stoves," Thea said with an attempt at humor. "It was sure nice to have them. I'll miss them."

"There'll be other stoves at Gold Lake," Evan assured her, as much to quiet his uncertainty as hers. "Better stoves, probably."

Thea looked up from the last of her packing, her face flushed with anticipation. "Everything will be better there," she announced. "You'll see."

CHAPTER 5

They went east into the sun with the morning, following the line of what they hoped was Haskins Valley, where once there had been a trail, and perhaps still was, deep under the snow. They went slowly, their path spreading out behind them, tracks huge from their snowshoes, looking like some long-fossilized monster had returned to haunt the mountains.

At the end of the first day they were exhausted, their legs leaden and deeply sore, their eyes shot with red from the fierce light off the snow. They made camp for the night not far from the ruins of an old mine, the most protected location they had seen all day. Their makeshift tent sprawled over the snow, suddenly rickety and uncertain shelter against the night.

"It'll be fine," Thea said, her conviction sounding forced, even to her. She barricaded one end of the tent with her pack, and strapped her crossbow to her arm.

"I don't know if we can get a fire going," Evan said after a moment. There were small bits of kindling at his feet, and they sat on the snow like an abandoned bird's nest, giving no promise of warmth.

"Then we can eat the meat cold. It's cooked enough," Thea said, determined not to be discouraged.

So they ate their cold food, huddling near the tent as the sun sank below the jagged horizon. Wind sliced at them as night fell. The trees, with their burden of snow, sang to one another in eerie harmony.

When they had finished their sparse meal, Evan buried the bones in the snow, feeling both foolish and frightened as he worked.

In the tent they lay near each other, wrapped like cocoons in heavy blankets, each trying to forget the aches in stiff muscles which were magnets to the cold. They had a long way to go, and the next day would be no warmer.

"Evan?" Thea's voice sounded far away in the little tent.

"Yes?"

"Remember when you were talking to Rudy Zimmermann about music and your father? Is this the kind of music you meant?" And she sang the few words in her small, quavering voice, words about love and betrayal: *"Sola, perduta e abbandonata/ In landa desolata . . ."* She stopped. "I don't know if the words are right, but is that what you were talking about?"

He was genuinely surprised. "That's from Puccini's *Manon Lescaut.* Where did you hear it?"

"I don't remember very well. I think my father used to play it, when we were still in Davis and had a record player. Sometimes my mom sang it, at Camminsky Creek. It always upset people when she did. It's been running around in my head all day." She made an apologetic sound. "I just wanted to know: what does it mean?"

Reluctantly, he told her. "It says, 'Alone, lost, and abandoned in a desolate place.'"

"Oh. I guess that's why people didn't like it. I just wanted to know." Then, after a moment she said, "There was another one, about a father asking his son to come home. It was pretty. Jack Thompson would sing it, sometimes."

"Do you remember any of it?"

"Not really." She pulled her blankets more tightly about her so that almost all of her face was covered. In a while she was asleep. But beside her Evan lay awake for long hours, listening to his memories.

*   *   *

The next day found them farther along their path. They knew they would have to find Sawmill Tom Trail if they were to get through the mountains quickly. Hobart had told them where it lay, but all the landmarks described were under the snow now. They struggled through the brightness, their eyes burning as the day wore on and the sun swung over their right shoulders. Once or twice they saw shapes moving through the trees, animals without features or definition moving silently over the snows, anonymous as shadows.

"Do you think they're stalking us?" Thea asked when two more shapes had melted away in the dark under the trees. The wind was moving mournfully, touching the forest with wisps of low-flying clouds which Thea watched anxiously. "It's piling up in the east. I think it will snow again tonight," she said when the clouds grew denser.

"I'll cover the tent with boughs. It will give us some insulation." Evan glanced at the compass as he spoke. "We should find a ghost town a few miles on. Oddle Bar, or something like that."

A cry from a cold, wild thing rose in the woods. "Maybe we can get there tonight? It would be good to sleep indoors again," Thea said, feeling gooseflesh rise on her arms as a grue touched her spine.

"That sounds like dogs: the wolves were killed off a long time ago, and I don't think there are coyotes up here," Evan said calmly as the sound came again.

The eerie wail was still moving through the trees when they stopped for the night. Oddle Bar lay too far ahead of them, hidden by the shoulder of the mountain, and lost in the coming night. They had waited dangerously long to make their camp and Evan worked in worried haste to cover the tent with rusty-needled pine boughs. Once more they ate their evening meal cold and in listening silence, burying the scraps deep in the snow before going into their blankets.

* * *

It was well into the night when they were awakened—sounds of a desperate fight dimly penetrated the pine boughs and canvas tent. First there were snarls, then whining challenges, then they heard the deadly struggle accented by yelps of pain and fury.

"Dogs?" Thea asked in a whisper which Evan silenced with his hand on her wrist.

Now the bodies of the fighting animals crashed against the tent, bringing down the limbs which had protected it. A sudden stench filled the air.

"Opened the guts, I think," Thea whispered, feeling sick. A stinking wet patch was spreading on the tent wall a few inches from her face. Abruptly the animals rolled back against the tent once more and the material pressed downward, taut under the thrashing bodies.

Involuntarily Thea let out a scream. For a moment the unseen combatants stopped their ruthless battle, but then the fight was resumed, more ferocious than before, and more desperate. Thea drew away from her side of the tent as the canvas ripped, revealing a dog's hind paw and the bloodied head of a raccoon that snapped its jaws spasmodically, closing on the dog's leg with an awful splintering of bone. The dog howled, jerking against the relentless raccoon, freeing himself at last as the masked muzzle lunged again.

"Thea! *Oh, God, Thea!*" The cry was wrenched out of Evan as he saw in the pale light, long stained fangs close on Thea's hip, sinking through the double layer of blankets to her body.

Thea twisted, shouting and striking out with the full force of her straight arm. The raccoon snarled, confused, then was dragged from the tent as the dog closed in for the end of the fight, whining as the raccoon met the attack with teeth and supple, grasping paws.

The sounds went on, then one of the animals coughed and the fight was over. The survivor began to feed.

"Thea?" Evan began anxiously.

She moved away from him, her words brusque to cover the nauseating hurt. "It's all right. I'll be fine. He got more of the blankets than me." As she pulled fruitlessly at the ripped tent, she went on. "I've got a couple of scratches, that's all."

Again Evan reached out. "Let me look at them."

Thea moved beyond his extended hand. "It's too dark, Evan. You can look in the morning, if it's still bothering me. Too bad about the tent. Do we have needles and thread?"

"I can fix it," he assured her, puzzled by her refusal to be helped. He knew she had been hurt; he had seen her face. He thought that perhaps she still could not bear his touch.

"We'd better do that in the morning." She pulled the blankets around her tightly and shut herself away from him, keeping her hurt to herself in the dark.

*   *   *

The morning was hazy, high ribbons of clouds taunting the sun, throwing soft, indistinct patterns on the snow.

The first thing Thea saw as she crawled out of the torn tent was the mauled body of the dog. Its stomach had been ripped away and the raccoon had made a solid meal of what he found. Near the remains there was a hole in the snow where the two animals had dug for the scraps from their dinner of the night before.

"So that's what brought them," Evan said slowly as he emerged from the tent. "I wondered about that last night." He turned to Thea, still concerned, still wanting to see what had happened to her hip. "How do you feel? Is the bite better?"

"I'm fine," Thea said, which wasn't an answer.

"Let me look at it," Evan persisted.

"I said I'm fine." Then she changed her mind. "Oh, go ahead and check it if you think it's that important. It's nothing more than a scratch. Really." Sulkily she opened her trousers and pulled the heavy cloth away from the gash on the top of her hip. She winced as the scabs tore.

"Is there some antiseptic in the first aid kit? It should help," Evan said steadily after examining the four deep furrows the fangs had left in her skin. Five years ago, he would have worried about rabies, but by now most of the rabid animals were dead and their disease had died out with them.

"Do you think it needs it?" she asked indifferently.

He began to find her attitude irritating. "That depends on whether you're planning to walk very far today. If you want to cover any distance, then I'd say you need something for it, yes." As Evan treated and bandaged the wound, he asked her, "Do you think you can carry your pack?"

"Of course," she snapped.

"I'll take some of your load, if you like?" He was bandaging the hip now, padding the hurt with gauze before sealing it with the last of their adhesive tape.

Instead of answering him, she said, "I remember when I was little, there used to be this stuff you could just spray on cuts and they'd stop hurting and heal over. Tissue cement, that was it. The vets used it for a long time before it was used on people. I sure wish we had some. It worked great. Better than this."

Evan finished his work. "You can button up your shirt now. It's all done. I'll help you on with the pack." This time it was not a request.

"Okay. But I can manage, Evan. I've managed before."

Stung, he said, "Then do it yourself."

She slung the pack over her shoulder, grimacing as she tugged the lower straps firmly into place. The buckles were awkward, but she soon had them secured and her pack properly balanced.

Evan watched her as she tightened the last of the straps. "From now on," he said, "you get help when you ask for it. You're right: you can manage."

Thea looked through lank strands of dark hair. "So can you."

* * *

By midday they had reached the ghost town of Oddle Bar. They had come upon it in a southward turn of the trail, down the side of a rugged river canyon, now lost under deceptive drifts. There, where the mountain made its elbow crook, the town was perched, the old buildings leaning dilapidatedly under their deep thatches of snow.

"I guess we don't sleep out tonight," Thea said as she caught sight of the town. There was unmistakable relief in her words. "They aren't much, but they're better than the tent."

"We'll have shelter, anyway," Evan said, trying not to feel too happy about their discovery. "Those two on the upper slope; they look most likely. Better keep your crossbow ready." Evan sensed something, an itch in his mind. He did not trust the town, or its appearance of safety. To justify his discomfort, he reminded Thea, "We aren't the only animals looking for shelter."

Thea nodded, beginning to feel the hurt from her bite all the way down her leg. She did not particularly care about the danger. The lure of the old houses, and the rest they represented, pulled at her. She notched her crossbow, setting the trigger, and reached for a quarrel.

An old voice, breaking from lack of use, announced, "You two creeps come one step closer and I'm gonna kill you." This was followed by the unmistakable sound of a rifle being cocked.

Evan stopped, his arm out to shield Thea. They looked at each other, and seeing the same wary fright in one another's eyes, they waited.

"How'd you get here?" demanded the old voice.

"We came over from Buck's Lake," Evan answered, raising his arms as he spoke, showing the voice that he was unarmed.

"There ain't nobody left at Buck's Lake."

"We came in before the snows, from the east. It was deserted then. We're going south now. To Truckee." It was a lie, of course, but Evan did not dare say too much to the old voice. He looked around cautiously, wondering if there were more than one person waiting in the old houses.

"You with that thing on your arm. Take it off and come closer. Both of you."

"I'm not giving up my crossbow," Thea whispered fiercely.

"Hurry it up!" the voice ordered impatiently.

"Look," Evan called to the voice in the house. "We can't leave our weapons out here. They'll be ruined. She'll take the quarrel out of the slot . . ." He motioned to Thea, and she reluctantly withdrew the quarrel. "There. It's unarmed now. It's not loaded." He took a cautious step forward, the quarrel still in his hand.

"You put that thing in your pocket, mister."

Evan did as he was told, keeping a surreptitious eye on Thea. "I've done that," he called when the quarrel was tucked away.

"Right. The lady got any more of them?"

"Yes. In my pack!" Thea shouted resentfully.

"Then you can start walking up here, real slow. No talking between yourselves. You can walk nice and easy so's I can get a better look at you. I don't want no damn raiders or Pirates in here."

Thea shot a look at Evan, who shrugged and started toward the largest house on the upper slope. He kept both of his hands in plain sight. Thea shook her head, but followed him through the snow, their progress marked by the undulating path of their shadows stark as ink at their feet.

When they were no more than twenty feet from the door the voice spoke again, sounding even more like a rusty hinge. "Come in one at a time: I want to check you over."

"No," Evan said quickly. "Both of us or none."

"Maybe the lady feels differently," said the voice slyly.

"I feel the same," Thea said immediately.

There was a rustle in the house and then the voice spoke from further back in the darkness. "Okay, you creeps, you can come in. But take it slow. No sudden moves. No talking. And no falling over or any of that. I know all those tricks. I'll shoot you if you try anything."

Thea and Evan exchanged one quick look, then entered the old house. The room they came into was obviously an old bedroom on the second story of the building. Flowered wallpaper peeled like bark from the walls, and two wardrobes flanked the door. The rest was monastically simple, having a hard chair, a table, and a small stove, which glowed now with warmth and added a soft, ruddy light to that provided by a branch of candles.

"You can put them packs down," the voice said from beyond the inner door. "But look you do it careful."

"Look, old man," Evan said, trying to be patient. "You ordered us up here. You're the one with the gun. What do you think we're . . ."

"I ain't no *old man!*" shrieked the voice. There was a loud clang as the rifle fell to the floor, and in a moment a wizened old woman, her face as dark and twisted as a walnut, stormed into the room. She was dressed in a violent orange skiing jacket and electric blue thermal pants, which were tucked untidily into beautiful high suede boots. Her sparse, filthy hair was elaborately set and cascaded around her face in greasy ringlets. She was almost as tall as Evan, and it was he she confronted.

"What do you mean, calling me a man. I am not, *not* a man."

"Yes, I can see that," Evan told her gently, wondering where she had got the clothes she wore. The smell of her was like a separate presence in the room.

She seemed to find Evan's reaction flattering, for she giggled girlishly and struck a pose. "Do you like this? Real special. No one ever looked at me, back then." She twirled on her toes. "Bet you haven't seen an outfit like this before."

"I haven't," Evan said truthfully. "Where did you get it?" He hoped that this strange old woman might be willing to give him extra information.

"This old rag? I've had it for years." She coquetted in the doorway, touching her hair. "They left them behind. When the Oroville Dam got blown up, before all that big flap about the radiation leaking in the dumps off the coast, all the guests left. . . . And they didn't take their stuff, not all of it. So I took what I wanted." Her old eyes grew dreamy. "It was wonderful, all those pretty things. And perfumes. And jewels."

"Guests?" Evan asked, incredulous. By no stretch of the imagination could Oddle Bar have accommodated guests in over a hundred years. "Here?"

"Of course not, silly man. I worked at Squaw Valley, the place where they had the Winter Olympics, a long time ago. It was quite a place for a while. It had some bad times, too. But all the best people came there, in their fancy cars and furs. Some of them had posh houses in the Valley, and some stayed at the hotels there. It was really something, mister. But when the dam went, the troopers ordered us out of there. I took my time leaving." She touched her hair again, a delicate, primping gesture that was as ludicrous as it was frightening.

"Took your time? Didn't the troopers make you leave with the others?" He knew that this was the question he was supposed to ask, and that her answer was something she would be very proud of.

"They couldn't make me go: they couldn't find me. Let me tell you, it was confusing there, all those rich people in their expensive cars, all of them scared about the bombs planted in the mountains. That's what the troopers said, that there were bombs in the mountains and that they were going to blow them up. They did, too. You should've seen them run. Leaving tons of pretty things. I helped myself. I got more'n three hundred outfits, some I haven't even worn yet. They're gonna last me a lifetime." She laughed quite suddenly, showing dark brown stumps where her teeth had been.

"Three hundred?" Thea stopped in the door, watching the old woman with increasing alarm. She could feel the hair on her neck rise as she watched the old woman pout for them before crowing, "And they're all mine! The prettiest clothes in the world!"

"You must enjoy them," Evan said, making his face smile.

But already the old woman had changed again. A crafty look stole into her bright eyes. "You said you come from Buck's Lake. Where were you before that?"

"Portola," Thea said before Evan could answer. "Out of Idaho." Her eyes dared Evan to contradict her.

"You come a long way," the old woman said carefully, measuring them from under her hooded lids. "I disremember the last time I got someone from Idaho. Must've taken a long time, coming all that way."

"Two years," Evan said, shrugging out of his pack. "We're trying for the coast; if we can get to Truckee, we can follow the highway down."

"Why'd you leave?" The question came like a gunshot.

Evan had an answer ready for her, but he hesitated, as if it were hard to talk of. "You heard about that poison gas? That the Army buried out in the mountains?" He felt glad weakness come over him as the old woman favored him with a guarded nod.

"Well," he said, deliberately pausing for effect. "It leaked."

"Yep." The old woman gave a rusty bray of laughter. "I know about that."

What Evan had told her was true enough. Some of the Pirates had drifted in from that part of the country, telling stories of dead livestock, of ranchers killed by the air, lying rotting in the open, their faces blistered and burned.

"That was some time back," the old woman recalled, reaching once more for her rifle.

"For the most part, it was. The big leaks, that is. But that gas spreads, like fog. In time it reached us. And some of the smaller containers didn't rupture until later. We thought we could hold out in the mountains back of Twin Falls, but then, year before last, all the sheep died and the people a couple of miles away started to get sick. So we left. There wasn't anything else we could do." Thea was always surprised at how easily she could lie. It was as if she were outside herself, and let another woman live in her for the lie. She almost believed for a moment that she had lived in Idaho raising sheep.

"Too bad," the old woman said perfunctorily. "But it won't do you no good to go to the coast. It's all dead down there. Been dead for years. And there's Pirates all over the roads."

"Pirates?" Evan asked, as if the word were new to him.

"Yep. You know, raiders. They come in, take over, loot and all. Then, when they've used the place up, they burn it down and go on." She chuckled. "But they ain't never found me. Don't know how to. Couldn't get up here if they wanted to. Come to think of it, they did get as far as Graeagle last month, where all them golf people used to come. But them Pirates didn't come up here." Abruptly she sat on the floor, patting it. "Sit down. Sit down. You can relax. I ain't gonna do nothing to you. You're okay, I can see that. Sit down."

Obediently Evan folded onto the floor, leaning back against his pack, seemingly at ease, but watching the old woman carefully.

"Tell me more about the Pirates. I haven't heard about them." He smiled as he said this while a cold fear gathered in him: he realized that the Pirates had to reach Graeagle through Quincy.

"They're a bad bunch, them Pirates. Mean, I tell you, they're so mean they skin people, yep, they do. And make leather with the hides." The old woman went on with her recital of the horrors the Pirates had committed, adding her own thoughts when the facts grew dull. She talked in the singsong way that people who talk to themselves often use. The words were so familiar to her that they had lost much of their meaning. Once started, she spoke in a rush, as if a dam had broken.

Thea listened to the babble in fear. The old woman was danger-ous. She could feel it in the air. She was wrong. Try as she could, Thea could not rid herself of the deep conviction that the talkative old woman would harm them if she could.

". . . And then there was the trouble on the Sacramento when all the insecticides got dumped in the river by accident, which made that big mess all the way down to San Francisco Bay. . . . Killed the fish, killed the insects, and then the birds died, most of them. I guess you noticed that. Don't see birds here but once in a while. I ain't heard birds in years. . . . Don't miss 'em much, up here. I got other things to think about. But it was a dumb thing to do. That's what I think. Nobody planned anything right. . . . But there," she interrupted herself at last. "You two are hungry, aren't you? Serving food, that used to be my job back at Squaw Valley. I'll get right on it." She bustled to her feet, the garish clothes like beacons in the darkening room. "Fancy me forgetting my manners like this. I got food here, and you folks are wanting a meal. I'm willing to share with you. I got more'n enough. Come on down and look for yourself. I'll fix some of it up for us. There's plenty of cans still. I took boxes and boxes of canned food, not just my pret-ties. I figured back then that Safeway was closed for good, you know."

"Thanks very much," Evan said guardedly as he got to his feet. "We'd be happy to share a meal with you . . ." He left the name he did not know up in the air.

The old woman let out a cackle. "Y'mean I ain't told you my name yet? Lordy, what you must think of me. I'm Margaret Cor-nelia Lewis. Ain't that a mouthful? Who're you?"

"My name is David Rossi," Evan answered, using the name he had given Thea when they first met. "That's Thea."

"Mr. and Mrs. Rossi, heh? Sounds kind of Italian. You Ital-ian?" she demanded, peering closely at Evan's sandy hair and faded blue eyes.

"Part," he said truthfully. He looked quickly at Thea, hoping she would not object to the lie of their marriage. "We're sure grateful for your hospitality," he went on rapidly, hoping to get onto safer ground.

"Well. Well, Mr. and Mrs. Rossi. You're my first guests in ages," Margaret Cornelia said happily, and went bustling out the door and down the stairs, calling as she went. "Give me a couple of minutes and I'll do something about supper."

"Evan, let's get out of here," Thea whispered urgently. "Something's wrong, I can feel it." She looked toward the stairs where Margaret Cornelia had disappeared. "She's crazy, Evan. Truly crazy."

"Yes," he replied. "But we've got shelter and a hot meal."

"I don't care. I wouldn't care if there was food enough for a year. We've got to get out of here. Promise me we won't stay. Promise. She's terrible. We aren't safe."

"Let's see how it goes," he hedged. He was hungry and he knew that Thea's bite was worse, for he had seen her go white about the eyes as they walked, though at the time she had denied the hurt. "If it doesn't work out, we'll leave."

"Promise!" she insisted as they heard Margaret Cornelia coming back up the stairs, her voice growing louder.

"Mr. Rossi. Mrs. Rossi. It's me."

Evan nodded to Thea. "All right. I promise," he said as he turned to greet their hostess.

"For the occasion. What do you think of it?" said Margaret Cornelia from the door. She had changed from her skiing clothes into a long dress bright with sequins. It was several sizes too large for her and the cloth hung in shiny folds between her shrunken breasts. Her shoes had very high heels and were of some shiny material colored an improbable red. "This being such a special night I thought I'd dress up." She turned provocatively in front of Evan. "Well?" she asked coyly. "What do you think of me, Mr. Rossi? Isn't this chic?"

"It's quite a dress," Evan said in complete honesty. Out of the corner of his eye he saw Thea move back from Margaret Cornelia, looking blankly at her.

"I bet you never saw anything like this, Mrs. Rossi. This dress, why there hasn't been a dress like this made around here for close on twenty years," Margaret Cornelia said to her, interpreting Thea's reaction as stunned admiration.

"Not ever. I never saw one like that."

Margaret Cornelia smiled complacently. "It's nice to dress for dinner, I always say. It's one of those nice things people don't do any more."

"There's a lot of nice things people don't do any more," Thea said.

"Yep. That's true enough." With a flirtatious turn of her head, Margaret Cornelia waited for Evan's hand. "Mr. Rossi, you'll be my escort down, won't you? It's always nice to go to dinner on a gentleman's arm."

As Thea followed the two to the stairs, she said suddenly, "Do you have an outhouse? Or a bathroom?"

"Sure do. Down the hall and to the left. It works fine most of the time. Just don't flush unless you have to. You know what ice does to the plumbing, and it's harder all the time to get replacements. Be gentle."

"I'll be careful with the plumbing," Thea said stonily, going where the ancient fingers had pointed while Margaret Cornelia swept on on Evan's arm.

* * *

The bathroom was filthy, as Thea had thought it might be. Years of excrement clung to the toilet bowl and the smell, deadened by the cold, still hit Thea like a muffling blanket as she opened the door. Feeling ill, she relieved herself in the sink, that being marginally clean. She was about to bolt out of this ghastly room when she saw a door on the far side of the toilet. Fighting down the bile taste in her mouth, she decided to investigate.

The room beyond had once been a sun porch, but was now a butcher's locker. Sides of meat hung from the ceiling on heavy hooks. There were hump-shouldered deer, what looked like the remains of a bear, and half a dozen limbless human carcasses. They hung, neatly gutted, still in the frozen air, waiting to provide Margaret Cornelia with variety in her meals.

Slowly Thea crossed the small room, numb horror making her steps jerky. At last she reached out and touched one of the bodies, and her senses recoiled as she felt the cold, clay-colored flesh. Blindly she turned away from the carnage, wanting to cleanse her sight with the chaste coldness of the snow beyond the window. She fixed her eyes on the purple shadow that lay over the side of the mountain, and it was then that she saw the footprints. There must have been eight, ten sets of them, all quite new, all leading to the ancient building next door. Panic thudded in her chest, in her brain, and she clapped her hands over her mouth, turning away from the new threat outside. She collided with one of the bodies and had to fight her own rising fear before she could steady the swinging carcass and reset the hook in the shoulder.

Carefully telling herself that any disturbance to the body would surely be noticed by Margaret Cornelia's bright, piercing eyes, Thea backed from the meat locker, revulsion flowing through her like strong acid. She made her way back past the encrusted toilet and ruined tub to the door, slipping out without touching anything in the room again. Once out the door, Thea leaned against it, as if to shut away forever the things she had seen there. She knew that she must tell Evan, that they had to leave, and soon, or they would end up hanging from hooks with the others. As she neared the bottom of the stairs, she was hoping fervently that it would be bear or venison on the table.

"There you are," cried Margaret Cornelia from the door to the kitchen. She was looking archly at Evan as Thea came into the room. "Sorry it's a little messy in the bathroom right now, but you know how it is. I've been so busy I haven't had time to clean up. It's hard to keep up, with the snow and all."

Thea gave some neutral answer and glanced at Evan, trying to let him know she had to speak to him.

"Oh, now, you mustn't be jealous, Mrs. Rossi," Margaret Cornelia said, wagging a finger at Thea. "You can't blame a girl for flirting with a handsome man, can you. Especially someone like Mr. Rossi. I do think a beard makes a man look particularly virile, don't you?"

It was a miserable meal. There were a few withered potatoes baked to near carbon in the stove. The meat, which was almost certainly venison, was lost in a thick brown sauce that tasted of rubber. All during supper, Margaret Cornelia kept up a flow of conversation that was so independent of her guests that they might not have been there. She told them how she had come to Oddle Bar from Squaw Valley, and how she had outsmarted all the people who had tried to trap or cheat or rob her over the years.

"I can tell when I'm safe," she said, wiping a dribble of sauce from her chin with a stained damask napkin. "I get feelings about people, you know? I knew you were fine the moment I saw you. I could tell just like *that*. Oh, now Mrs. Rossi is a little jealous of me. That's because I've got all these fine things that she don't. She'd like my pretty dresses, wouldn't you, Mrs. Rossi? You don't have to worry. It shows you got good taste, is all."

"If it's as dangerous here as you've said," Thea began, ignoring most of what the strange old woman told them, "why don't you move on? Or join up with some others? You won't have to keep hiding then. You could fight the Pirates and anyone else off." As she spoke, she was acutely aware of the terrible room almost directly overhead.

"I couldn't do that, Mrs. Rossi. Dear me, it wouldn't be smart. You know what it's like when a lot of people get together to guard something? They become a target, a real easy target. I'm not ready to be anybody's target, oh no. The Pirates spend all their time looking for places where people are. They wipe 'em out. Kill 'em all. Now, me, here by myself, no one knows I'm here. I keep it that way on purpose. I'll make it on my own, thanks, and let the others be the sitting ducks." Gleefully she beamed at Evan. "'Course, one more person, though. I could manage that. I ain't stingy."

"Margaret Cornelia," Evan said sternly. "There are two of us. We're married."

"Ah, that don't mean much any more. You're as married as you want to be." She turned to Thea, challenging her. "You can't make him stay with you, Mrs. Rossi. I got a lot more to offer. I got a house, and food and pretty things . . ."

Evan stepped into the breach. "We Italians are Catholic, Margaret Cornelia. Marriage is a sacrament." He had got the tone right, startled at how much like Father Bowen he sounded. He had not seen Father Bowen in more than thirty years.

Margaret Cornelia had flared her nostrils, but dropped the subject with a sour smile. She returned to more stories of herself, of the glorious days at Squaw Valley. When she rose at last to serve coffee, which was the color and texture of glue, Thea made an impatient pull at Evan's sleeve, all the while being careful not to let Margaret Cornelia see her fright.

"What is it, Thea?" Evan asked loudly enough for the words to carry as their hostess moved between dining room and kitchen. "Oh, I see. Let me help you with that." On the pretext of doing something to her boot, he leaned over. "What's wrong?" he whispered.

"Not here. Later. It's bad."

Evan nodded. "Let me check the other boot for you," he said loudly.

"It's dangerous, Evan. There are maybe ten people in the next building."

"Right." He pulled himself up straight. "I think that's got it now."

"Thank you," Thea said, stretching out her mouth grotesquely to a smile as Margaret Cornelia came back with the coffee.

"You'll like this," she promised as she set the warped tray on the table. "After a long walk like you had, a cup of coffee really hits the spot. I make it good and strong. You'll see."

*   *   *

As soon as they were alone in the cramped bedroom, Thea told Evan what she had seen. The tale came out in disjointed whispers as they pretended to undress.

"Damn," Evan said softly. "I thought we might be able to stay here—kill her and take over. But she's not alone, after all."

"Sssh! She's listening, Evan. I know she is." Thea glanced quickly at the door. "She must have signaled them earlier. We can't stay here."

"You're right." He touched his pack absently.

"Evan, we could end up hanging on hooks in there."

He nodded. "Get your pack ready, but carefully. Make it look like you're going to undress," Evan said very softly as he pulled his pack nearer. He put his snowshoes over his arm, afraid to strap them on while still in the house.

With silent acceptance, Thea finished packing, pulling her load onto her back with stiff reluctance that told Evan her hip was worse.

"The door is barred: she'll hear us if we try to open it," Evan said as they prepared to leave. "It's dark out. We're taking a big chance."

"We're taking a bigger chance here. I don't care about out there, so long as we get away from here. I'd rather fight bear." Thea shouldered her way past him to the door, grabbing the heavy bar that held it closed. With one tremendous surge of strength she lifted it free of its holdings. The thing made a sound like the breaking up of a ship on rocks.

"Go!" Evan urged, pushing her out the door ahead of him.

The snow was deep, but two days of bright sun had turned it crusty and that crust held them up as they ran.

Behind them a window shot open and a voice screeched after them, "You creeps! You *creeeeeeps!*" Moments later a rifle coughed, but the shot went wild.

The slope grew steeper. Evan shoved Thea, yelling, "Roll!" and threw himself sideways onto the snow.

Two more shots cracked, one coming quite close, as they tumbled helplessly down the hill. Arms and legs flailed, churning their wake into gouges and pockets of cold. Ahead in the dim moonlight Evan saw planks reaching up above the snow, as dangerous as shoals, ready to rip them, break them as they slid away from the range of Margaret Cornelia's rifle. Desperately he moved his legs forward, praying that they would not catch and break before he could absorb his momentum. His feet came solidly against the hidden wall, his knees forced hard against his chest as he reached out for Thea. To his amazement, he not only grabbed her but held her as well, keeping her from rolling farther down into the snowbound ravine.

For several minutes they lay together, panting in the moon-bright snow while Margaret Cornelia's screams faded away. When all was silent and they breathed normally once more, Evan turned to Thea, releasing his grip on her arm. "Put your snowshoes on," he said gently. "We have a long way to go."

*   *   *

They made little progress that night, climbing to the ridge east of Oddle Bar, and throwing themselves, exhausted, onto a few cut branches. The next day took them along the drifted slopes to Onion Valley. They went quickly eastward, stopping the following night on North MacRae Ridge, in the full force of the wind, coming now with an illusive, distant promise of spring. Evan cut branches while Thea built a fire, shielding it with a clumsy lean-to. There they huddled, engulfed in cold and the vast emptiness of the mountains while the trees writhed in their distress, shedding snow as the wind buffeted them. Occasionally there was a sound like gunfire, and another tree would fall, broken, a sacrifice to the poison that waited to claim them all.

The wind continued to blow the next day as they made their way around the shoulder of the mountains to Johnsville.

"What's that?" Thea asked as they saw the ruined buildings clinging to the mountains, high on the side of the slope.

"It says Johnsville." Evan pointed out a badly weathered sign. "Johnsville. Johnsville . . ." he said to himself, as the name triggered a memory.

"What about it?" Thea asked. She was grateful for the chance to stop. Her hip was still sore and she had limped the last three miles.

"I think this was the mining town the British owned. They were Cornishmen, the miners. Here for the golden glory of Her Britannic Majesty, Alexandrina Victoria." He chuckled. "I'd almost forgot about it. The Second Gold Rush, in '81 put the town back in business. Before that, all it had was a hotel, and, I think, a restaurant. I remember reading about it, a long time ago. Something about its never being properly admitted to the state, and so it was not legally part of the Union. The things we used to worry about . . ."

"Is there anyone left?" Thea asked as they came into the hollow with its pathetic trimmings of delapidated houses.

"Not for a long time, now," Evan said quietly, hoping it was so. Oddle Bar had been a ghost town, officially, and he would not make the same error twice. He went a few steps into the town, all his senses alert. He turned to Thea. "Keep your crossbow ready. And wait here."

"But, Evan . . ." she protested as she fitted a quarrel into the groove.

"I need you to cover me." He turned once more to the buildings hidden like strange dark mushrooms under the snow. Only the wind moved here, teasing the snow into fantastic shapes. Fallen trees had wrecked two houses, and the spire of the church leaned crazily, threatening to topple the whole building. The afternoon shadows were slanting across the town, long areas of purple and blue that made the snow much shinier in contrast. Evan was grateful for the shadow, and welcomed its relief. His eyes were sore, his head ached, and he was lightheaded with hunger and exhaustion. He stood in the silent town, slowly lowering his crossbow. After a moment he gestured to Thea, and waited as she came through the snow to his side.

"I think it's sad," she said as she came up to him.

Evan studied her. "Sad? How do you mean, Thea?"

"I don't know. It just feels like it should have people in it, and it's lonely for them."

Around them the wind picked up, making a shriek like a cat. It was a demented, abandoned cry.

When the eerie feeling had left him, Evan said, "Well, tonight we'll be indoors. And we can probably find a bed or two if we look carefully." Now that the long walk was almost over, Evan felt his body thrum. He thought fleetingly that he was getting old, and remembered with some surprise that he was forty-seven. "I don't know about you, Thea," he said softly, "but I'll be glad for the rest."

She turned a wan face to him. "We've come a long way," she said as she unstrapped her crossbow. "I guess we'll get to Gold Lake, soon, though, and it will all be over." She added then, so wistfully that Evan was touched, "It's near here. It's not far. We'll check the map Hobart gave us as soon as we're settled."

* * *

It was the ruined restaurant that gave them the space and the warmth they wanted. The couches in the lounge were so large and bargelike that they promised to be excellent beds. There was a soft, fungus-flavored air to the place, and the ancient flocked wallpaper was muzzy with dust. Some of the old lamps tilted precariously in their sconces, their fuel discolored scum in the glass reservoirs. Other lamps were still on the tables, thick coats of dust and spiderwebs robbing them of their sheen.

"You know, Thea, if this weren't so close to Graeagle, it might almost be worth staying here," Evan remarked as he stoked the stove. There were still stacks of wood in the kitchen, as well as several boxes of candles. He had fixed up three or four candelabra, and now the main room glowed with warm hospitality, and the fire in the Franklin stove was making a little headway against the cold.

"I don't like being so close to the Pirates, even here. They could be up here in half an hour, if they wanted to."

"Not at this time of year," Evan reminded her. "Not with their vans. They can't get through the snow."

"We're too close to them," she insisted, but added, "It *is* nice here. I can see why you want to stay." She pulled two changes of clothes from her pack and went toward the kitchen and its large sinks.

Evan tossed her two thick wool shirts. "While you're at it. I'm going to check around, in case there's anything we can take with us to Gold Lake besides bandages, matches, and candles."

"Knives," she said practically as she opened drawers looking for soap.

"That's a thought." He had discovered the door to the cellar, and taking one of the branches of candles, he disappeared into the basement.

Thea was startled to hear him let out a whoop a few minutes later. Dropping her wash, she reached for her crossbow and went fearfully to the stairs, calling down, "Evan?" She waited. "Evan? Are you all right?" and cocked the crossbow as she waited.

"I'm fine," he called back happily. "There's tons of canned food down here, dried food, too, and Thea, there's a wine cellar."

Shortly afterward he appeared, clutching cans and dusty bottles; there were cobwebs caught in his hair.

"What did you find?" She had unstrapped the crossbow and was once again busy with washing.

"Look at this." He held out a bottle to her, making a useless attempt to wipe the label clean. "Mondavi Cabernet '86."

To his amazement, she said, "The '78 is better." Then, seeing the incredulity in his face, she laughed. "My father was a virologist, specializing in vines. He developed the plants that were grafted all over the Napa Valley. I'd almost forgotten about the wines. We didn't have them at Camminsky Creek. I haven't seen wine in years." She reached out and touched the bottle. "To think that was picked the year I was born."

"You never mentioned your father . . ." He stopped, not wanting to think about what other things she had not mentioned.

"I don't think of it much, any more," she said apologetically. "It was a long time ago, Evan. A lot's happened since then."

He knew this was so. He changed the subject. "Tell you what: you leave me to do the cooking and you get yourself washed up. We'll celebrate tonight. It's Gold Lake tomorrow, and the worst will be over. If the community is operating . . ."

"If . . . ?" she asked, becoming defensive.

He made a self-deprecating gesture. "Don't mind me, Thea. I've seen so many things go wrong, I can't believe the way you do. I keep waiting for a catch to come up."

"You don't think . . ." She did not dare to say more, as if putting her own doubt into words would somehow give them reality.

"No. I don't. Now go get yourself scrubbed. A hot bath is a luxury, and so long as there's a twenty-gallon soup kettle in the kitchen, we might as well fill it up with snow and stick it on the stove for a bath."

She nodded, excited. "There's still soap left, too."

"Great. If you get the snow, I'll start to work on our meal." So saying, he shoved her out of the room, smiling at the cans and pots that waited for him. He wished he could take some of the kitchen appointments with him, for the people at Gold Lake could surely use some extra utensils. And these were the best he had seen in a long time; fine French cookware—even a broad, flat copper crepe pan. At the back of his mind there was another niggling doubt, one that asked why, if Gold Lake were so near, the people hadn't taken these things out of Johnsville a long time ago. "They don't want to call attention to themselves," he answered his doubts aloud as he rummaged through the spice shelf. "They know they have to be cautious." It didn't make sense, but he pretended it did as he turned his attention to their food.

*   *   *

They had dinner by candlelight, Evan recalling the long-vanished days when candles were romantic, glamorous additions to elegant rooms rather than lighting necessities. He had made a kind of lasagna, using some crusty ancient cheese he had found in the cellar with the wine. Instead of fresh meat, he had used canned, and added some chopped sausage to improve the taste. The tomato sauce was thick, and the canned mushrooms added more texture than flavor. Pearl onions glistened in the sauce, as well, and these were so pungent that they were almost impossible to eat.

Wine was served in fragile glasses of fine crystal. It glowed warm in the outsized glasses, and the glow was reflected in their faces. It was a sweet night, shining with the ghosts of lost graces which Evan had almost forgotten and Thea had never known.

Their talk was pleasant, lightened by the warmth around them as much as the wine. Toward the end of the evening Evan had trimmed his beard with the poultry shears he found in the kitchen, and decided that the years he had been clean-shaven were wasted. Thea watched him, amusement in her face at odds with the fatigue that pulled her toward sleep.

"What do you think?" he asked when he was satisfied.

"It's fine."

"Really?" He turned to regard himself in the long mirror over the bar. "I used to shave every day. I was very particular about that. I never thought I'd look good with a beard. I thought I had too much jaw—you know, too wide."

"It's fine," she repeated, nibbling on some leftover lasagna.

He checked his reflection once more and decided that the beard made him look younger. Not that it mattered. Then he caught sight of the twenty-gallon pot. "You know, someday, I'd like to have a bath in a tub again. It's been months . . ."

Her face clouded. "There are a lot of things I'd like to have. But they're gone, Evan. They're gone."

* * *

Bleary-eyed and sluggish, they started out late in the morning, climbing slowly above the creek, which gurgled happily where the ice had worn away. The way was steep and they went slowly, feeling weighted down by the two large meals they had had.

They had come around to the leeward side of the mountains again, and the snow was harder, and the drifts more treacherous. Between the snow and their food, it was late in the day when they came to the Lakes Basin tucked into the gouges at the crest of the range. The sun hung low on their right, and the rustling in the trees down the mountains promised a rising night wind.

Gold Lake lay at the far end of the Lakes Basin, the largest and most protected of them. As they approached it, Thea said, "I thought there'd be guards before now. They must patrol the place. . . . Do you think they use some kind of monitors?"

Evan firmly slapped down his doubt again. "With the Pirates as near as Graeagle, they'd probably put their guards at the other road," he said, wanting to reassure her.

"That must be it," she agreed uncertainly as she strained her eyes to see where the community might be.

At last they rounded the bend and Gold Lake lay before them, wreathed in ice, stately in its isolation. There were no signs of fences, of outbuildings, of barns, or greenhouses, or any other structure that would show that people lived there, worked there.

Then, on the far bank, they saw a cluster of darkened houses, forlorn, hollow, burned-out. The snow had almost buried them, and the skeletal remains of the homes were surrendering to this, breaking, falling, crumbling away to unrecognizable charred pieces.

"Oh, Evan," Thea cried out from the desolation that filled her as she saw what lay ahead. "There's nothing there, nothing. Evan, *nothing!*"

CHAPTER 6

Evan stopped walking, suddenly overwhelmed with fatigue. His arms dropped to his sides. This was not the fatigue of long walking, although that was part of it. This was more; the fatigue of continuous struggle which had brought him so far and lost him so much. "F— it," he said dully.

Thea had sunk into a drift, her eyes vacant, looking unseeing at the remnants on the other side of the lake. She had no words now, and she did not know what to do.

Evan took one of the cooking pots he had lugged from Johnsville and threw it away from him, suddenly disgusted with his own disappointment.

"I always wanted to be here, from the first time Dr. Ho told me about it," she said to the wind. "He promised there would be a place for me . . ."

"Oh, Christ." Evan jammed his fists together, and took a certain satisfaction in the ache it created in his hands.

"I . . . I wanted it to be here. It had to be here. . . . I've been coming here for years, years. And all the time, it was gone." Only her nervous fingers toyed with her crossbow, as if denying the rest of her body, showing that the calm was not calm. The wind whipped her hair, blowing some of the feathery dark strands over her face, hiding her eyes. She did not brush the hair back, but took refuge behind it.

Abruptly Evan pulled her to her feet. "Come on."

"But why?" She shrank back, seeking the snowdrift again, and its cool, comforting quiet.

"Because it's coming onto night and we have to sleep somewhere." He jerked savagely at her arm, hoping to see understanding, acceptance, fear, any emotion at all come into her pale, serene face.

"I can't," she said, pulling away.

"Yes, you can; you're going to." The harshness in his voice startled her, and for a moment she saw him as the man who had led the Pirates for those destructive years. His face was set and under the tangle of his beard his jaws were clamped tight. "We are going over there, we are going to find ourselves a place to sleep, and when the morning comes, we're going to search the place from top to bottom. We'll take anything we can use. And then we'll leave."

"Leave?" she asked helplessly. "For where? Where is there to go?"

"Somewhere."

"But how? How, Evan?"

"The same way we've been doing," he said, rather more gently. "Day by day, until we find a place. We'll go south for the time being. To Tahoe, or maybe Yosemite. But we have to get out of here. If the Pirates can find Graeagle, they can find this, and when they do, we'd better not be here. They'll find Johnsville, too," he added regretfully. It would have been pleasant to go back to that snug kitchen and large wine cellar.

"But why not stay here for a while?" she said, more animation in her face. "We could make the community happen again. We could set it up, do some farming, maybe . . . find others to help us . . ."

"Farming? Up here? In this?"

She started to shake her head, but he took her by the shoulders, ignoring her protests. "Evan!"

"Listen to me, Thea. If we stay here, we're going to die—maybe from cold, maybe from starvation, maybe the Pirates will kill us. It doesn't matter how. We'll be dead. We can't farm here in the snow. You know yourself that there's too little game in the mountains for us to live on. And the Pirates are half a day away after the thaw. I haven't come over a hundred miles through these mountains for the privilege of dying. You can stay here if you really want to"—his tone told her that he would not leave her behind—"but I'm going on. Anything else is surrender. And I've gone through too much to give up now. You've never abdicated before, Thea. Don't do it now. If we die, we let each other down, Thea."

Sighing, she leaned against him, resting her head on the tough canvas of his jacket. "It's just that I wanted it so much," she said at last, looking across the frozen lake to the wreckage. "I really did believe in it." Turning, she studied his face. "You never did, did you, Evan? Not really."

"Let's say that I hoped," he answered kindly. "Come on, we've got to get around the lake before all the light's gone."

*   *   *

Morning showed the full extent of the damage, the gutted houses revealing ominous bits of charred bones scattered through the rubble like pieces of some terrible puzzle.

"It happened a long time ago," Evan said as he held up a rusted hinge. "Perhaps as much as five or six years."

"I can't get used to it," Thea said. They were in the seventh ruin, and she was scooping away snow to see what lay below. "I didn't think this would happen. I thought somewhere would be safe."

Evan tossed the hinge aside and paused to blow on his cold, gloved hands. "There never was an Oleana."

"Oleana?"

"There was a song once, about Oleana. It was supposed to be a wonderful place, fantastic and pleasant, where there was no work and no trouble. It turned out to be a land swindle. But the song was sung, long after the fraud was exposed." The simple, enthusiastic melody jigged in his mind. "There never was a Big Rock-candy Mountain, either—that was another one of those songs, about a place where everything was perfect."

"But this wasn't perfect, Evan. It was a chance, just a chance."

He was about to say that a chance was as close to perfect as they would ever get, but held back. Even if it were the truth, he did not want to face it. "I know," he said very softly.

"But there isn't even a chance any more, is there?" Thea waited for a reply, and when none came, she went back to work, sorting necessary things from the unnecessary. She moved through the building emotionlessly, betraying little of the deep loss she felt. She went as if she were exploring another world, an alien place that had no meaning for her but the satisfaction of her curiosity. Evan knew that she was using the work to shield herself from shock, as she had shielded herself from so many other shocks before. She even had the guts to whistle once when she found several long-tined cocktail forks with barbs at the points.

"Look, Evan," she said as she brought them to him. "What

quarrels they'll make. I've salvaged all the whole ones." She studied the forks as she turned them over in her hands. "Whatever possessed them to keep these things? I'm glad they did, but *why?*"

"Maybe they couldn't give them up. Maybe they were special. Maybe it made it easier for them to live up here. How do I know? But we can use them, so maybe it's good that they were here."

"There are some other forks too, but they're heavier. They won't carry as far."

"Never mind them. These will do fine. And those fondue prongs you found. They're good, too." He shook his head, unable to understand why anyone would have brought such needless luxuries into the mountains. He stared at the rumpled snow and the few metal bits that had escaped burning.

"I guess it is hard to give up nice things. I remember that Mom had some good china that she insisted we take to Camminsky Creek. She almost never used it, but she kept it."

"Yeah," he said, recalling some of the senseless trophies the Pirates had taken when they were looting.

Thea saw the new strain in Evan's face, and her disappointment at the loss of Gold Lake lessened. She touched his arm fleetingly. "It's not important," she said, and even she was not sure what she meant.

*   *   *

They stayed at Gold Lake one more night, then followed the road down to a place that had once been called Bassetts. It had been burned out long before Gold Lake was. Another, wider road merged with the Gold Lake road there, leading south and east out of the little valley along the beginnings of the north fork of the Yuba River. It was now early February, or so Evan figured, and the winter storms were at their worst. Three days of heavy snow stranded Thea and Evan at Bassetts, and it was more than a week before they left the old hut in which they had taken shelter.

"We could go back to Johnsville," Thea suggested as the storm ripped the shredding sky. The three layers of canvas which was their door boomed and bellied like sails.

"We could. And the Pirates might come up the mountain. Or we might run out of food, even there. We can't go back, Thea. We wouldn't be safe."

"No," she said dubiously.

"Look, Thea, one more good storm and the winter will be almost over. Traveling will be easier. We'll find a good place, some place that's protected, where we can stay without Pirates coming." There was a forced enthusiasm in these words, and he wished that she would not remind him of how vulnerable they were.

"But we won't get a thaw for a while, Evan."

"Maybe we will. You can't tell." It was a vain hope, he thought, as the darkness deepened.

"All right. I can't tell." She turned away.

*   *   *

At Yuba Pass they found a survival station, and in it several cases of food and other vital supplies.

"How long can we stay here?" Thea asked as she looked at the bright room with its shiny cabinets and wonderfully stacked cardboard boxes. Only three of the boxes had been damaged, their contents long since scattered. But the rest waited in army-made lockers, just as they were when they had been put there. The stamps affixed to the boxes dated them as 1982; over thirty years before.

"A week, maybe two," Evan said, wondering how to find out if the contents were still good.

"It will be better in a week. There's another storm coming up, I think. But it should clear up." The uncanny sense that warned her of changes in the weather was touching her bones. "But it's going to be a wet spring."

"A wet spring it is, then," Evan said, prepared to delve into the treasures they had found. "Ten days from now, you see how you feel. We'll be rested then, and fat and sassy. I sure wish we had a bathtub. But sponge baths are a lot better than no baths."

"Why?"

"Don't you like to be clean?"

"Sure. I just wondered what made bathtubs better." She sat wearily on the edge of an olive drab metal table. "Hot water's fine."

"I've always liked to soak . . ." He broke off. "God, it's funny what you miss. I miss hot baths and good food and music. But there were other things that were more important."

"And now we can be tired and hungry and scared. You might

as well miss nice things as any others." She moved away from him. "Make us a meal, Evan. And tell me how good it used to taste."

* * *

"Quincy, north; Truckee, south," Evan said as they looked at the rusted sign by the old highway. There, in the Sierra Valley, the snow had turned slushy as warmth came back into the mountains and the trees armed themselves against the spring with long, leaking icicles. The creeks and rivers were growing noisier under their layers of snow.

"Quincy," Thea said, feeling a draw to that pleasant place she had tried to forget. "Do you think . . . I hoped we could go back there . . ."

"Thea, the Pirates are at Graeagle." His words were harsh but his face shadowed with sorrow. He tightened his hands on his pack straps and adjusted a smile. "Come on. We'll do better going south."

"I know. But it would have been nice." She cast one swift glance over her shoulder, then turned her back to the north.

* * *

Keeping to the old ranchers' road that skirted the base of the mountains which rose around the marshy expanse of the Sierra Valley, they avoided the open places where unfriendly sharp eyes might be watching. They could see buildings in the distance, white buildings that looked well kept, almost prosperous in their austerity. That might mean safety and a welcome. More likely it would mean hostility and danger. They decided not to put the matter to the test.

As they approached the town, Thea pointed out the crosses that stood at the peaks of the roofs of many of the buildings. "What are they for?"

"I don't know," Evan said, casting his mind back, trying to remember if there had ever been a religious community here before.

"Well? There's sure a lot of them. Even that barn over there."

He paused, looking through the snowy brush toward the town. "I don't like it," he said slowly.

"Neither do I," she said, plainly relieved. "Let's stay away. We can avoid the town, Evan. We've got enough food to last us a couple more days. There's no reason to stop here."

Evan nodded his agreement, and tried to ignore the persistent flicker of worry that stung his thoughts.

"It's too special there," Thea said, putting words to his fear. "We don't belong here."

*   *   *

They found a comfortable hollow for the night, between the cemetery and the bulk of Randolph Hill. A few miles away the town of Sierraville kept to itself, announcing the passing of the night with a mournful bell and strange chantings.

Snug in her blankets, Thea asked what the music was that drifted toward them some time after midnight.

"It's called *'Veni, veni Emmanuel.'* It's a Gregorian chant, about seven hundred years old, more or less." He wondered why they would be singing that particular chant, when he remembered that it was near Lent, the season that promised resurrection, the return of Christ and the sun and the green things of the earth.

"It sounds sad," she said after giving it some thought. "What's it about?"

"It's calling Emmanuel, the Savior, to come to them."

"Gaude, gaude, Emmanuel captivum solve, Israel." The music rose in the night, a celebration lost in the wilderness.

Evan reached up and tightened the flap; he had heard rustlings in the trees and he wondered if there was any danger of raccoons, dogs, or even larger animals troubling them. He hoped that hazard would not arise for a while, until they had something more durable than a tent to protect them.

"Are they going to do that all night?" she asked, irritated by the monotonous patterns of sound.

"They may," Evan allowed, thinking back to the endless services he had heard in Rome when he was twelve years old. He had been very devout then, and had found inspiration in the singing of hymns. It was three or four years later that he realized it was the music, and not the religion behind it, that had held him transported. "Sometimes, at special holidays, the services go on for hours."

"Great," she said, pulling the end of her blanket over her head.

Evan lay back, listening to the chanting, and thought about the men who were singing. Eventually he recalled that there had been a monastic order getting started in these mountains, years ago.

Something like the Trappists, he thought; very strict, very severe. He could not remember if they had included a vow of silence in the Rule. When the chants he heard now were new, a monastery had meant sanctuary, but Evan doubted that these singers were very charitable. No one could afford to be now, not even monks.

When the singing stopped at last, he fell asleep to dream of lost Easters and the world that went with them.

* * *

They were still at breakfast, listening to the solemn tolling of the bells across the valley, when the five monks arrived; somber, dirty men with unkempt beards. Their robes of dark sacking were so filthy that it was difficult to tell what color they had been before grime had turned them brown-gray, and stiff with grease, the way the Pirates' leather outfits were.

"In the name of the Father, the Son in His Suffering, and the Penitent Spirit, we give you good day," said the tallest and gauntest of the five.

Evan had almost crossed himself as he heard the greeting, but saw that Thea had reached covertly for her crossbow. Evan restrained her with a quick gesture, seeing that the monks were stern-featured and carried heavy walking staves. He guessed that a practiced blow from one of those thick sticks could and would break bones. He did not want to invite their antagonism, or their fear. "Good day to you, Brothers," he said.

One of the five monks frowned. He pointed his walking stick at Thea. "Is this woman your wife, or are your souls in peril for fornication?"

Evan knew this was not a promising beginning. "She is neither my mistress nor my wife. We travel together, agapate, as the early bishops of the church did." He hoped fervently that deliberate ignorance was not part of these monks' existence, and that they knew of the agapate traditions.

The leader nodded in what looked like approval, although his face was as stern as ever. "You are taming the fires of the flesh, which is good in the sight of God, and works to forgiveness of sin and error. We, Penitent Sons of an Angry God, scourge the imps of desire from our bodies with flail, prayer, and fasting."

As she tried to catch Evan's attention, Thea felt the back of her neck grow warm, as if there were other eyes on her, unfriendly eyes that marked them for destruction. She moved away from the cowled men.

"Your woman does not speak," said one of the monks with curious satisfaction. "It is good for a woman to remain silent. St. Paul praises silent women. St. Anthony wanted to strike out the tongues of women so that they could not indulge in idle, godless chatter."

Now Thea wanted terribly to speak up, but saw the warning in Evan's face. Religious these men were, and their faith made them dangerous.

"I see you have broken your fast," said the leader monk, looking at their tin army plates with food scraps in them. "If you are willing to accompany us, you could spend the day in prayer, and share our evening meal, for the good of your souls and the duty you owe to God."

"We do not wish to impose on your holy retreat," Evan said, thinking there was something dreadfully wrong with the monks. He saw that the formidable walking staves now formed a barrier around them, and that they had no choice. He turned slowly to Thea, moving as carefully as he would have moved in front of hungry animals. "We have had a long journey, Thea," he said tentatively, hoping that she would not refuse now, when their vulnerability was at its greatest.

"Thea!" thundered the smallest of the monks. "That name is sacrilege!" He was about to raise his staff when his leader stopped him. "That will do, Brother Roccus. A name does not prove heresy, but ignorance. Her name is the sin of her parents, the sin of pride, for which they surely burn in hell."

It was all Thea could do to keep from running, her hands covering her face as she saw the ferocity in the monk's eyes.

"Forgive Brother Roccus' impetuosity. His zeal is commendable, but it leads him into error. The temptation to error is strong in him, and he has not subdued it." Was it Thea's imagination, or did Brother Roccus shrink at his superior's words? "He knows that he will have to ask pardon of you and of Our Lady and Her Son Who Suffered Martyrdom for him."

Evan said quickly, "We recognize that all mankind is filled with sin."

The leader nodded gravely. "It is well that you do, for your sin is great."

"But . . ." Evan was prepared to explain his chastity, but the old monk interrupted him.

"Yours is the sin of pride, for you tempt yourselves with the flesh and think that you will not fall. There is much error there." He turned. "We are returning to the monastery. You are to come with us now."

"May we bring our packs? And our tents?" Evan did not think they would be refused so reasonable a request.

"They are objects of vanity," the leader pronounced after giving the matter his consideration. "You have chosen to go in the world, but have not trusted to God to feed and shelter you. This you reveal by your packs and tents, which is vanity. We cannot have such objects within our walls, for they might lead us into similar vanities."

"The packs have our food and supplies, Brothers, that is all." Evan hoped that their definition of vanity did not include food.

"Was the food provided to you?"

"We found it by . . ." Evan realized he could not credit chance. He let his pause lengthen. ". . . By the Grace of God. We were lost, and our steps were guided to a place where this food was."

Again the leader fixed Evan with his angry gaze. "And you did not acknowledge your debt then. You should have thanked God for His care, and given all this freely, as it was given to you." He studied the packs. "Brother Odo will take them." The leader indicated a brawny monk with shifty, stupid eyes set in a moon face. Reluctantly Evan handed the packs to him, knowing that it was unlikely he would ever see them again.

Taking a chance, Thea turned to the leader, her eyes on the ground and her voice as soft as she could make it. She understood these men now, knew their severity that grew from hatred and fright, men who had fled the world, certain that they would be devoured if they did not flee. She also knew that they wanted women to be complacent, submissive, and weak. "What is your name, Father?" she asked, taking a chance on his title.

Her gamble paid off. "I am Father Leonidas. I succeeded Father Gervase, the founder of our Order."

"It must be a grave task, guarding the spiritual good of so many," she murmured. "Your willingness to open your monastery doors to us is beyond our merit. I fear we will bring too much of the world within your walls."

She saw a rictus movement of his mouth that could have been a smile and knew that her bluff had failed.

"That is the devil that speaks in you, woman. You are not to turn away from the Glory and the Agony of God for the midden of the flesh."

She cursed her luck as Father Leonidas stood aside, motioning to them to pass.

*   *   *

They were left in the chapel by the Brothers, with the instructions that they should purify their minds for the questions the monks were bound to ask them for the good of their souls. Brother Odo had closed the door on them, slamming it with a satisfied, fatalistic thud.

The chapel was small, made of stone, unheated, bare, forbidding. There were a few rough-hewn benches for the monks, set on the uneven stone floor. Lit by a solitary skylight, the altar showed stark simplicity that was watched over by a crucifix that twisted itself in a grim reminder of the Passion. Two small candles burned by clumsily carved statues that flanked the altar. One statue showed a saint holding his flayed skin in his hands. The other was a young woman wearing a martyr's crown as she was stretched mercilessly on a rack.

"I don't like this place," Thea whispered to Evan as they walked toward the altar.

"They've certainly gone in for all the bloodier aspects of Catholicism," Evan agreed, trying to keep his voice light. The words came out cracked-sounding, showing his fear. He swallowed hard and spoke again. "You're right about this place. I don't like it either."

"What do they want us to do?" she asked as they neared the altar.

"I think we're supposed to kneel and pray. I'll show you." He dropped to his knees and joined his hands together under his chin, remaining that way for some time. "You do it, too." At that moment he wished he could remember the ritual of the Mass. He had so often heard them sung, the big glorious sounds of Berlioz,

Fauré, Verdi, Mozart, and Bach. But he had long since forgotten the ceremony.

"How long do we stay like this?" she asked after they had been kneeling for a quarter of an hour. The cold came from the floor into their bones, and the uneven stones bit cruelly into her flesh, making her legs and back ache.

"Ask them," he said bitterly. "However long it takes."

* * *

It took three hours. Just as Thea whispered, "My bladder's going to burst," Father Leonidas came into the chapel, his robes whispering around his grimy sandals, and his face set in stern lines.

Evan crossed himself in what he hoped was the right form and rose to face the monk. Pain squeezed his legs as his cramped muscles strove to support him. "Good Father," he said as evenly as he could, "it was kind in you to grant us this time of prayer and solace."

"So it is when one comes to the Mercy Seat," intoned the monk, who then crossed himself and knelt before the altar. He murmured in Latin, again made the sign of the cross and rose, saying to them, "Are you now prepared for the ceremony?"

"What ceremony?" Evan asked, schooling his voice to sound respectful.

"Your marriage ceremony," Father Leonidas said, as if surprised that Evan was not aware of it. "We cannot question you until you are man and wife: man and wife are one flesh, so repentance and contrition must be the same for you both, for you have traveled and sinned, by fornication, or lies, or pride, as one. No, do not deny it. For though you have not polluted your flesh with her, or so you claim, yet you are a man, and all men are stirred by the lusts and the senses. Your thoughts have been carnal. In the world there is no way to escape this sweet poison, the lure of this charnal being. What is this thing you seek, but carrion and the gates of hell and eternal damnation." He motioned to the other monks who had come into the chapel. "We will witness your vows and hear your confessions. Then, when you are one in the Sight of God, you will answer our questions, and whatever one is condemned of, the other will be so, too."

Glancing at Thea, Evan saw her face had taken on the frozen

look of fear. They had been trapped into co-operating with the monks, but he knew now they had to have time. He turned to Father Leonidas. "Before we place ourselves in your hands for this sacrament, let us attend to our bodies." He took a chance, adding, "You have the holy strength of your Order in you, but we are not so. For us, the demands of the flesh will distract the mind from your sacrament."

Nodding, Father Leonidas indicated the side door of the chapel. "You will find what you need there. Brother Odo will watch from the door, that you do not profane these grounds."

So they don't trust us, Thea thought as she followed Evan into the tiny enclosure where the outhouses stood. She felt herself long for escape and understood the monks' precaution.

They entered two of the stinking, cold stalls side by side. Evan tapped the wood, whispering, "I don't know what they're up to, but I know it's bad. I wish I could see our way out of it."

She snorted. "It doesn't matter what we say, does it? They've made up their minds."

"Thea, you've got to be careful," he said to the thin wood that separated them. "This is my mistake. We should have pushed all the way through the valley last night. That way we could have avoided them altogether."

She was tempted to agree with him, remembering the ice that had filled her spine when she had caught sight of the spires of Sierraville. But he had not blamed her when she had been wrong and had not condemned her for the dream she had lost at Gold Lake. She also admitted to herself that he knew much more about these strange men with the burning eyes than she did.

"Thea?"

"I'm thinking. Maybe you're right. But we're here now. We can't change that."

"I'll think of something, Thea. I promise you. I won't let them go through with this."

Brother Odo tapped ominously on the door, his staff making the cramped cubicles echo like the inside of a drum. "It is time for the ceremony. You must not delay."

Evan emerged, trying to hide his worry. "Ready, Thea?" he called, pretending not to notice the glowering Brother Odo at his side.

Thea appeared, keeping her eyes downcast as Brother Odo led them the little distance back to the chapel.

"Here are your garments," announced Father Leonidas. He held out two shapeless robes of rough sacking. From their smell, they had once held grain. "It is fitting that you should be new-dressed, for we are all to be new-dressed at the Wedding Supper of the Lamb. What you have been shall be judged, and upon your expiation of sin, shall be blood-washed in the sight of heaven." He made a gesture and three young monks came forward. "Strip them," said Father Leonidas.

Thea's stricken eyes met Evan's as the clothes were pulled from them. The icy air of the chapel bit into her as much as the eyes of the monks, those eyes filled and drugged with denied hunger. When her underclothes were taken off, Father Leonidas approached her. "A devil's Mark, and in a place of Lust," he said, fingering the scar where Lastly's knife had cut away her nipple. "A lure, a lure to take men from purity. See this, my brothers, and be warned of the lure that is woman."

With his clothes half torn away, Evan pulled himself free of the monks, moving between Father Leonidas and Thea. "You must not do this, Father. In your compassion"—he spat the word—"you cannot do this. She has been raped. That is the mark of a brutal man, not the devil."

An expression of pity came into the monk's flinty eyes. "So she has deceived you, my son. Her words of honey have led you into error. There is no rape, my son, there is only the Sin of Eve. For why does a man surrender to the flesh but that the woman tempts him to it. Woman is the seat of Sin, my son, and her ways are full of lies and wiles. If she was taken as you say, it was she herself who caused the crime."

Evan choked back a retort as he saw the glint that came into Father Leonidas' eyes when he saw his regenerated arm. "So," whispered the monk. "So the unpure has come again, full blown with pride as a corpse with flies." He stared at the tawny orange skin below the scar, and a scowl darkened his face. "I have prayed that we might see the impure brought low. This is the great Sin of Pride, for it is against the will of God. That which is dead must not rise again but in the Name of the Lord, for it was Jesus who called Lazarus from the tomb. All else is wickedness. This is the work of the Anti-Christ, who has come among us in the last days."

Both Thea and Evan were naked now, their bodies shivering in the cold, which did not come from the air alone. Father Leonidas made an abrupt gesture and the two shapeless garments he had called their wedding clothes were thrown over their heads and pulled roughly into place. The habits were surprisingly warm, but were woven so coarsely that they chafed the skin wherever they touched.

One of the monks began to chant, the others joining him. Among the voices were the high, strong sounds of *castrati*. Evan shuddered as he heard them, knowing what had been done. "I did not know you took such young men into your Order," he said carefully to Father Leonidas, for he was aware that the sweet, sexless soprano voice could only be kept if the singer was castrated before puberty.

"We take all who come to us purely. If you remark our choir, nothing is done without the conviction for faith and a willing heart. The monks do this as a sacrifice, keeping themselves forever beyond the chains of the flesh. At the same time, they preserve the glory of their song for the Most High."

Thea stared. "You mean they do it to themselves?"

"It would not truly be a sacrifice otherwise, would it?" Father Leonidas asked gently.

". . . *misericordiae, vita dulce* . . ." the choir sang. Two of the monks came forward to face the altar. They held up a chalice as they sang.

"You prostrate yourselves before the face of God," Father Leonidas informed them, motioning Brother Odo to force Thea and Evan to the floor.

"Ad te clamamus exulis filii . . ."

So they lay on the uneven stone floor, face down, arms outstretched with the fingers of one hand touching the other. The monks marked out their places with candles, as they would for the dead, singing still as they worked. ". . . *gementes et flentes in hac lacrimarum vale. Eia ergo advocata nostra* . . ."

"What do we do?" Thea whispered to Evan, and before he could answer, Brother Odo cuffed her ear. "You must remain silent, meditating on your sins," he said angrily, his huge hands clenched over her head.

"Et Jesum benedictum fructum ventris tui, nobis post hoc exilium . . ."

"Wait," Evan said.

"O clemens, O pia . . ."

"Wait," he repeated, more loudly now. The singing stopped raggedly as Father Leonidas turned on him savagely.

"You interrupt the Praise of the Lord and the Holy Virgin!"

Evan pulled himself onto one elbow. "I do not wish to profane the House of the Lord. I cannot marry this woman, not here and not in your way."

"Heresy!" cried the terrible old man.

"No." Evan held up his hands in proper supplication. "No, Father Leonidas. This is your rule, not mine. Were I free to do so, I would be glad to marry this woman, for we have endured much together and she has the warmth of my heart, though I have never taken her body."

"Free?" asked Father Leonidas, and the other monks waited, eager.

"I cannot marry this woman because I already have a wife." As he said it, he felt ironic satisfaction that it was the truth.

CHAPTER 7

They waited alone, scarcely breathing. Sound and light left the chapel and it grew colder in the gray stone room. Only the light on the altar flickered, a baleful eye hanging over them.

"I hate them," Evan muttered at last, pulling his beard where Brother Odo had struck him with his crucifix. There was blood matting the hair, making his face stiff.

"What will they do now?" Thea watched him uncertainly. There had been venom in him that she had only glimpsed fleetingly before. Now his face was rigid and his eyes colder than the stones of the chapel. "Evan?" she ventured, lifting her hand toward him.

"They have no right. *No right!*" Furiously he wiped at the blood with his sleeve. "Isn't it enough that they ruin themselves? *Castrati,* in this world, in this place. And they call that a sacrifice. Filthy, stupid, sadistic . . ." He spoke softly, the words hardly carrying as far as Thea, but each was laced with acidic hatred.

She pulled herself nearer him, taking his hand. "Don't let them see your anger. It gives them strength against you. They'll twist it, Evan. Don't show your anger. Please."

He ground his knuckles together as he watched the candle waver in the drafts which teased through the chapel. "We should have stayed away from here. We should have gone through the valley if it took until after dark."

"Look," Thea said softly, "there might be enough time for one of us to get away, hide out in the mountains until the other can . . ."

"Shit, Thea, they'd be after us in a moment. And if one got away, you know they'd take it out on the other. They're looking for an excuse to do that right now." He softened then. "If you think you can get away, go on: this was my mistake and I'll pay for it. They want more than ten Hail Marys, though." His laugh was achingly sad.

"Evan?"

He moved away, sitting heavily on one of the benches, his head lowered and his eyes hidden. He sat that way for some minutes, not looking at anything but some indistinct spot on the floor. Thea watched him, knowing that he had isolated himself and wished to keep her away. She made herself as comfortable as she could, tucking her legs under her and pulling the rough garment more tightly around her. Silent, worried, she waited.

"The monks really scare me," he said at last, like a small boy admitting to breaking something valuable. "I've seen this kind before. Some of the Pirates are like this—Cox, Mackley, that crew. They're fanatics and because of that they feel totally justified to force their position on others." He shook his head, keeping his face turned from her too-probing eyes.

Puzzled, she moved closer. "They think they're right: it makes them crazy."

"They don't *think* they're right; they *know* they're right. No doubt about it, no questions, no unpleasant suspicions that other people might have something for their point of view, too. They have their damned Truth with a capital T to back them up." Bitterness came from him like an infection.

"There's more, isn't there?" she said, as much to herself as to him. "What is it? What happened?"

He didn't answer immediately, and when he did, it was in short, bruised words. "There was a time, maybe thirty years ago, when most people knew that things had gone wrong. The air was bad, the food was lousy and jammed full of chemical garbage, there wasn't enough power, there were too many people, and the backup systems were breaking down faster than new ones could be thought up." He stopped, thinking back to his childhood. He felt young and old at once then. "I was a bright kid. I traveled a lot with my father. I don't think I spent four months of the year at home after 1978. Between school and his work, I went everywhere. When I was about fifteen, in '82, things began to get very bad in Europe. Everyone wanted the easy way out, and why not? No one had told them there wasn't an easy way out. So they gave up some things and rode the bus to work and grumbled about the service and the phone and the taste of the water. And they thought it made a difference."

Thea moved back as he got to his feet. "That isn't all, is it? That isn't what hurt you." She knew that he had talked around his pain so that he could bear to speak of it.

"No. No." He turned away from her again. "Anyway, a lot of people decided to take another way out, and revel in their guilt. That also kept them from having to do anything. My older . . . step-brother got religion. He found the Truth, capital T, and after that, he knew all the answers and didn't have to worry about things, because no matter what new atrocity occurred, he had handed out the guilt and that negated any responsibility he might feel. He knew sin when he saw it, and he convinced a lot of people. They kicked him out of the Church the week of the bombing of Montreal. His Madrid followers got killed in the Power Riots in '94."

While Evan paced, Thea watched him, her mouth set and her body held tightly against itself.

"It wasn't that he believed in guilt, or that he had faith. That wasn't it, Thea. Most people that cared about anything survived on faith alone, in the worst years, when nothing else could save them. They found a strength to hold out. I admire that strength. But Raoul didn't have strength, he had arrogance. And he made his followers arrogant as well. These monks are like that." He stopped pacing to glare at the altar. "They know their austerity, their perversity makes them superior. They feel that they have the right to judge the world by their standards and their conditions. And they know, they *know* they need never show compassion or kindness or charity or love because their one right way exempts them from their humanity. They need not be responsible. They aren't affected by anything but their own narrow world." His hands were knotted at his sides, and he was breathing quickly. Then he bent over as if he were in pain, and when he spoke again, it was in a tone Thea had never heard him use before, coming out of a sorrow he had kept locked inside of him for too many years. "Jennifer believed him. And Eric, too. After he was born, she believed."

"Jennifer? Eric?"

"My wife and my son." The words were harsh.

For a moment they were both still. Then Thea rose and tentatively touched his arm. It was an uncertain gesture drawn out of her fright and his suffering. Her eyes strayed to the bolted door of the chapel. "Then you are married. It wasn't a lie."

"I was married twenty-two years ago. In Milan, in April, during the opera season, where Jennifer was singing. We were married in the cathedral, a year before it was wrecked." He remembered the huge building and the sound of the choir and the glorious happiness he had felt on that warm day as the Nuptial Mass was celebrated. Jennifer had been wearing ivory lace over creamy silk, and her eyes were as bright as the brilliant windows. "We were quite happy for a year. My career was doing fine, and hers was beginning to branch out. She was singing internationally. Then we had Eric." The muscles in his jaw worked, standing out under his beard. "Eric was badly deformed . . . and after a while, Jennifer began to listen to Raoul and his talk about sin and guilt. She came to believe . . ." He forced himself to look at Thea, to let her see his face as he said, "She came to believe that our marriage was a sin and that our son, because of his deformity, was her punishment."

"But there's lots of deformed kids," Thea said reasonably, not quite understanding. She had never seen families who, if they had children at all, did not have at least one child who had not turned out right. Even in her controlled environment where each of the pregnancies had been tended with precision and care, her brother Davey had not been normal. For a moment she could see him again as she had last seen him, nine years old, lying in his bed and crying as he flailed his spidery arms about, futilely trying to grasp something, anything, with his limp bony hands.

Evan drew an uneven breath. "Do you remember what happened in Baltimore? Those cannisters of poison gas that ruptured offshore? The ones that killed the coast from New York to Georgia?"

"Jack Thompson said something about it, I think. Twenty years ago, or less. No, more like fifteen." She studied Evan's face and saw a confirmation in his misery-filled eyes.

He tried to control himself once more. "Fourteen years, Thea. Jennifer had taken Eric with her to Raoul's national center in Maryland. He was holding a conference there. Everyone come and confess. When that first cannister broke, Maryland got the full force of the gas. That was at the time of the conference." He threw his head back, eyes closed. "I was in Phoenix when it happened, making some arrangements for passage to New Zealand. There was nothing I could do. I couldn't even look for them to see that they were decently buried. If they died."

"Evan," she said, wanting for the first time to comfort him, to hold him gently until he had rid himself of his hurt.

"I don't know even that. Raoul's last broadcast said that some of his followers had lost faith and fled. He didn't say who they were, only that they were cursed." He shook his head. "I couldn't find out . . ."

Beyond the door the sound of chanting rose and the slow cadence of footsteps drew nearer.

As the bolt was pulled back, Thea moved closer to Evan. He took her hand firmly in his as the door swung open, and together they faced the monks.

"Have you meditated on your errors and transgressions? Have you prepared yourselves to answer God?" Father Leonidas intoned, reciting his questions with ritualized perfection.

"Do we have a choice?" Thea asked as anger waked in her. "You have already decided that we are in error and sin: you want proof so that you can decide on a punishment. Any proof will do."

"Blasphemy!" announced Brother Roccus with ill-concealed satisfaction. Turning to Father Leonidas, he said, "The woman betrays herself as the seat of evil."

Father Leonidas gave a signal. Four of the strongest monks came forward, holding their staves across their chests. In a moment they had pulled Thea and Evan apart.

"It is well," declared Father Leonidas. "Take them to the barn and chain them. On opposite walls, not together."

* * *

The barn was small, and for that reason alone it held some trace of warmth. It smelled of sheep and two pathetic old cows as well as rotting hay, which littered the earthen floor. An icy wind raced through the cracks in the building, shrieking its infernal joy.

They were manacled to opposite walls and both quickly discovered that their bonds gave them very little room for movement, and certainly not enough to touch.

"What do we do now?" Thea asked when the monks had left them alone. She had wanted it to sound like a joke, but she did not succeed.

"We wait."

"We'd better pull down some straw from the loft, or we could freeze to death tonight. There's not enough hay here." She scuffed at the damp wisps at her feet. "We can't keep the cold out."

"You're right," he said, looking up to judge the distance to the hayloft above them.

"Can you reach up?"

"Not that high." He looked at the barn walls, searching for a place that might give him access to the hay. There was nothing near.

"I wish we still had that rope," Thea said slowly as she pulled, testing her fetters to their limits. She felt the cold bite of metal on her wrists and ankles, uncompromising, cruel. She moved experimentally and found that she could reach farther up to the left than the right, and she concentrated her search that way.

"Look," Evan said as he watched her progress. "There. Near the byre. It's a rake. If we can reach it . . ."

For a moment Thea stared, then she saw the tines poking up. "It's too far away for you. I don't know if I can reach that far."

"Try. Try."

She pulled against her chains, hearing them chink as they reached tautness. "No . . . I can't . . ."

Grabbing up a short board that lay at his feet, Evan threw it into the loft, cursing as it missed the hay and thudded back to the barn floor.

"Evan! Kick that over here."

"What?" He was aware of an ache in his feet; the cold had bitten through and was gnawing at his flesh like a ravenous animal. "Why?" He reached out and found that the board was now out of reach.

"Kick it, then."

"What for?"

"So I can get the rake."

Evan looked at her. "I'm a fool. You're right." Carefully he pulled himself to the length of his chains, then touched the board tentatively with one foot. "I don't know . . ."

"You've got to." She pulled at her bonds in sympathy.

He moved his head uncertainly, judging the angle of the board. "Here goes," he whispered, and slapped his foot down.

The board slid, turning, sliding over the straw, then caught.

"I can't reach it," Thea wailed softly as she strained toward it. "It's too far away."

Evan saw that one of her ankles was starting to bleed. "Thea, don't."

"I can't. I can't . . ."

"Neither can I," he said bluntly, sinking back against the wall, letting the hurting cold seep into his legs. He had heard that freezing to death was not too bad, that in the end you felt warm again. He hoped it was so.

"No, Evan."

"Thea, shut up," he said, and turned away into his own self-loathing.

She stared at his distress, strangely frightened. She started to say "You mustn't . . ." but the droop of his head and shoulders and the deeply scored lines by his mouth showed her that he would not listen. She waited, thinking, then decided to take a chance. Slowly she flattened herself onto the stinking earth floor of the barn, edging her arm and leg out as far as she could, letting the merciless iron chafe her. This was little enough to pay for the straw that would keep them from freezing. When she had reached as far as she could, she began to pull bits of the straw toward her, tiny handful after tiny handful. Her hand and foot were soon caked with mud, which made the penetrating cold hard to bear. But she would not give up. Pressing herself more tightly against the matted straw, she snatched at the wisps more desperately.

At last the board began to move, inching its way toward her, pressed closer to her hand by the gentle nudgings of her foot. Occasionally the board would be hung up on an uneven part of the floor. She knew despair then and wanted to scream her vexation. She kept her silence and continued her dogged work. She felt she had been after that board her whole life, that eighteen inches of board was more precious to her than clean water. She ground her teeth with the effort and felt grit in her mouth.

Then she could touch it with one finger. She restrained an impulse to grab at the board, fearing that her touch would move it further away, not nearer. Three more handfuls of straw brought it close to her hand, and a shove with her knee sent more straw up behind the board, so that it rolled forward into her open hand.

She lay there panting, almost sobbing with relief. Even the muddy wetness soaking the front of her robe could not bother her.

Stiffly she got to her feet, hanging stubbornly onto the board, unwilling to let it go.

Once on her feet, she took it firmly, going once more to the length of her chains and stretching out. She reached with the board, hoping it was indeed long enough, not willing to fail.

With a crash that startled the cows into lowing nervously and brought Evan out of his melancholy withdrawal, she fell heavily, overbalanced by the chains. And the rake fell across her.

"What in the name of . . ." Evan began petulantly. Then he saw the rake. The death that had been so close to him retreated, leaving lightheaded relief. "Thea." His life was in her name.

Muddy, shivering, straw clinging to her, her face and hands scraped raw and her manacles stained with her blood, she sat up, triumph in her face. Carefully she got to her feet, and carefully she reached up with the rake, pulling down the musty hay from the loft, scattering it like confetti over them both.

*   *   *

With the sun came the chanting monks as they began their devotional day, singing the praises of their Savior, who had set them apart from the rest of corrupt humanity.

From their straw cocoons Thea and Evan listened, afraid to think what the day might become for them when the monks discovered they had not died.

"We're alive," Evan said when the monks had gone into the chapel. "That's something."

"Maybe," Thea allowed, her temper now as ragged as the skin of her wrists and ankles. "I wish I knew more about them."

"Father Lundsford tried to teach me about monasticism." Evan shook his head. "I wish I'd paid more attention."

*   *   *

Brother Demetrios appeared later that morning with two bowls filled with a pale yellow, gelatinous cereal mush. These he placed near the prisoners without a word, and then left hastily, as if afraid of contagion. He pulled the barn door shut behind him, crossing himself as he went and muttering a prayer.

Evan stuck two fingers into the mush and gave the stuff an experimental taste. "Millet," he announced, pleasantly surprised. "It's pretty good nourishment, considering."

Wordlessly Thea took her bowl and began to eat. She thought

the mush tasted like paper, but did not mention it. Food was too scarce and she was too hungry to think about taste.

"There," said Brother Demetrios as he pulled the barn door open once again. "As you see, their cunning has saved them." He was speaking to another monk, a small, pinched man with a narrow, pointed face. "You must question them, Brother Philian. It is not possible for them to have gotten the straw by themselves. They must have been aided."

"Aided?" Brother Philian asked in a voice that was full of dust. "By whom? Who among us would do this?"

"None of us," Brother Demetrios objected, horrified. "But Father Leonidas is forever warning us of the wiles and tricks of the devil . . ."

Brother Philian laughed, and it made the others squirm. "First we must eliminate all the possibilities. Human agencies first, Brother Demetrios. After that, we will investigate the others." He moved into the barn. From his crablike walk Evan gathered that Brother Philian was clubfooted. "God be with you this morning, blasphemers, and lead you into His Light."

"Good morning to you, too," Evan said dryly.

"Perhaps you would be good enough to tell me how you got the straw you lie in?" Although the words were polite and mildly spoken, there was a serious threat behind them.

Evan decided that evasion was useless and unwise. "Thea pulled it down with that rake." He pointed to where the rake lay between them. Brother Demetrios' eyes widened and he hurriedly grabbed it.

From her nest in the hay Thea snorted derisively.

"Have more respect before the Officers of God," Brother Philian snapped. "You say," he went on smoothly, turning back to Evan, "that you used the rake?"

"I said Thea used the rake."

"How did you get it? It was in the byre."

"Ask Thea," Evan recommended.

"I am asking you. She is of no importance—chattel only."

"I disagree." Evan pulled his fingers around his food bowl, sucking the last bit of mush from them.

Brother Demetrios sighed. "How did she get the rake?"

Thea spoke then. "There was a board on the floor. I used it to knock the rake over. Then I pulled down the straw." She got to her feet, facing Brother Philian defiantly. "Were you disappointed that we lived? Is that it?"

"Be silent, woman. It is not your place to speak."

"You wanted to know how we got the straw: I told you."

Brother Philian controlled himself with a visible effort. "You will not speak. It is not appropriate for a woman to speak in the House of God."

Thea glanced significantly around the barn. "Your God certainly has strange taste in houses. But the worshipers are about right," she added as she looked at the two cows and the sheep.

"Thea," Evan said, warning her. "What else do you want to know, Brother?"

"Many things, my son. All in good time." He licked his lips furtively. "You have been away from the Church for a long time, my son?"

Evan thought of the cathedrals he had seen in Milan and Paris and London and Moscow, and remembered the music he had heard there. "You might say so."

"It is lamentable in these sad days that there are so few left to administer the sacraments to the faithful."

Evan nodded absently, covertly watching Thea. She was standing back from them now, and she was upset; Evan knew it from the way she held her head, from the tautness in her hands and her rigid posture that brought her chin up.

There was nothing she could say. She had been watching Brother Philian and saw that he had an erection. She knew with the certainty of fear that as soon as he became aware of it, he would blame her. She begged her thoughts to go elsewhere, not to notice what had happened to Brother Philian.

" . . . To return to Church life, this community is always open to you," Brother Philian was saying to Evan even as his eyes strayed to Thea.

"I appreciate that," Evan said, not thinking about what he was saying. He knew something was wrong with Thea, and did not know how to help. He wanted the tiresome old monk to leave.

"This is a simple matter, my son. You have only to live our life for one year, take our vows, and be secure in this place."

"Ummm."

Brother Demetrios had stood back, listening to this exhortation, and at last bent to pick up the food bowls. As he bent, he saw the other monk's excitement. His face whitened and he crossed himself. "Brother Philian!"

"Yes, Brother?" the old monk asked, annoyed at being interrupted.

"Your flesh . . ." Brother Demetrios could say no more.

Brother Philian stared, and then, in realization, he felt the swelling under his robe, horror in his eyes as he stared at Thea. "Devil!" he shouted at her. He turned back to Evan. "You see what that woman of yours has done to me?" As if in confirmation of this, the erection grew.

"I didn't . . ." Thea protested, though she knew it was useless.

"Even vile, even confined, she is a devil!" He screamed this, and hurled the two wooden bowls at her, crying out with her as one struck her face.

It had been automatic, the closing of her nictitating membranes, a protection like the flicker of an eyelid. She stood still, knowing that both monks had seen. The cut on her cheek where the bowl had hit her began to bleed and she felt the warmth on her face.

"Anathema! Witch!" Brother Demetrios had gone chalky all over, and his body trembled.

"Leave now, Brother Demetrios. Else she contaminate you as well," Brother Philian ordered, a sly expression in his eyes.

"But can she do that?" He was wild now, verging on panic.

"She can," Brother Philian assured the other monk. He turned back to Evan as Brother Demetrios fled from the barn. "You did not mention this"—he gestured to the front of his robe—"why did you not mention this?"

"I didn't think it mattered. I thought you knew." Evan had not moved, but his whole body was tense, coiled like a cat.

"But you know that interference with the works of the Lord is blasphemy. All else is Heresy. You have heard Father Leonidas. You are of the Faith."

Evan spat.

"I see." Brother Philian stood straight. "It is a pity. Obviously you have chosen to ally yourself with her and the flesh. If I may say so, this is a foolish mistake."

"I doubt it."

Again Brother Philian felt himself through the robe, a glazed satisfaction in his eyes. "Heresy . . . heresy is punished with flames, my son. . . . Only fire can take away that sin. . . . You will burn: you and she."

* * *

When Brother Philian had left, Thea had sat with her back to Evan, not speaking. She was too wrapped in her hurt to hear the few words he had said to her, and the cut on her face was like a seal on the document of her shame. While rage and humiliation burned in her, she shut him out.

"Thea?" Evan said quietly, then sat still.

Brother Odo arrived to milk the cows, remarking that it was fortunate that the witch had not dried up their udders. He rubbed the teats with holy water to protect them from that peril. When at last he gathered up the pails, Evan made a hooting noise and rattled his chains to speed the monk on his way.

At last Brother Roccus had come, shortly after midday. He held a book and carried a crosier. "I will hear your confession now, given of your own free will, without instruction or coercion."

Thea remained immobile in the straw. Evan looked at the monk, one eyebrow raised.

"Your confession is necessary."

"Is it?" Evan pulled himself to his feet, taking advantage of his stocky build. For although Brother Roccus twitched with energy, he was both short and thin, and Evan's solid strength was more imposing than his greater height.

"We must seek out error. You must acknowledge that error before the Throne of God so that what we do is for His Greater Glory, and not the Sin of Man."

"You're a sadistic bastard," Evan said calmly as he crossed his arms. "You get nothing from me."

"It is necessary," the monk insisted. "Brother Philian says there is grave error here. He will pronounce anathema on you if you do not repent and confess."

"I don't give a damn. You've hurt Thea and you've already made up your minds to kill us. And don't pretend it's otherwise," he went on, making the most of Brother Roccus' confusion. "You want a show of a burning . . . it was burning, wasn't it?"

Brother Roccus' brow darkened. "It is ten days until the Lord's Day. Father Leonidas has said that on that day your guilt will be offered up."

"Charming."

The anger in the barn grew denser, almost palpable. The cows moved restlessly, sensing emotion, and a few of the sheep began to mill in their tight little pen.

"I will have your confession. I do not need to hear the woman—we know her sin already."

"Get out."

Brother Roccus stood his ground with a visible effort. "You must confess. I have been sent to hear your confession, and if you do not . . ."

Evan finished it for him. "If you do not hear my confession, Father Leonidas will give you an Act of Contrition to perform, won't he? He must give you a lot of them." Evan remembered that it was Brother Roccus that Father Leonidas had reprimanded the morning before.

"That is not in question."

"Isn't it?"

The sheep had huddled together in the far side of their pen, bleating nervously.

This was too much for Brother Roccus. He had endured more from Evan than he was able to stand. He charged this tormenting prisoner, his book upraised, making a gobbling sound as he came.

Evan moved back against the wall, but not in fear. He was getting as much play as possible in the chain that held his wrists. When he had enough, he swung it expertly, almost casually, across Brother Roccus' face and shoulders.

There was another sound from Brother Roccus now, one that sent the livestock milling, distressed. Brother Roccus fell, lying slumped at Evan's feet, his face torn away where the chain had hit it. Evan leaned back against the wall and waited.

"Evan?" Thea said after a moment.

He looked over at her, lowering the chain. "Are you all right?"

She nodded, touching the scab that had formed on her cheek and was at the center of a massive bruise. "It'll heal," she said.

*   *   *

It was almost an hour later when the monks came to find what had happened to Brother Roccus, and by that time the body was cooling. In horror they looked at their murdered brother, and then at Evan, who twitched the chain suggestively as he grinned, his eyes ferocious.

A monk was sent running for Father Leonidas and when that austere man arrived, he reddened visibly under his filth. "This is the Great Second Crime!" he thundered.

"Take his feet and drag him out. I don't want to smell him any more." Evan gave this order as the old monk came near. "And if any one of your men try to touch me or Thea, I'll do to him the same thing I did to that vermin."

Brother Odo was given the task of pulling the corpse from the barn, and the monks retreated hastily to prepare for the Requiem.

*   *   *

That night there was no bowl of gruel or anything else for them to eat. From the chapel came chanting and the recitation of the long vigil for the dead. In the barn, Thea and Evan listened, counting off the hours of the night as the cycle of prayers continued.

The sun had been up for some time when Evan heard the first sound, like a distant cannon; a crack that echoed across the valley and brought him upright in his chains.

"It's the thaw," Thea said after a moment. "The ice is breaking up in the river. Maybe it's March already."

"What about the snow?" Was it his imagination, or had the smell of the air changed, too, promising the green scent of new grass?

She listened critically. "This is in the valley still. Maybe a week at most before it spreads higher up."

"That means the passes will be open," Evan said, a deep frown settling between his brows. "Graeagle is too close."

"It won't matter in a couple of weeks," Thea reminded him. The sharp hurt of the chains had become a persistent ache and she moved with difficulty.

Evan considered the bound cloth leggings they had been given to serve as shoes, testing them with his hand. He scuffed speculatively at the wall. "How far do you think these would last?"

"I don't know."

"Could we walk out of here, if we were out?"

"It depends on the cold," she said when she had thought about it. "It would be chancy. Frostbite is worse than rocks."

Through the day the distant river boomed for spring.

*   *   *

After sunset Father Leonidas appeared in the barn once more. "In ten days it is the Lord's Day, when He Rose Victorious," he informed them. "On that day, you who are in sin and without repentance, you shall surely perish. And the body of Brother Roccus shall stand as sentinel over your deaths so that his murder will accuse you as you die."

"Delightful. Do you think he'll keep that long?" Evan murmured.

Father Leonidas quivered, his face suffused with red. "Infamy. Infamy. Iniquity."

In response Evan's chains chimed together. He had the satisfaction of seeing Father Leonidas back away from him, reciting prayers as he went.

*   *   *

The rising moon dappled the barn with soft light a week later. There had been clear skies for two days, and the hills sang with freshets. The chanting had continued in the chapel, and occasionally three stave-armed monks would bring a bowl of gruel to the barn for the prisoners. The air was cold, but not the deep biting cold it had been before. With no latrine and little room to move, the barn had begun to stink.

"You awake?" Evan asked softly as he watched the moon through a crack in the wall. He reckoned the time near midnight, but he was not tired, though inactivity had made his muscles sore.

"Yeah. You too?"

"I was thinking," Evan said dreamily, "what it used to be like, a soft winter night like this with spring just coming on. Usually we were in London, and we'd walk along Old Brompton Road, looking in the dark shops. Most of the time it rained, but once in a while it would be clear and cold. Or there'd be just enough snow to make the city shine. God, I loved London. I remember in '85, the Thames froze enough to skate. You should have seen it. People everywhere. It was like a festival."

"It must have been very pretty," said Thea, unable to picture it.

"It was beautiful. A lot of things were beautiful."

"Get some sleep, Evan."

He shook his head. "I want to see this. I want to remember it." He added, very softly to himself, "I want to remember you. Thea. Thea."

* * *

After the monks pronounced formal anathema on them, they were left alone once again. Thea scrambled up in her chains holding a rusty crowbar. "I found it under the floor boards behind the byre," she said. "I think I can get loose if I work at it." She paused. "If there's time, I'll do you."

Evan didn't feel noble and didn't attempt to fool her. "I'm not looking forward to burning," he said. "I hope there's time. But if there isn't, get away."

She looked toward him across the barn, feeling a rush of pity for the dirty, ragged man he had become. "If I can, I'll get us both out." It was a promise. Then she set to work with the crowbar on the shackles that held her chained to the wall.

Outside the monks bustled about gathering wood for the *auto-da-fé*, taking care to choose branches that were green and would burn long and slowly. They worked with more animation than they had shown before, so it was not until the Pirates reached the gates of the monastery that Evan realized what had happened.

The first gunshots blended with the breaking up of the ice and the moaning of chains as Thea struggled with the crowbar; Evan did not hear the sound of the attack when it began, or if he did, he paid it no attention. He did not want to think of the monks, or of what they were doing beyond the confines of the barn.

Then one of the Brothers outside gave a yell and rushed off, shouting for help to his fellows.

"What is it?" Thea asked, pausing in her sweat-drenched work.

"An attack," Evan said slowly as he separated the sounds in his mind. "Pirates, I think. We knew they had to break through soon."

"Then we *can* get out," she said as she went back to work on the chains.

"Not if they see us, we can't. Cox wants my head and you're a Mute. Cox and Father Leonidas would agree about that: they both hate Mutes. Cox might be a little harsher, perhaps, but the end would be the same. And they'd flip a coin for the pleasure of cutting out my liver." He leaned back and listened.

Thea stopped working once more to look at him, seeing him clearly now, seeing his face, thin under the tangle of sandy beard. His eyes were hollow and there was a tightness about his mouth that told more than the short sound of his words. She could see the gray in his hair, sprinkled more heavily than when she had last studied him. She could not see her own face, the deep lines that had been drawn by the ordeal that was her life. There were streaks of white she had not seen growing in the dark shadows of her hair. The winter was over now, she realized. Her birthday had long passed, while they were at Quincy. She was twenty-eight years old. She felt fifty.

"Get back to work, Thea," he told her as gently as he could. "You haven't got much time. They're working on the gates."

"And leave you to Cox or the monks?" she asked, pushing harder on the crowbar. "You're crazy."

"Never mind." He watched her work as he listened to the fight growing louder. There were shouts and screams now, and the occasional splintering of wood, the rupture of gunshot and impact. Then there was the smell of smoke, drifting on the gentle wind.

With a shout Thea broke free of her leg bonds, shaking her feet and pulling the metal around her ankles. "Look, Evan!" She drew the chain from the huge staple that held it to the wall. "We can use this for a weapon if we have to."

"Take it with you," he said, trying to keep the envy from his voice. To see her so close to escape tasted of gall to him, and as much as he hated the feeling, he knew he would rather have been the one to be free.

"Just wait. I think I can get out of this one easier," she said as she started confidently to work on the upper chain that held her wrists.

The smell of smoke grew stronger, and from the chapel the bell began to ring, a wild desperate clanging in counterpoint to the determined snarl of engines and shouting. The Pirates were winning.

"How are you doing?" Evan asked when the smoke had begun to sting his eyes, making him cough. He knew that if he inhaled much more smoke he would be ill, and mucus would fill his nose and throat.

The sheep and cows were milling, almost mad, terrified by the smoke, the rattle of vans, and the crackle of the fire. They pushed against the walls of the barn, trying to break away from the threat around them.

"I'm going to make it," Thea grunted through clenched teeth. Tears almost blinded her eyes, slowing her work and streaking her face with soot and grime. Using her whole body she leaned with all her strength against the chain and finally was rewarded by a small seam in the link. The smoke was growing thicker, and the animals battered at their enclosures, breaking boards with their hoofs and butting their braces until their heads streamed with blood.

"Quickly," Evan told her as she worked. Two gunshots had come nearby and the monks were rushing from the chapel into the farmyard where their stores were gathered.

The metal groaned with Thea as she forced herself against the crowbar. Slowly, slowly the gap widened.

"Keep working, Thea," he said as the smoke made him cough steadily. He felt a searing pain in his chest from the smoke, and thought that life was too sweet to end this way. He had come too far and endured too much.

The wood on the far side of the barn began to smolder.

"Got it!" she shouted as the link gave way at last. Then, sobbing from the effort and choking with smoke, she fell forward onto the hay.

"Get up! You've got to get up, Thea!" The urgency of his voice brought her to her feet faster than the sight of the first lick of flames on the wall. She drew the rough fabric of the habit across her face and stumbled toward the door of the barn. Evan watched her go with regret.

She flung open the door and stood back as the maddened animals bolted through it, their panic sending them into the mass of monks who were running for the storage sheds on the opposite side of the yard.

There was a great crashing roar as the bell tower collapsed, and with it came the shouts of the Pirates as the first of their modified vans rushed into the farmyard.

Thea grabbed a hatchet off the wall by the doors, then turned and scrambled back through the smoke to Evan. Without a word, she began to chop at the couplings that held his chains to the wall. The fire moved hungrily nearer and the heat became intense.

"Thea," he said as she hacked at the wall. "Thea, please, get out of here." As he said it, he knew he meant it. The smoke was making him dizzy now and the heat prickled his skin. She paid no attention to him.

Outside, the Pirates started to run down the livestock that had bolted from the barn, and they slung the carcasses into the beds of their vans as they pursued the monks.

Most of the far end of the barn was on fire now, and the beams above them were charring, ready to kindle. Evan tried to push Thea away, but she shouted at him. "You fool! Stay still!" She staggered back through the smoke and returned with her crowbar. Gasping for breath, she gave it to him, motioning him to help her.

They worked together against the metal as the fire ate its way nearer. At last she kicked the gouges she had made with the hatchet and part of his chain came away, a piece of the wood still attached to the cleat. With this break came fresh air, and it eased their breathing as it fed the fire in the rafters.

From the open door there came a yell. "Hey, Davidson! There's a couple of monks in the barn! Tell Mackley!"

"How many?"

"Two, I think." The Pirates were as close to the door as the flames would let them come. "That fire's going great."

"Let 'em fry!" was the answer and the Pirates hurried away toward the valuable food stores.

In a final effort Thea threw herself against the wood, shoving Evan and the crowbar hard on the weathered boards. The old wood splintered and came away in jagged sections. So great was the force of her attack that she tumbled through the hole into the slushy mush of the poultry yard. Dazed, she lay on her side, bewildered, her face inches from the melting snow that framed the muddy patch where a few bedraggled chickens clucked nervously. Her hands were scraped; the manacles had opened the sores in her ankles and wrists. For the first time she felt the pain of it as she pulled herself onto her knees and stared back at the barn. She was out. She was free.

CHAPTER 8

It was a moment before Evan realized what had happened. His head was muzzy and thick with smoke and the first resigned cloudings of death. He stood at the edge of the hole, staring stupidly while Thea got to her feet and brushed at the stinking mud that plastered the habit she wore.

"Come on!" she shouted to him hoarsely, for the sound of the fire and the battle were growing louder. "We can get away now!"

A new burst of gunfire brought him to his senses. He grabbed the wood which held his chain and flung it through the hole, then clambered out himself. He skinned his knees as he almost fell.

The air was acrid with burning and the hot breath of the fire scorched them. Not far away, stretched on the ground, were the mangled bodies of three monks, caught from behind by Pirate shotguns. To the right, the remains of the chapel, now burning the last of its wood, sent occasional sparks into the air as it was consumed. Thea stood watching the fire, her face showing mottled fear that surprised Evan until he realized that she, just like himself, was seeing the way she would have died at the hands of the monks.

"We'd better hurry," he said in a croak.

Shaking herself, she turned toward him, making an effort to shut out the sight of the flames around them. "You're right," she muttered, then cast about for the safest way out of the valley. "There's a pasture through those gates. And then the hills. That's best."

"We'll go that way, then." He pulled at her sleeve. "We can follow the highway if we have to. The Pirates won't clean up here for a couple of days yet. They're after the grain stored in the sheds and any metals and tools they can salvage."

"The crowbar!" she cried out suddenly.

"Right here." He lifted it, his chains clanging against it. Although he did not want to, he cast a look back over the wreckage that burned behind them; then, gathering up the chains, he started away from the barn toward the gate and the pasture beyond.

Thea stopped long enough to grab some rags drying on the fence, then came quickly after him, not taking energy and breath to speak as she fell in beside him.

"Don't look back," he recommended, knowing what a temptation it was, and how good a target they made crossing the open pasture. "If they get us, they get us. Don't make it easy. Don't stop walking."

She nodded and moved faster, gritting her teeth against the hurt.

That pasture stretched out like eternity, and the twenty minutes it took them to reach the safety of the red-needled pines felt to both of them like the journey of days. The smell of burning followed them, and the sounds of slaughter mixed with the soft chorus of monks who had given up to their captors and were praying. *"Inflammatus et accensus per te, Virgo, sim defensus . . ."* drifted up to them as they at last found the welcome shadows of the trees where they could lose themselves.

*   *   *

The first rise of land that led over the next pass slowed them down, but in a matter of yards they were in the scrub and could afford to stop for breath and take stock of themselves. Smoke from the burning monastery drifted above them and in the distance, barely competing with the rattle of the fight and flames that now consumed the barn where they had been captive, was the distant sound of the river and breaking ice.

"What have we got?" Evan asked when he had caught his breath and wiped his streaming face on his sleeve.

"You've got the crowbar and I've got some rags for our feet." If she was discouraged, she did not show it.

"Anything else?"

She bit her lip. "That's it."

He nodded and found solace in her challenging eyes. "Then we'd better find some shelter." He turned up the slope. "There's a lot of snow around."

"We've been in snow before," she said easily, knowing that they did indeed need shelter, but not worried or beaten now. She re-

membered the years she had survived alone, with little but her wits
to sustain her. She was not frightened. "Snow's better than that,"
she said, pointing back down the hill toward the ruined monastery.

"Yes," he agreed before turning his back on it forever.

*   *   *

The going was hard, for although the snows were melting the
ground was icy wet underfoot and the water quickly soaked
through the rags that bound their feet. Just under the surface the
earth was still frozen and there was little relief from either the
hardness or the cold. Most of the trees had shed their burdens of
snow and now swayed, whispering, in the north wind.

As they climbed, Thea watched the ground ahead of them and
once brought them both to a halt.

"What is it?" Evan asked, seeing a soft indentation at the edge
of a shaded snowbank.

"Bear," Thea answered, her eyes dark with concern. "They
must be coming out of hibernation now. I hope there are deer
around for them."

He understood her implication, and at the moment he bitterly
missed their lost crossbows. To have hungry bear about was a serious danger, and to be unable to hunt brought hunger back to him
with crushing rapidity. He remembered then that they had had no
food that day. The monks had not fed them well after he had
smashed Brother Roccus' head with his chain.

"We'd better keep moving," she said as he paused, deep in
thought.

"Keep your eye out for dried wood." He gave her what he
hoped was a friendly smile. "We'll need some protection, and the
monks did all right with their walking staves. God, I wish we had
matches."

She nodded, but said nothing. She, too, was hungry, and knew
far better than he the risk they had taken. But it was better than
dying in the monks' fire, or at the hands of the Pirates. She set her
teeth against the pain in her ankles and wrists and kept walking.

*   *   *

Nightfall found them above the snow line once more, with Sierraville far behind them. Thea pulled down pine boughs and
wrapped them around Evan and herself for the night; the cold and

the rustlings of animals in the brush kept them half awake as the long hours ran their course.

She found her thoughts straying, not back to the community at Camminsky Creek or her years of wandering, but to her first meeting with Evan, and for the first time she felt an odd, anguished regret that she could not bring herself to accept Evan's body. The few times he had suggested sharing even so little a thing as a mattress she had recoiled as if she had been branded. Her loathing of Lastly grew, and she began to have contempt for herself. She felt maimed, disfigured, and she despised it.

Evan slept heavily, seeking the oblivion of dreams that were insubstantial fragments of the world he had lost.

They woke shortly after dawn to a distant muffled roar that seemed to come from the very bowels of the mountains, a sound that penetrated to their bones, that made even the trees bow and tremble, to silence the few pitiful cries of little animals that had echoed forlornly across the morning.

"What was that?" Thea asked as she scrambled out of her pine nest. She was haggard and dirty and the mark that Brother Roccus had left on her face was sullen purple. The manacles on her wrists caught the morning light and flashed back at her, dazzling her eyes.

"It's not gunfire," Evan said after a bit. "I don't think it's dynamite." He got awkwardly to his feet, trailing his chain and the wood with the cleat. "It must be some kind of blast, but who would be blasting? And what?" He wondered if the Pirates were trying to break through the passes, but knew that this was a greater explosion than anything they could have achieved.

"Maybe there's someone in the mountains back of Sierraville? Someone who saw the Pirates come to the monastery yesterday? It could be that, couldn't it? They might want to close their passes. Seal themselves off from Pirates."

"But why? The noise would only call attention to them." He shook his head and draped his chain over his shoulder to make the carrying easier. He listened as the bellow of the explosion lost itself and the ground steadied.

"It's over, whatever it was." Thea pulled the crowbar out of the pine branches and handed it to him. "Find a stump or a rock. I'll get you out of that thing. I can't get rid of these yet"—she shook the manacles that she wore—"or yours, but I can get the wood off and the chain broken, maybe."

Absently Evan nodded, his mind divided between the strange sound that had wakened them and the job of putting his hunger out of his mind.

It was while they were breaking through his chain that the strange sound came again, the same roar, but this time longer, more sustained, a little more as if it were a cry of the earth itself. Shortly afterward another tremor shook the mountains, like a giant turning in its sleep, and a heavy pall of high smoke spread itself over the sky, drifting on the upper winds and giving the sun an evanescent halo.

By midday the distant sound was fairly constant and the ground quivered underfoot. Smoke clouded the northern sky as Thea broke through Evan's chain. Her determination had almost outlasted her strength, and she sagged when the task was done, only then permitting herself to ask, "Do you know what's happening?"

He stared at the sky. "Maybe," he said, his eyes narrowing. He took up the chain as a weapon and they headed along the old highway, keeping out of sight in the brush, but staying near the road. He felt that it was their only hope now.

*   *   *

The stream ran in front of them, an unexpected break in the scrub-covered slope. It was bright, shiny, living on the melting snow.

"We can drink now," Thea said after sniffing the water carefully. "Some water isn't good even when it's this fresh. And we still can't eat snow. There's too much risk of freezing."

Evan had already knelt to drink when the sound burst through the mountains again, rolling down the spine of the Sierra in awful intensity. He stopped, his hands full of water. "Lassen," he said quietly. "Or Shasta. Probably Shasta. But they're both possible." He found that his hands were shaking and he had to fill them with water again before he could drink. "Christ," he said as he lifted the water to his mouth.

"Lassen?" she asked.

"Lassen and Shasta. They're both volcanoes. Lassen is closer and it was still in business. Even fifty years ago they would occasionally close down the park around it because it was belching smoke and ashes. Shasta did that, sometimes. There was a real scare in the late seventies. I remember reading about it. They thought Shasta was going to blow then."

She scowled, looking back over her shoulder to the obscured sky. "I think Jack Thompson said something about that. There's a whole chain of them, isn't there? Right along the Pacific coast?"

He had busied himself with the water, washing the dirt from his face at last, and so did not answer her immediately. He could feel the grime peel away like a mask and it heartened him. "Yeah," he said at last. "All the way from Alaska through South America. You wash up, too, Thea. You'll feel better."

She did as he bade her, but refused to put aside the question of the volcanoes. "What's the nearest one? Are we too close?"

"Lassen's the nearest, probably, and it's still a long way off." A frown pulled at his brows and mouth. "I'm trying to remember: with all the pollutants in the upper atmosphere, will this make the weather warmer or cooler? And how much of an eruption is it?" Suddenly he pulled his beard. "The first place we find scissors, this gets trimmed. And my hair. And *your* hair." The last place he had been efficiently barbered had been Quincy. Since then he had hacked with scissors and shears, but he knew that the effect was ragged, making him even more shaggy.

"What about the volcanoes?" she persisted.

He made an impatient gesture and started away from the stream. "I don't know. I'll tell you when I remember."

"Will it make things worse?" she asked gently.

"It sure as hell won't make them any better." He turned abruptly and faced south once more, motioning her to come with him. He held the crowbar awkwardly, as if it were a scepter.

"You could sharpen one end," she suggested when they had walked a few miles farther.

He made no answer.

*   *   *

The sunset that night displayed itself spectacularly through the smoke, lighting the whole sky with glowing radiance that turned even the dying, desolate mountains into a place of rare beauty. From the edge of the meadow Thea and Evan stopped in their cutting of pine boughs to watch, each admitting that it was a wonderful sight. The sun's rays flaunted like banners across the sky, and the intensity of color made it almost unreal.

But there was no food that night, nor the next morning. There was a bear, snuffling around the pine nests, curious and hungry.

Thea lay in her branches, her body wet with fear. The bear was pulling at the boughs, still not sure that it was worth his while, but scenting the sharp sweat. His stinking breath bore down on her neck and she could feel the movements of the branches above her. She wanted to call Evan to help her, but the sounds died in her throat, and she knew that any additional noise might be enough to make the bear come after her in deadly earnest. So she lay still, alone with the bear and her fright.

Then there was a movement, a sound, and the bear rose and turned away from her. Evan, brandishing his chain, whirling it around his head like a single lethal propeller, came toward her, yelling for her to get away.

The bear rounded on Evan, teeth bared and a growl in his throat. With a vicious underhand swing, Evan brought his chain upward, full force against the bear's jaw. There was a snapping sound, a yelp of pain, and the bear moved back, but only for a moment as rage and fright brought him onto his hind legs, curving claws ready to disembowel, to mutilate. Evan retreated a few steps.

"Thea! Thea! Get up!"

In a rush the bear charged Evan: he stepped back hastily, bringing the chain around again to crash against the bear's head. This time the impact was harder as the force of the chain cracked bone, and the bear faltered before pressing the attack, giving Thea just enough time to struggle free of the pine branches and to bring the crowbar into play. Following Evan's lead she aimed for the head, using the crowbar for a club. Her first swing went wild and she came within inches of the long, yellowed claws as the bear reached out for her. Evan shouted, and the bear, confused, swung back his way as the chain whistled through the air again, wrapping itself around the bear's neck.

The bear lunged forward now, and Evan knew his danger. He tried to jerk the chain free, to get beyond range of the huge, angry animal, but the blow had been good and the chain held. The bear came on toward Evan, ready to kill. His powerful jaws gaped, showing blood where Evan's first strike had broken teeth. Thea screamed as she wielded her crowbar with both hands. Pressing in close behind the furious bear, she swung the crowbar up, pounding the bear on the back of the neck so that the metal thrummed.

Now the bear hesitated, wanting Evan as his ready victim but plagued by Thea's drubbing. He paused, swaying on his hind legs, pawing at the air and making a coughing growl. Evan saw his chance and leaped for the chain, and as he pulled it, Thea's crowbar connected for the last time. There was a thick, liquid crack and then the bear waddled one or two uncertain steps before he fell forward, twitching as he died, paws reaching for something he could never catch.

"I thought he had you," Thea panted as she felt her knees turn to water. The surge of adrenalin that had carried her left her and weakness took its place, making her feel quite sick. She sat down abruptly.

"I was afraid he'd get you," Evan said almost at the same moment, his hands now shaking terribly.

"Well, maybe we can eat it," Thea said in what she hoped was an optimistic tone. "It would be good to have something to eat."

"It'll have to be raw," Evan said as he touched the bear with his foot. The rags binding it were fast disintegrating and there was a patch of blood near his heel.

Seen dead at their feet, the bear was thin and mangy; one fang had broken and rotted away to a dark stump, and the grizzled muzzle showed his age.

"We don't have a knife," Thea reminded him, lifting her crowbar. "Can we do something with this?"

In the end they had to settle for strips of meat torn from the uneven lacerations the crowbar had made on the neck and shoulders of the bear. The meat was strong, gamy, and the fibers tough, but it gave them an energy they had not had for days. They ate determinedly and fought down revulsion as they drank some of the blood before it congealed. When they had finished their meal, they pulled a few more strips from the carcass and regretfully left the rest: they had no way to carry or store more than a little of the meat.

*   *   *

That day they passed through the wild scrubby mountains where once there had been a National Forest. Perhaps forty years before Congress had voted to increase logging in the hitherto protected woods. Now the ruined land bristled with scrub stretching away for miles. There reptiles and a few insects lived, but the chemicals that were supposed to speed the forest regeneration had made the place uninhabitable for all but the smallest and most voracious animals. Of the pine and fir which had been planted in the wake of the logging there was no sign.

When night came there were no boughs to wrap in, nor any need for them. Thea and Evan found a hollow near a contaminated stream littered around its banks with small bones. And there they slept, close to the snow, serenaded by the poisoned water.

*   *   *

By the middle of the next day they found the town—a few huddled buildings and the remains of a sawmill. The road cut through the cluster of buildings, as if casting them aside in its hurry to be somewhere else.

"Do you think it's safe?" Thea asked Evan. She was looking critically at the chafing on her wrists where the metal of her manacles had left deep welts of infection, and she knew that Evan must have the same trouble. "We have to get some rest. And some shoes. And these off."

Evan thought for a moment. "It doesn't seem right, on a road like this. . . . You'd think . . ." But there was no sign of habitation, no indication that the Pirates had come through. The snow that melted around the buildings was undisturbed, showing nothing but small tracks of animals.

"It's in the middle of nothing," Thea said unhappily, casting a glance around the snowy, scrub-filled waste.

"Yes." He lapsed into silence. "We'll have to try, though."

She grabbed her crowbar, shouldering it with a shrug. "Anything you say."

They circled the town through the patches of snow and underbrush, occasionally sinking into the shallow drifts when the spindly branches underneath gave away. They came in from the west, having gone halfway around the huddled buildings, carefully avoiding the road or the snow that lined it, knowing that footprints there would advertise their presence. There was no sign of life, even when they came closer to the houses. At last they stood on a snowy, overgrown dirt road a few hundred feet from the nearest house.

"Booby trap?" Thea asked.

"It doesn't look like it," Evan answered, but he did not put his chain down. He knew that if he were in one of the houses, he would not show himself. He would wait silently, holding back, keeping his peace, his invisibility, until he could pick off the invaders.

"Shall we go in?" she said, giving her crowbar an experimental heft.

He nodded as he made up his mind. The few yards to the back door were all that they had to cover. He went ahead and pushed carefully on the weathered wood. The door swung open. It had not been locked.

Inside they found what was left of the householders: four partly decayed bodies lay sprawled in the living room, a strange phosphorescent mold on their peeling skin.

"Chemical contamination. They must have tried to farm the forest after it had been sprayed," Evan said as he knelt by one of the bodies. "Too bad. It doesn't look like anything else went wrong, though. This isn't leprosy. It isn't cancer."

"It doesn't have to be," Thea said dryly. She had raided the kitchen for knives and found two or three with fine sharp blades, as well as the bonus of a meat cleaver. "There's also some canned food," she reported carefully. "Home canned. No dates."

Evan rose from the side of the nearest body. "It could be contaminated too, of course. That's what you're saying? If they did the canning after the forest was sprayed. And there's no way to tell."

She nodded her confirmation before turning back to the kitchen. "No way."

Evan followed her, furtively rubbing his hands on his fraying habit. "We'll have to take a chance and eat. There isn't much choice."

"What if we don't eat?"

He opened his hands hopelessly. "Look out there. It's a long way to other food. If we don't eat, we starve."

"I see." She leaned against the kitchen table, looking at the disorder around her. "There's no wood. We'll have to break up furniture if we want any heat. And the water doesn't work. I tried that already."

He put down the chain. "We don't have to stay here very long. Only until we're out of our chains and our feet heal a bit."

"Or until we die, like the others."

So it was settled.

* * *

In the house they found files and after long work they were free of the manacles. A salve in a tube left in the bathroom turned out to be good medication for the abrasions on their wrists and ankles: after a few days they felt better and the marks began to fade.

They buried the bodies, then set to work sorting out the food jars, and worked out a program for a systematic raid on the other houses for shoes and clothes, ending up with a choice and variety that was almost intoxicating. Evan found proper scissors and trimmed his hair and beard. After some powerful persuasion he talked Thea into letting him cut her hair.

"You can't want to have it all matted and flopping in your eyes," he said gently, touching her head. "It's silly, Thea."

"I like it." Her chin was out mulishly and there was discomfort in the back of her eyes. She said truculently, "You don't have to do it. I can manage."

Then he understood. "Look, Thea, I'm not going to trap you. I'm not trying to force you to do anything you don't want to. It's your hair, and you can wear it any way you want. It's also very dirty and scraggly and a damn nuisance. You said so yourself. But if you want to keep it, fine. I know I want mine cut off."

"Good. All I've got to do is wash and comb mine and it will be fine."

He handed her the comb he had found and watched as she tried to drag it through the tangles.

"Let me cut your hair, Thea," he said once more when the comb had broken.

"I just want to make crossbows," she mumbled, but Evan could see that his suspicions had been right, and that she still feared his touch, even his nearness. Her body kept an uneasy truce with itself and she went on this precarious way to avoid the fear which still lived in her. The scar on her cheek where Brother Roccus had hurt her was only a pale line, and her breast had long since healed. But there were other wounds, wounds of the soul, still open, festering, hidden deep inside her. Evan wished then that he did not want her as much as he did, that he was indifferent to her, that he could hold back from her without regret.

She sat stonily as Evan wielded the scissors.

*   *   *

Four days later, with new clothes and canned food and newly made crossbows, they set out to the south again, for Truckee and the mountains around Lake Tahoe. Two days brought them near Truckee, but the drifting soot on the wind told its own story, as did the eight impaled bodies of men at the entrance to the town. They had not been dead long and the oppressive stench was ghastly.

"This is a new wrinkle," Evan said as they saw the ominous stakes with their grisly burdens.

"Pirates?"

He looked at the impaled men, but there was little human left in their faces. "I don't know. Maybe. But they can't have come from Graeagle. Maybe from Auburn. Cox wanted to have a base there last year. It was one of the things that he promised when he took over. If these are Pirates, they might be at Tahoe ahead of us as well as behind us." He gave a scowl to the stakes. "They mean to keep people out. These are warnings not to go any farther. They will probably have patrols out. They mean it, Thea." He could see Cox again, his face reddened by the sun so that the freckles were lost under the burn. He was so inoffensive-looking, Cox was, until you took the time to watch his eyes and saw the muddy hatred there. If Cox had ordered the impalement, it was because he enjoyed watching it.

"I don't like this: let's go, Evan." Thea started down the road toward the town. "We can make it if we're careful."

"No, not that way. We can bypass the center of town and cross the highway this side of Donner Lake. There's a long bend in the road, according to the maps we've seen. They can't watch every inch of the road all the time, and they'll be sticking close to the town." He looked at the sky. "It might snow soon. They'll stay indoors."

"Snow or rain," Thea corrected him as she studied the clouds gathering overhead, shoved one on top of the other by a south wind.

"Or rain." He adjusted his sack slung over his back and got his crossbow ready. "Slot up a quarrel. If we have to fight, there won't be any warning." He looked one last time at the hideous pales. "I wonder who taught them that?"

Thea had fitted a quarrel to the slot and set the trigger, then fell in beside him. They went silently, keeping away from the patches of snow that would leave tracks. The sun crept across the glowing sky, and they marked their progress by it, that bright smear behind the clouds.

Finally they approached the highway that lay curving below them. There were a few building shells, long ago destroyed, and the rusted remains of cars between them and the highway. "What do you think?" Evan asked as he watched the road, tense, alert.

"I can't hear anything. There's nothing moving."

"Umm." He tightened his crossbow another notch.

In a moment she said, "That business with the stakes—that wasn't your idea?" She looked at him for an answer.

"Impalement?" He raised his sandy brows, more surprised than anything else. "You think that I would do that?"

She shook her head, relieved and guilty at once.

"I knew about it. Anyone who'd read history knew about it. But I never used it. Never." He looked down at her, at the white in her dark hair, at her face that never smiled. He knew deep sadness for her, that she should be born into the world where men impaled one another, where joy was gone and only the hardship remained, where even hope was impractical.

"I'm glad you never did that. I'm glad someone else taught them to do that," she said, meeting his horrified eyes only fleetingly before she fell silent once more, her face closed to him, remote, alone.

He could think of nothing to say to her. Raising his crossbow he moved toward the highway.

* * *

It turned out to be easier to get across the road than they had thought it would be. There was no one about, and in a while it began to rain, a slow, sleety mizzle that reduced all the world to shades of gray.

On the far side of the highway they found what had been a hospital, gutted and looted, a grim testament to the presence of the Pirates.

"I think they might have left medicine in here. We could use it, if there's any left. Even bandages, we need bandages." She turned to him. "Should we look? Do you think anything's left?"

"We've got a couple of hours until nightfall, we might as well use them here."

Keeping his crossbow ready, he led the way through the shattered doors into what was once an emergency room. Three partitions separated gurneys from each other, and shelves, although raided and pulled apart, still had bandages and a few basic first aid supplies. In one corner an armored door stood open, crazily askew on its hinges where the explosives had ripped it away. Obviously it had at one time contained drugs.

"Here," said Thea as she gathered up the bandages. "There's tape, too, and some doctor's knives. We could use them. We still need knives and they make good tips for quarrels."

He picked up the scalpels without comment, packing them away with the blankets he found. Then, quite by accident, he found two flashlights, obviously the sort that had been used by nurses, and with them a sealed box of batteries.

"Will they work?" Thea asked him when she saw him loading the batteries into one of the flashlights.

"I'm going to see." He knew he was trusting to luck and was very much afraid that the reason they had been overlooked by the Pirates was that they were useless. But to his amazement the flashlight did produce a feeble beam. "Here," he said, handing her the first flashlight and loading the other, "only use it for emergencies. You'll be glad to have it then."

She took the flashlight wonderingly. "I haven't seen one of these since"—she thought about it—"years." The word was lame, as if she wanted to shut the memory away. She had been seventeen when she had last had a working flashlight. She had left it in a steel pipe that fed an irrigation canal. She had clung to that flashlight as its beam faded, then sat in the dark, listening to the farmers searching for her outside. There had been rats in the pipe, and once the flashlight had died, she had used it as a club to fend them off. She shuddered as she recalled it.

"Keep it with you," Evan said flatly. He had seen her face change and knew that he must not force her to share her thoughts with him.

They made a last search of the hospital, hoping to find some-thing more that had been left behind. And it was then that Evan found the bodies stuffed in a closet. They had been dead for many weeks and had died terribly.

"Pirates?" Thea asked as Evan moved back from the closet, gagging.

"Yes," he said when he could speak. "That one, the one with the skin off his arms, the one with the extra finger"—he pointed to a viciously mangled body—"that's Cox."

Thea stared. "Cox? But I thought . . ."

"So did I. But I guess the mutations have caught up with them." He studied the rotten corpses, willing himself to be impassive. Along with the burns, the abrasions, the marks of torture, he saw new fingers, regrown tissue, still its tawny-new color in spite of decay. "This changes things," he said.

* * *

Late the next day they heard the sound of engines. They had chosen to follow the highway south to Lake Tahoe, hoping to find Squaw Valley, for if crazy Margaret Cornelia had been right, they might be safe there. And if Margaret Cornelia had been wrong, they would be no worse off than they were already.

"Vans?" Thea said, uncertain.

"I think so." He was already heading into the underbrush sprouting by the road. "Quickly, Thea."

In a few moments a pair of vans sped into view, each with a driver and a man riding shotgun. They went up the broken road with grim efficiency, making only a few necessary signals from one vehicle to the other. Evan watched the signals carefully and when the vans had rumbled out of sight, he said to Thea, "It seems they're taking over part of Tahoe."

"What does that mean?" She was cold with fear inside.

"It means that we stay away from the lake until we know more." He thought of Margaret Cornelia and her madness again, locked away in the mountains as surely as she would have been locked away in an asylum decades ago. "I hope she was right about Squaw Valley. We need a place like that. We can take a few days to comb the mountains west of here. It's got to be around here somewhere. We can find it, check it out. Maybe we can stay there."

"But what will we find? Will we be able to defend it from those Pirates you taught so well?" Even as she said it, she knew it was not fair to him, but the words were out; there was no recalling them.

More than he wanted to admit she had hit home. "They were my Pirates once, but not now. Remember Chico, Thea?"

She wanted very much to apologize, to ask him to forgive her, but she avoided his eyes and said, "If we're going to find that valley, we'd better start looking now."

*   *   *

That night as they ate a frugal meal, he tried again to sound her out, to discover what had upset her, but she remained stubbornly silent. She slept as far away from him as she could and still be near the embers of their small fire.

She remained silent the next day as they climbed through thick undergrowth that tangled itself between the red pines. Her face was blank and she would not look at him. She spoke only once, and that was to point out the rutted and broken bits of road which dead-ended at an old landslide.

"What do you think? That it's the valley?" Evan asked with ill-concealed excitement.

She shrugged, saying something indifferent while she wished she could touch him without hating herself.

"I think it is." He watched her, thinking of the long climb over the slide which might end in disappointment.

"And if it isn't?" Her years of loneliness were in that question.

"Then we keep trying until we find it, Thea. It's all we *can* do."

"Until the Pirates come."

"Oh, Thea." He reached out his hand in comfort but she shied away, stepping well out of reach. He dropped his hand. "We'd better get going."

*   *   *

It was dusk when they reached the other side of the landslide. Away in the gloom, surrounded by snowy slopes like cupped hands, lay the valley. At one side three large buildings reared up, unkempt but untouched. The steep slopes were dotted with houses ranging from mere cabins to substantial homes. From one of the buildings at the far end of the valley there rose a series of flimsy towers, wrapped now in broken and rusted cable from which bits of wood dangled. In the radiant afterglow they could see enough to know that this valley had survived in isolation, hidden and secret, safe from the horror all around. Winter and a landslide had protected it.

"Well, Thea," Evan said as they walked toward the center of the valley. The snow was marked with a few animal tracks, but there were no human footprints in the soft drifts. The valley floor was wide and fairly flat, easy to walk on. Evan indicated the houses on the valley floor and on the lower slopes, picking them out with the weak beam of his flashlight. "It's up to you to choose. Where do you want to live?"

As they went further, they could see that time and winter had taken a toll. Some of the houses had caved in under the weight of the season, some were leaning precariously, their perches on the mountain no longer supporting them, and a few others, better located and built with forethought, stood intact and waiting. At last the thread of light picked out a house, an octagonal one with a high railed porch that squatted on the side of the mountain. Instead of great panes of glass, which many of the houses had once boasted, this sensible wooden house had only high, narrow windows at each angle of the octagon. The chimney, which stuck up from the sharply sloping roof, promised a wood stove, and one pipe above the frosting of snow was of accordion plastic, unruptured in spite of temperature changes and severe weather.

"That one," Thea said, starting away toward the octagonal house.

"There are larger ones around," Evan said, offering her the chance for room and luxury.

"They'd just be harder to heat," she said bluntly, and continued through the crusty slush on the valley floor. She watched the house as she walked, as if it were a lighthouse, marking safe harbor in the middle of a storm.

Evan knew she was right. There was no longer a place in the world for luxury. He made his way steadily through the silent valley, following Thea to the octagonal house on the side of the mountain.

CHAPTER 9

The octagonal house was well and thoroughly locked. It took some time to find the garage door, which was still partly buried under the snow, and then even more time to loosen the lock so that they could lift the door enough to squeeze under it. From the garage it was an easy matter to take the lower door off its hinges and to climb up into the house itself.

Thea was the first one up the stairs, and found herself in a room that took up half the octagon. There was, as she thought there would be, a large, partly open fireplace, with wood neatly stacked near it. No drafts chased them round the room; the flue was closed. Whoever had planned and built the house left little to chance, and Thea was impressed.

To one side of the fireplace there were stairs leading to the second floor, and at the back of the stove, in the other half of the octagon, was an ample kitchen, again with a wood-burning stove, and next to it, standing in its antique glory, was an ancient water heater, one that was filled by the sink pipes and heated by the warmth in the lighted stove.

"That's incredible," Evan said when he saw the water heater. "Those things weren't in common use for about eighty years. I wonder where they found it?"

"I don't care," said Thea, "as long as it works."

A search of the pantry off the kitchen revealed well-stocked shelves and safely sealed bins of flour, all carefully labeled. There was even a large jar of honey, now crystallized with age, but keeping its amber color and the rare promise of sweetness. A spice rack hung on the wall, its fifteen neat bottles stopped with cork. Beneath it a coffee grinder waited.

The unoccupied, musty smell hung in each room of the house, a sad, neglected scent, as if the house were in mourning. This odor permeated everything, giving a staleness to the rooms, making the big throw pillows in the living room seem flat, the kitchen less friendly, the upstairs like an attic. Thea put aside her caution and opened two of the windows in the small bedroom above the kitchen.

While Thea explored, Evan got a fire going, and after two or three determined belches of smoke, the chimney began to draw properly as Evan adjusted the draft of the flue. The fire leaped merrily and began to banish the dark of twilight.

When the house was warmer, Evan left the living room for the kitchen to fire up the stove there and prepare their evening meal. He was delighted to find enough canned goods to let him turn out what seemed to them a sumptuous meal. He had taken canned chicken, thinking as he did that he had not eaten chicken for a long time, though he had seen a few. To this he added canned peaches, mace, and allspice. The aroma was dizzying. When he had set this in the oven he opened cans of Boston brown bread and string beans, heating them in separate pots of bright enamel. To complete the celebration, he also made a kind of hot chocolate from powdered milk, sugar, and baking chocolate. There were also five bottles of brandy, but these he set aside for later, when they might need the warmth more than they did now.

When they had eaten they sat for a few minutes, saying little, while the large, scented candles fought the somber darkness.

"Do you want a bath?" Evan said as he gathered the plates into a pile.

"I want some sleep." She was staring into the dregs of her chocolate. "I'm tired."

"Maybe in the morning, then?" He rose, carrying the plates to the sink.

"We don't even know if the water works or not." But she got to her feet and joined him at the sink.

He turned the tap and a trickle of rust-colored water ran out. "Not much," he allowed. "Maybe I can fix it. There's a pump out back . . ."

"Try in the morning."

Upstairs they found fresh linen in cedar chests, with lightweight acrylic-filled comforters that were wonderfully warm. After a brief debate Thea took the smaller room because it was warmer, although Evan suspected that she did not want to sleep in the double bed. Certainly the bunk beds in the smaller room were more closed, less exposed, than the big bed in the second room.

"It was a good dinner, Evan," she said, very sleepy, as if the contentment of the meal had released a spring in her.

"It was," he agreed awkwardly.

"We used to have chicken at Camminsky Creek, sometimes. I'd forgotten how it tasted. That smell. Nothing else smells like roasting chicken. It was like being back in my mother's kitchen."

"I know. There's more cans of it. The people who lived here before must have thought they'd get snowed in all the time. There's enough food for three months down there in the pantry."

"Three months."

He laughed. "We don't have to worry yet. Even if we stay longer than that, there are other houses. We can get things from them."

"We start tomorrow," she said, turning into her room.

"All right," he said to the closed door. "Tomorrow."

* * *

Thea awoke slowly the next morning, and for a moment of panic, could not remember where she was, or what had become of Evan. But as she touched the soft comforter and smelled the friendly aroma of something cooking, she felt all of the previous day come back to her, flooding her mind. She wanted to shout, or cry, or run, to show how she felt rather than fight to find the words. But she did none of these things. She pulled the comforter more tightly around her, and with more care than was necessary she climbed out of bed and hesitantly started down the stairs. She was barefoot, thinking that she had rarely dared to move anywhere without shoes, but that here she was safe, and could move around in a comforter, unarmed, unshod. And she did not want to wear her grimy, stinking clothes. The comforter was nicer, cleaner.

"Good morning," Evan called as he saw her. "There's breakfast in about ten minutes, but you'll want a bath first." He gave her an encouraging smile, carefully keeping his distance. "There's hot water, I fixed the pipes, and the bathroom is waiting. I've put out soap and towels for you. Go on, Thea. I had mine earlier." By the looks of him, he had scrubbed himself with laundry brushes, for his skin glowed and his hair hung damply around his face. His beard was newly trimmed and even his fingernails were clean.

Unspeaking, pleasantly apprehensive, Thea went into the bath-room and looked skeptically at the tub. It was large and bright red, standing on gilded claw feet. Obviously this was the one room where the otherwise austere owners had given their fancy free rein. The sink was also red, and above it a broad mirror was fogged and showing the path of water drops, left over from Evan's use of the room. A few sandy hairs were still in the sink, and Thea found this almost disturbing. The room embarrassed her; she had never seen anything like it before. In all the places she had wandered the bathing was Spartan in its simplicity. Now this, and the little re-minder of Evan's presence made her shy and awkward.

Gingerly she went to the tub and looked at the handles. Then, very slowly, as if she were afraid the whole thing might explode, she turned the handle of the tub marked *hot*.

Water and a warm cloud of steam gushed out, making a happy splashing sound as it cascaded into the red tub. Belatedly she real-ized she had not put in the plug, and she tried to stop the water, scalding her hands in the attempt. She let out a little shriek.

In the next moment Evan was at the door. "Are you all right, Thea?" he asked with quick concern.

"I don't know what to do," she said miserably, turning to the door. "Help me. I don't remember how these things work."

He nodded and came into the room. Following her pointing finger, he went to the tub and pulled the handle, shutting the water off. The gushing stopped. Then he picked up the plug from the soap dish. He held it out to her, but she would not take it. He put it in place for her and turned on the taps again. The tub began to fill. "How warm do you want it?" he asked, careful not to look at her. It was getting terribly difficult to keep his distance from her, particularly now that they were safe for a while, and had time to learn to know each other.

"Warm?" she ventured, still rationing herself by the number of buckets of hot water it would take to fill a tub like that, as she had done as a child.

Evan adjusted the handles to a comfortably hot level and watched while the water rose. When it was deep enough, he turned the water off and stepped back. "That ought to do it," he said, and left the room abruptly.

It had been more than nineteen years since Thea had had her last hot bath in a proper tub. She could vaguely remember the house outside Sacramento with the shiny appliances and cool rooms that defied the heavy heat of high summer with purring efficiency. At Camminsky Creek they had still had tubs and hot baths, but those were filled by the bucket from water boiled on the stove in huge pots.

She sank into the steaming water, the unfamiliar warmth feeling almost evil. She had been cold for so long that now it hurt to be warm: this was a forbidden pleasure, to use so much water and heat just to wash more comfortably. She stretched out, feeling the filth leave her and the knotted tension in her muscles release its grip on her. The soap smelled sweet and it spread softly over her, unlike the grainy stuff she had washed with so often, when she could wash at all.

She came out of the bathroom at last, wrapped in the engulfing towel Evan had put there for her. She felt like another person, one who had always lived in a warm house and took hot baths and ate chicken for dinner. Her hair clung in tendrils around her face, her skin was pale coral, and she moved easily. The first suggestion of a smile hung at the corner of her mouth.

"Breakfast is ready," he said, presenting her with muffins and jam, some canned fruit, and condensed milk to take the place of cream. There was even coffee, a thing he had not tasted for years and which she had never known.

"Do you like it?" Evan asked when she frowned at the bitterness.

"Not yet," she said, determination in the line of her jaw. "But I will. I will."

"You don't *have* to like it. I found some tea. You can have that," he said as he refilled the mug.

"Oh, yes I do have to like it," she said, closing the subject.

*   *   *

Because she wished it they raided the other houses nearby that day, looking for food and other supplies they could use. The people who had kept houses at Squaw Valley had not wanted monkish lives, and there were many valuable things that lay strewn about the rooms, things Thea had never seen, and some that Evan remembered only remotely. There were paintings on the walls ranging from amateur efforts to signed masterpieces, books were plentiful, there was a wide variety of decoration, electronic systems sat with silent speakers flanked by vinyl libraries.

There were jackets and coats made of furs of animals that no longer existed. There were jewels like sections of the rainbow in chests that rivaled their contents for beauty. There were boots and shoes in so many shapes that Thea grew disgusted with them.

Musical instruments littered one house, strange flat things with buttons and wires as well as strings. These were hooked up to amplifiers and speakers, forever voiceless now that the power was gone from them.

It was there that Evan looked through the record collection, for this one was much more vast than those they had seen before. He pulled them out at random, shaking his head and returning the cardboard envelopes to their designated slots.

Then he came across one that he took out very slowly. He was dazed as he turned to Thea. "Look," he said, handing her the album.

"What's that?" she asked, not particularly interested. She was fingering a jacket of soft mink the color of apricots. It was very warm and almost the right size.

"That's my father," he said unbelievingly. "That's my father."

Interested now, she put down the jacket and came nearer. "What's he doing?" she asked, seeing the photo of a middle-aged man waving a long thin stick with his right hand and making a fist with his left. Even though the photograph was old and faded, there was an energy to the man, and a kind of beauty.

"He's conducting." Evan's voice was thick and the words did not come easily. "Mozart's *Jupiter Symphony*."

"Conducting? You mean leading the orchestra? And the Mozart is the one you and Rudy Zimmermann talked about?"

"Yes." Without warning he threw the record across the room and rushed from the house. The door slammed behind him.

*   *   *

Thea found him some time later back at their house. He was sitting, staring into the fire, a glass filled with pungent amber liquid in his hand and a half-empty bottle of brandy beside his chair. There was a bleariness about his face, a loss of focus, and his words, when he spoke, were slurred.

"Why did you leave?" She kept her usual distance from him, but there was real concern in her voice. "What went wrong?"

"With my father?" He refused to look at her, at the beaver jacket she wore over a sensible wool sweater. "He died."

"But I didn't mean . . ."

"At London. In '98. When the chol . . . cholera broke out. When everybody died there. The bodies got as thick as . . . It stank, London did." He took another mouthful of the brandy and let his face sag. "It was such . . . such a great city. The sickness got it. Destroyed it. Destroyed the people."

She moved a little closer to him. "Evan, why haven't . . ."

But he interrupted her. "It was a waste." His voice was harsh. "A whole city died because too damn many people lived there. They all wanted things. Another car. Television. Wash-after-one-wearing clothes. Freezers full of food. *Everyone* wanted that." He stopped long enough to finish the brandy in the glass and pour more. "It wasn't their fault, though. It wasn't. No one told them the truth. No. Not the truth. Truth"—he wagged his finger at her—"doesn't win elections. Or sell papers. Truth isn't popular. So they died." Suddenly he stopped. "So we're like Goths, living in the ruins. The Dark Ages come again." A racking sound filled his throat. "I'm going to be sick," he muttered. He lurched to his feet and shambled from the room. A moment later Thea heard him vomit into the toilet.

"Evan!" There was alarm in her voice as she ran to him and found him bent over the bowl, his face gone from flushed to pasty. He stopped her at the door. "I'm drunk, Thea. Keep away."

She hesitated, then, worried, started toward him.

"I said keep away!" The sound was like a blow and she reeled under it.

"But why? You need help, don't you? Evan, what's the matter?"

Even in his condition he could sense her concern and confusion. Slowly he wiped his mouth on one of the fresh, soft towels, and threw it down with a grimace. He sat on the edge of the tub, gesturing to her to come nearer, taking her hand when she did. "I wouldn't say this to you if I were sober," he began, making an effort to keep his words crisp. "No, don't draw back. I won't hurt you. My word on it." He could see she was poised to flee from him. "You're perfectly safe. I'm not that drunk. If I were going to take you against your will, I would have done it a long time ago. I couldn't do that to you, Thea. But . . . but, Thea, I'm not a stone. I know you and I want you. That's all. I couldn't . . . hurt you, Thea. I know what hurt is and I know what it does to people. All right. Maybe I don't understand what it was like. But I wouldn't *do* it, Thea." He rubbed at his eyes as if wanting to wipe alcohol or his memories away. "It's been almost a year since we started traveling together, since you saved my life in that silo. We've been through a lot together. I could not have survived without you. I would have died months ago. And now I know you, Thea. I know the kind of woman you are. I value you. I want you. I won't lie about that." His fingers tightened as she started to pull her hand away. "Maybe it's not possible. Maybe there's no way. But promise me . . ." With an effort he released her hand. "Don't say no yet. Promise me you'll think about it."

She nodded, frightened, but not with the blind terror he had seen in her before. Then she was gone from the room and Evan felt himself sinking into a hopelessness that was as engulfing as night. He knew he should not have spoken to her, that she wasn't prepared to deal with his need. It wasn't lust, he told himself. Or if it was, it was only a small part of it.

In a little while she was back, holding a cup of cold coffee out to him. "I think it helps. I remember my mom saying that once."

Wordlessly Evan took the cup and drank the coffee, not aware of the dreadful taste. It was much easier to drink the coffee than to talk with her, for now he was becoming more sober by the minute, and he felt the first discomforts of a hangover even more acutely than he felt shame. When the cup was empty, he handed it back to her, watching her lean, strong fingers close around it.

* * *

The next day they explored the old stadiums and dormitories. There was a little shop filled with winter clothes and another, next to it, that displayed pretty, useless things that were for people to keep or give as mementos. "Souvenirs," Evan explained, picking up a tiny, badly done statue of a deer with Squaw Valley scribbled on its side. "People used to buy millions of these things." On one rack there were faded paperback books, most of which had fallen to pieces. Beyond it, a stand with toothpaste and aspirin, shampoo and tanning lotions.

"What did people do here? Why did they come?" Thea asked as they walked to the foot of the dilapidated ski lift.

"Winter sports. Ice skating. Skiing. All the sports that go with winter. Hockey, downhill and cross-country skiing. It was fun.

They came up from the Coast and the valleys and exhausted themselves in the snow. Then they went back to the cities, tanned, stretched, almost smug. I used to play hockey myself, in college." He looked up at the mountains rising around them, to the snow that clung so tenaciously to the crags, the shaggy fringe of trees defying winter, the redness of their needles reaching toward the sun. It was not a place for playing now.

*   *   *

But it was pleasant as the spring came on, timidly at first, and then with a fragile energy giving a kind of beauty to the place. There was a shining in the air, a freshness that not even the new pall of volcanic smoke could obscure. The streams grew their own kind of peppery watercress, and miner's lettuce poked out of the ground, more stunted than before but still tangy and good. The days became weeks, and a month went by.

"What about the animals?" Thea asked as she sorted out boxes of canned goods. The regular meals for the last month had taken away the tight hollows of her body; the bones that had pushed angrily at her skin were changed to sweet, angular curves that erased the brittle look she had worn for so long.

"Too near Tahoe, probably," Evan answered. He was busy cleaning a couple of small traps he had found in another house. With luck he thought he might catch something on the western ridge of the valley. He, too, had put on flesh, having now something of the indomitable solidity that had marked him once as the most respected of the younger general directors, shuffling the bookings of six opera companies and fifteen symphonies all over the world. He had done his job well, then, and cleaned his traps with much the same care that he had used in contract negotiations. "We can try, though. There's been bobcat tracks by the upper creek once or twice. They're predators, and they must be living on something."

"Not bobcat." She said it with finality, seeing again the bobcat at Buck's Lake as it sank under the ice.

"All right. No bobcat. What about raccoon?"

She considered this, recalling all the strange meats she had eaten to stay alive; rats, when there was nothing else, and rattlesnakes. "Evan, there's enough food to keep us going for a while, isn't there?"

"Sure," he said.

"Then let's wait for a bit. Don't put traps out yet."

He glanced up at her in surprise. "Thea? I thought you were the one who didn't want to take all this for granted. You said we shouldn't get used to living like this."

Half-frowning now, she made a complicated gesture. "I don't know. It's just that there are so few of them left. We don't need them yet. We don't have to kill them, do we? Not yet?"

"No, we don't have to. Not yet." He gave her a gentle smile and felt himself ache for her.

"Then put the traps away, okay, Evan?" she pleaded.

"Okay. Until we really need them," he promised.

*   *   *

Over the next few days the smoke in the sky grew darker and occasionally the air would echo eerily with the distant sound of the volcano. The light grew hazily colorful, even at midday, and turned violently bright at sunset, as if the fire in the earth were reflected in the sky.

"Why did it happen?" Thea asked as they trudged toward their house in the glow of a spectacular May sunset.

"Who knows? Volcanoes have always been a puzzle. Lassen was threatening sometimes, and Shasta was a potential hazard. It was bound to happen someday. It was now rather than another time."

Thea looked at the vivid display in the west. "I don't think I'd like to be any farther north. Lassen and Shasta are north of here, aren't they?"

Evan remembered once stopping in Iceland, when the volcanoes there were active. He had seen a lava snout poke its way into a village and watched as the buildings burned like matches. "No. I wouldn't want to be any farther north."

*   *   *

At night, seated by the fire, Evan would read to her, picking the books at random to entertain her and himself with a great variety of stories.

"What's this one about?" she would ask, handing him another book, then sit back to listen while he read. Occasionally he would have to explain some detail, for Thea knew very little history, and her knowledge of geography and politics was sketchy at best. Because much of what was in the books was strange to her, she shied away from reading aloud herself, but was always delighted to hear him read.

He was in the middle of *Pride and Prejudice* when she stopped him after one of Elizabeth's more cutting observations, asking with a clouded face, "Did people really live like that? Spending all their time wondering about money and marriage and clothes and parties?"

"Well," he answered, holding his place in the book with his finger, "I guess they did, yes. This is a satire, so Austen emphasizes it, but it is pretty much the things people at that level of society worried about. It was different for the titled and landed and the wealthy, like Mr. Darcy. The poor were the way the poor always have been, and that's outside the scope of this book. But for women like Elizabeth and her sisters, yes, their lives were fairly limited. Remember, this was two hundred years ago. And then, marriage was the most important thing in their lives, and husbands were very hard to find."

"But all those words and all that plotting just to have two people end up together."

He stifled a laugh. "Yes." To a large degree it had still been that way when he was young. Some few determined and talented women had broken away from the pattern, and the resurgence of feminism had forced a few reforms in law, but even then, for most women, marriage was the framework for their lives. "It didn't change a lot," he said in a moment. "People used to get married, you know. I did."

She scowled at him. "Is it that important?"

"What? Marriage?"

"No," she snapped. "Sex and children. Do people really care that much? Does it make that much of a difference?"

There was a look in his eyes that made her turn away, wishing she could take back her questions. When he could, he answered her. "Yes, when there is time, it *is* that important." Clumsily he opened the book and began to read again, but his attention had wandered and he soon found an excuse to stop.

*   *   *

But that night, as he lay in bed, staring at the darkness, he became angry. It had been one thing to keep to himself all those months in the cold and danger, when he could not afford to think about wanting Thea. Now that they were safe things were different. Now, he thought bitterly, because we have time and opportunity, because we're not starving or shot at, it is important. It is important. He was so preoccupied that he did not hear her come into his room: her light touch on his arm startled him and he sat up abruptly.

"Evan?" said her small, still voice. "Is it that important to you?"

He waited a moment, gathering his thoughts, wondering if he had understood her. "Is wanting you that important? Is that what you're asking?"

She made a little sound and a nod.

He took a chance. "Yes. It is."

Although her hand shook and grew cold, she resolutely kept it on his arm. "I don't know if I can. But I'll try."

"I don't want a sacrifice, Thea," he said, hating himself for giving her a reason to leave him again. He thought he might still be asleep, and this his dream. He flexed his toes and felt the sheet move.

"I'm not trying to sacrifice myself. I just thought that maybe it was right, or it could be right, after all." She started to draw her hand away, but he caught it in his. Gently, kindly, he touched her arm. "All right. We can try. If you want."

"But what do I do?" she whispered.

"You let me touch you," he told her as he untied the belt of the robe she wore. Her body felt stiff as he pulled the robe away, and the urgency that had risen in him calmed, so that his hands were slow and careful. He drew back the covers, moving to give her room. "Come here, Thea. It's warmer here."

She dived gratefully into the bed, wrapping the covers around her like bandages or blindfolds. She felt her nerve fail now that he was beside her, warm and hairy. She set her teeth and forced her hands to her sides. "Go on," she said.

"Oh, no, Thea," he said between laughter and sorrow. "Not that way." He took one of her small fists in his hand. He kissed the fingers one by one, then the palm, opening her hand like a flower.

"Why did you do that?" Some of her tension was lost to curiosity.

"Because I want to. Because it's pleasant. Because you're dear to me. Because it's better if you enjoy this as well."

She pulled one of his hands to her lips. "Like this?"

"Well, not quite. I'm not a sandwich." He kissed her hand again. "Like that." He rolled closer to her and waited while she conquered her fear. Then he turned her face to his, smoothing the wayward strands of dark hair back from her face. He kissed her forehead, her eyes, her cheeks, and finally her mouth.

She stiffened, pushing against his shoulders, trying to get away from him. "Don't. No. No."

He stopped immediately. "God, Thea. I don't want to frighten you. I won't hurt you. Let me try again. If you don't like it, I won't do it again." He knew he was going too fast, that his body's insistence was too strong. If only her body were not so sweet, if he were not so hungry for her.

"You scare me."

"Me?" He held back from her. "Do I frighten you?"

"Some," she admitted.

"It is kind of scary the first time," he said, forcing his hands to move easily, softly.

"This isn't the first time!" She said it with such fury that he felt the weight of her fear.

"Yes, Thea, it is," he said, pulling her toward him, wrapping her in his arms, holding her tenderly, as he would a child. "Rape isn't like this, Thea. But you don't know that yet. Please, please let me try."

She set her jaw. "All right. Go ahead."

It wasn't very promising, he thought as he stroked her with his big hands. He eased her legs open slowly, and found she was not ready for him. And when he touched her labia with moistened fingers, she turned her face away. Her distress confused him, and he felt a spark of anger; anger at himself for doing this to her, anger with her for making him feel guilty for loving her. "Thea, I don't want to hurt you. But I might. If I do, tell me."

She nodded, unable to speak. She fought her revulsion as he held himself poised over her, willed her hands not to strike out as he eased his body into hers. He did not rush her, moving slowly inside her, trying not to startle her as his passion mounted. But then he moved faster, and his breath became panting and he held her fiercely. Then he cried out hoarsely and she felt his warm moisture overflow between her thighs.

Is that all there is, she thought as he moved off her, falling close beside her. There had been discomfort, but no real pain. He had kept his word. She held her lower lip between her teeth until the urge to weep was past.

"Thea," he said thickly. "Next time will be better for you. The second time is always better."

"The second time?" She was ready to leave the bed, to return to the narrow bunk in her room, knowing that he was satisfied now, and that she could endure his touch if she had to.

But his hands were on her again. "Stay, Thea, please." He put his hand over her breast and felt where the nipple had been. "At least let me try to give you pleasure."

"It's all right," she said stiffly, turning from him.

"No, it's not." He began to knead the muscles of her back, massaging the rigidness out of her. He worked thoroughly, taking plenty of time, letting her body learn his hands without hurry. After a while a gentle languor came over her, and she turned to him of her own volition. Now he caressed her, soothing her, drawing her out of the frightful armor her body had become.

"Can I touch you?" she whispered, half afraid of his answer.

He smiled in the dark. "I would like that." He lay still while her strong hands explored him, discovering his flesh like a foreign land. Somewhat later, she said, "Will you try again? I mean, in me?"

"Yes." And because this time he loved her with patient understanding, and because he had freed her from the prison of herself, that part of her she had never known opened to him, and she clung to him while she cried for joy. The specter of Lastly retreated in her mind as Evan's nearness, his warmth, began to heal her.

*   *   *

Smoke from the volcano hung over the mountains for a long time and the days did not warm as they should. By late spring, although the snow was largely gone, afternoons were cool and the nights still shone with frost. There were sounds of animals in the woods now, but those they saw were strange, starved things, looking more like specters than animals.

"Is it the volcano?" Thea asked, watching the sky before resuming stacking the freshly cut wood.

"Partly. There's been a lot of pollutants poured into the upper atmosphere and it's filtering down in the rain. The junk from the Valley didn't reach this far a couple of years ago, but now . . ." He shrugged. "It's going to get worse, too."

"Isn't there any way to change it?" She had set up the rest of her split logs and was getting ready to load them onto their improvised sled.

"Not now. The time to change it was before you, or even I, were born." He put the last of the wood onto the sled, waiting as Thea trimmed back the loose bark with her hatchet. "That's enough for the time being. It should keep us for the rest of the week."

She gathered up the ax and saw, going ahead of him down the hill, clearing a path for him and the load on the sled. Dusk was gathering by the time they got back to their house, and the sky overhead glowed with streamers of orange and yellow.

"Too bad," she said over her shoulder to him. "Look at that. It's beautiful and it's killing us."

He stopped before hauling the sled into the garage, taking a good look at the sky. "That's not enough to have a lasting effect. It'll make the next couple of years rough, but we can handle that. What would be bad . . ." He thought about the chain of volcanoes stretching north and south along the Pacific Ocean, covered in snow in Alaska, lying in the drowsy heat of Guatemala. "It would be bad if one of the big ones really blew. Not just erupted, completely blew up."

"Do they ever do that?" Thea held the door open and found that her hands were shaking.

"Rarely, but they do. It plays havoc with the weather around the world when that happens, too." He could half remember reading as a child about an island in the Pacific somewhere west of Java. It had blown itself right off the map, and had changed world-wide weather patterns for five years and more. Krakatoa, that was the name. It had been an island one day, and then it was gone.

"Maybe there are some books on volcanoes around," she said as she began to unload the wood. "Could you find one, Evan? I want to know what they do."

He was already starting up the stairs to fix dinner, but he stopped, hearing the fright in her words. "If you want, Thea."

"Please." Then she turned her attention to the wood once more.

* * *

Late that night as she lay tucked in the curve of Evan's body, Thea asked, "Evan, how long do you think we can stay here?"

"Getting bored?" he asked her in a rich chuckle.

"No, not bored," she said impatiently while she adjusted the angle of his arm across her shoulder. "I"m worried. What if the Pirates find this place? We can't hold out against them, can we?"

"We can hold out against anything," he said reassuringly.

"Evan, listen to me. I don't want to hear that. I wish it were true, but it isn't and I want to know what we'll have to do." She turned a little, moving back from him, trying to see his face. It was a moment before her eyes adjusted enough, and in that time she gathered her thoughts. "We can't stay here forever, Evan."

"Why not?" But he knew that this was not the answer she wanted.

"I saw tire tracks near the landslide," she said steadily. "Big tires. I think the Pirates are looking for this valley. Someone is, Evan."

"I see." He took a deep breath. "All right, it's true enough we can't stay here forever. Maybe we can last out the summer, or all the way through next winter. Eventually Mackley or whoever is in charge of the Pirates now will get a scouting party in here and then there'll be trouble. We'll have to fight or move out fast. Is that what you wanted me to say?"

"I didn't want you to say it, but I have to know. Oh, Evan, don't you see? If I have to give all this up, I've got to prepare myself. I feel like we belong here, I *want* to stay here. But we can't, not really." She reached out and touched his face, feeling the line of his beard and the soft texture of his hair. "It's going to hurt so much to leave, but we'll leave, just the same. Won't we?"

"You sound like you'll go alone if you have to." Anxiety made the words snap. He took her arm and held it tightly. "Is that what you meant?"

"No." Her voice was very low. "No, I didn't mean that. It's just that here I have you and I have a red bathtub with hot water, and books and a soft bed with clean sheets, and four fur jackets, and enough food that really tastes good, and time for you and me. I've never had that before, not all those things at once." She moved closer to him, still somewhat awkward with their intimacy.

His arm closed over her, drawing her near to him. "What a shitty world this is, Thea. All right. If that's what you want we'll make plans to leave now."

"It's not what I want. But what if the Pirates come in the winter? What if we have to spend more time in the snow? I didn't know how much I hated it until we came here and I didn't have to sleep with every bone aching. If we leave now, maybe we can find another place before it snows again. There are other places. Maybe not like this, but, Evan . . ." With a curious little cry she went into his arms, holding him tightly until they lost themselves in sleep.

* * *

They made their plans and gathered their stores, watching for a sign that winter had at last given up its icy grip on the valley. But another two weeks went by and still there was frost and freezing nights. The flowers that had tried to appear withered and died incomplete. The grass was sere and no birds came there.

"Where can we go?" Thea asked when they had made their final plans to leave. Now that the time was so close she found, perversely, that she did not want to, that she would rather face the Pirates and be killed here, in a place she knew, than die out in strange country. Twice she decided they should set out, and twice she found an excuse that postponed their leaving.

"We can take this route," he explained, pointing to the ancient topographic maps he had found some time ago in the lodge. "We go west and south across this ridge here, and this trail brings us to Tahoe at Emerald Bay. We can see everything that's going on down there long before we're close enough to be spotted. Then, if things don't look right, we can keep on the ridge trail and head south for Tuolumne and Yosemite. There's places along the trail we can stay, if we have to." Idly he wondered if there was going to be any trouble. They both had two crossbows apiece now, and a large variety of quarrels. They had rigged the sled to be a kind of wagon, and it would carry most of their supplies, or could be taken apart and made into back packs for them. In an emergency, it could make part of a lean-to. He knew they were as prepared as they would ever be.

"What about here?" she asked, pointing to the peaks behind Fallen Leaf Lake. "One of these might be okay for the winter. You and I could stay there if we had to." She was eager for him to agree, to see the possibilities, to promise her she would not regret leaving Squaw Valley. "There's a lookout station here, see? At Cathedral Rock. We don't have to go near Tahoe if we don't want to. We've got enough things to last us most of the winter if we're very careful. We'll make it just fine," she said too cheerfully.

"Yes. Of course we will." He hoped it was true. There had been more tire tracks on the landslide that morning, and he knew they no longer had a choice.

* * *

It was almost warm the day they left, starting west, out of the valley and into the high country where the snow still lingered and the wind bit endlessly at the stern granite faces of the mountains. They went quickly away from their home—for now it was their home. They had locked it up carefully, laughing sadly at the gesture. The sled was well laden, having knives, traps, and their crossbows at one end, blankets, food, and a few books at the other. Thea had improvised new runners on the sled, so that it moved easily, even over the rocks.

By nightfall they were far above the valley, sitting in the lee of a rocky outcropping. They munched the last of the meal of chili and canned artichoke hearts.

"Are you sad we left?" Evan asked, seeing the faraway look in Thea's eyes. Since they had started sleeping together, he found he was becoming intensively sensitive to her moods.

"Oh. Yes." She toyed with the last of her food, then, dutifully, she ate it. "I think of it as our place. It isn't, but I want it to be."

"We can go back, Thea. If you want."

She shook her head. "No. I couldn't bear to see it go up in flames when the Pirates find it. They will find it. By now they're too close to miss it. And it would have been more than losing a house. They would kill you. And they would kill me." She stretched out her hand to touch him, as if gaining strength from him. "We'll find a place that isn't so vulnerable. We'll be safe there. We'll make it right for us."

*   *   *

It took them four days to cross the high country: the snow was deep near the crest and it made passage difficult. This time hunger was not driving them, and they did not have to wear themselves into exhaustion. They did not know what to expect at Lake Tahoe, which they could see occasionally, lying lead-colored to the east. Sunset colors, reflected in its waters, took on acidic tints and gleamed evilly. Using the field glasses that Evan had taken from one of the houses, they watched the shores of the lake, but there was no sign of Pirate activity. No vans roared on patrol along the shore, no methane processer crouched over sewage ponds. No group of summer houses flew the Pirate flag.

"What happened?" Evan asked the day before they began their descent to the lake. "The place should be crawling with them. Cox wanted to use this lake for a command post. They can't have thrown the base away with Cox."

"Maybe the people who live here chased them off?" Thea suggested, not believing it herself. She had seen Chico, Sierraville, Truckee. There should have been a row of impaled reminders along the road, not this strange stillness.

"We'll have to be careful when we go down there," Evan said. Whatever was wrong, it had kept the Pirates away. Nothing else had done that so far.

*   *   *

Coming down the mountain took time, and at last they decided to stop for the night some two miles short of the shore. "We don't know what we're up against," Evan reminded Thea, as much for his own benefit as hers. "We'll be more alert after a good sleep."

Thea needed no coaxing. The feeling that raised her hackles had been with her all day. She moved warily, as if expecting to spring a trap with every step. She watched the lake as they drew nearer, and she liked it less. She resolved to investigate for herself later that night.

So it was that she crawled out of her sleeping bag some time after midnight. Below her, at the end of the ravine, lay Lake Tahoe, a pale haze of phosphorescence hanging over it—the same haze that hung over the Sacramento Valley, that cast its pall over Chico, clinging to bodies buried in nameless towns. "It's poisoned," she said quietly, turning her face away from it. She looked back at Evan, soundly sleeping in the tangle of his bag, and she considered waking him to tell him. But even as she did, she knew he would want to see for himself.

With a sigh she went back to bed, moving carefully so as not to wake him. There would be time enough in the morning to talk about the lake, to see what had become of it, what had driven off the Pirates. She knew that when she slept, she would dream of Squaw Valley, so she did not sleep.

CHAPTER 10

Shortly after sunrise they went undisturbed to the shore of Lake Tahoe and looked out at the desolation there. Slime floated just below the ash-colored surface and occasionally nests of water spiders would drift by. These deadly creatures were enough by themselves to keep the Pirates away from the lake, but the poisoned water made a Pirate camp impossible.

"Look at it," Evan said in a hushed voice. The winds that blew across the lake were sour-smelling and scoured the lungs with chemicals. Where the thickened wavelets lapped sluggishly at the shore they left a scummy residue behind that burned the fingers of those foolish enough to touch it.

"How did it get this way?" Thea stared, for as dreadful as the lake had looked by night, by day it was much worse. The miasmic veil that hung over the water had by day, instead of its glow, a kind of leprous silver that made her skin crawl. There would be no resurrection for Lake Tahoe.

"Who knows? They used to dump garbage into it, then they dumped things in to kill the garbage. What did they expect? It's a sewer." He turned away, his mouth a thin line above his beard. He gave the sled a savage jerk, pulling it away from the water, back to the pitted highway that threaded along the shore of the lake.

"Aren't we going back up the mountain? There's nothing here."

"In a bit. There's a junction at the south end of the lake. Before we do anything else, I want to find out what's there. If the Pirates retreated, they might have gone there, and that's too close."

"Let's try the south." She had already reached for her smaller crossbow and was strapping it to her wrist.

At first they kept in the brush at the side of the road, where there was brush, but soon it was obvious that this road was never traveled, so they walked down its center, but kept careful watch on the trees and brush around them.

It took no more than three hours to get to the junction and there they found nothing but the ruins of five large motels. There had been a city here at one time, but the contamination of the lake had taken its toll of the people as well as the buildings, and now the place stood deserted, a few façades pitted and scarred as mute testimony to the terrible effects of the breeze off the lake.

"Have you had enough?" Thea tugged anxiously at Evan's arm, looking westward to the crown of the mountains they had left. "We can make the climb in a day, Evan. We don't have to stay here any longer. You know the Pirates are gone. We can go, too. I don't like it here."

"Neither do I. But there are still the casinos on the south shore. If they had people in them three months ago, they still might have some now. I want to know about it." There was no fighting the set line of his jaw or the coldness in his blue eyes. Thea sensed that there was more than he had admitted in his desire to see the lake, to find out the full extent of its ruin, so she kept silent and followed him, her crossbow ready and her senses alert. What they were doing was dangerous, and she knew that she had to be doubly cautious, since Evan, for some reason, was being reckless.

* * *

Late that afternoon they came to the state line, well marked by six tall casinos and a rusted sign that had once welcomed the traveler to Nevada. Broken windows and crumbling walls made it clear that the big buildings had not been cared for, and Thea thought the places were abandoned.

But around the buildings were fences, bizarre conglomerations of roulette wheels, crap tables, felt-covered pool tables, and other tokens of the fantasy world that the gambling empire of Nevada had been. One of the casinos had hedged itself with slot machines, and their shiny fronts were now patched with rust.

As Evan led the way toward one of these phenomenal piles, there was a sudden shower of rocks, tiles, bricks, bottles, and pool balls, accompanied by angry shouts from behind the litter.

"Stop," he said to Thea, never looking away from the surface of the barrier. "Who's there!" he called, keeping his voice level and sure, as if talking to restive animals. "Who are you?"

"Go away!" several voices chorused back. "We don't want you here." This last was followed by individual voices adding their own insults.

"There's only two of us. We can't possibly hurt you."

The rain of missiles was renewed.

Evan stepped back, motioning Thea to get out of range. "Are you the only ones left around here? Have there been men in vans? Men with guns?"

The outraged shouts that accompanied the thrown things told Evan more than he wanted to know about the men in vans. One of the fragments of brick that had been thrown was lucky and glanced off Evan's forehead, leaving a trail of blood over one eye. He did not give ground.

"Where are those men now?" he persisted, raising his voice.

"Gone!" they shouted at him, adding glasses to the other assorted paraphernalia that came over the wall.

A soft sound made Thea turn. Not four feet away was a pathetically thin man of uncertain age. His skin was scabbed over with phosphorescent patches that Thea had seen too many times before. His clothes were matted with filth, his hair was wild, and there was a look about him that told her this man was not sane. She lifted her crossbow.

"Stop right there," she said clearly, the quarrel lined on the middle of his chest. "I've put this bolt through three bales of hay: you aren't anywhere near that thick."

The man stopped, his eyes on the sled. "Food? Have you got any food?" He pointed, grinning, to the sled. "Food?" he repeated as if speaking a foreign language.

"Not for you," she said calmly, but her eyes flickered nervously. If there was one man, there could be more. She made her voice louder so that it would carry to Evan. "We have company, Evan. He wants food."

"What?" Evan turned, his eyes widening faintly. With sudden compassion, he reached into the packages on the sled, handing the strange man one of their day's rations. "Here," he said gently. "You can have this. But will you tell me about the men in vans? Have they been here?"

With straining eyes fixed on the package Evan had handed him, the man said, "They were here. Yes. Now they're gone. Try Carson City. Over the mountain. East. Go east."

"Carson City?" Evan repeated. "Out on the desert?"

"The head man, called Mackley, ordered them over the mountain. He said it was better there. Safer. He said it would be hot. He said they'd grow food there."

"Mackley." Damnable Joel Mackley: tall, gaunt, his face belonging to some ruthless medieval ruler. "I thought he did in Cox. It must have been Mackley. He's the only one left."

"There's others," the man said. "More Pirates up north. Mackley has the south bunch now. They had a fight here last spring." He could stand it no more and clutched the package to him, turned and scuttled back toward the barricade of slot machines.

Evan stood for a moment looking after the pathetic little man. "Mackley. I wonder. Who's got the northern group now? Where are they?"

"Is it bad do you think?" Thea asked gently.

Evan nodded, considering Mackley and Cox. "It's bad. Cox was after Mutes and Mackley's after everyone else. With Cox dead, the rest would have to fight. I'm surprised it didn't happen earlier. Gorren might have the north now, or Spaulding." He wiped the blood from his face, not letting her see the damage. "Come on. We'll get out of here. I've learned what I want to know."

"It's getting late," she warned him.

"We'll find a place. We've always found places before." He dragged the sled after him as he turned away from the casinos.

*   *   *

That night they slept in a tumble-down service station which had long since outlived its usefulness. They ate quickly and set up watch rotation so that they would have one or the other of them awake all night. As Thea took the first watch she remarked, "My father used to have watchdogs, shepherds and stag hounds. They took care of all this."

Evan finished packing the dishes and the pots before saying, "I don't think I'd want to have a dog now. Most of them have run wild, and they aren't feeling all that friendly toward people any more." He adjusted his sleeping bag on the broken concrete. "I've been more comfortable," he said as he rolled into the bag, putting his shoes next to his head. "Wake me in four hours."

For all their precautions the night passed easily enough. Once or twice there were rustlings in the bushes that had sprung up around the station. On Evan's watch he was sure he had heard words just beyond the station that hissed and whispered as he patrolled the limits of their area. These, he knew, could have been the workings of his mind, and so he waited as the hours stretched on into morning.

Thea rolled out of her sleeping bag at dawn, an unfriendly frown on her face. "I wonder what's buried down there?" She glared at the jumbled concrete.

"Probably old filling station tanks, or maybe one of the hydraulic lifts they used to have for raising cars." His affectionate smile disarmed her.

"Then why's the concrete all broken up, and why is it shoved together? I tell you, there's something down there. I know it. There's no reason for breaking up the stuff like this otherwise."

To humor her, he said, "All right. After breakfast we'll pull up the slabs and see what's there. But we can't waste much time here. If we don't find anything in a couple of hours, we've got to move on."

*   *   *

There were five slabs to be pulled up and they ranged in size from a foot square to a monster that was almost two by four feet. It took more than two hours to drag the concrete aside so that they could dig into the ground underneath. They had dug for less than ten minutes when Thea's shovel hit something solid with a decided *thunk*.

"Well, whatever it is, we'll have it out in a bit," Evan said, his face shining with sweat in the cool morning. He stepped into the hole they had dug and began clearing the dirt away with his hands.

"Do you need help?" Thea asked as she put the shovel back on the sled.

"No. I can manage." He bent to his work again. What he found made him whistle. There, under the slabs and the earth, were a dozen rifles, seven shotguns, and twenty-four boxes of shells. He rubbed his head slowly, calling to Thea. "You win. There was something under us," he said quietly as he showed her the find. "These go with us. One shotgun and one rifle apiece and all the ammunition."

Her eyes sparkled. "Where do you suppose they came from?"

She knelt on the edge of the hole, reaching down to touch the guns. "Who left these? Do you know?"

"I'll bet you anything that these belong to my old friend Joel Mackley. This is exactly the sort of thing he'd do. The guns are wrapped in oilcloth and canvas and the ammunition is in waterproof boxes. He always wanted to leave caches of weapons when we were spreading out. He wanted to be sure we could defend ourselves quickly, if we had to retreat." He sighed. "I used to tell him that if we did, someone else might dig them up, and we'd really be in trouble. Turns out I'm right."

"Then he'll be back?"

Evan climbed out of the hole, four of the oilcloth and canvas packages under his arm. "Who knows? He might or he might not. There's no way of being sure of Mackley. That's what makes him so dangerous."

Thea took the packages from him and loaded them onto the sled. For a moment she was busy arranging the things there, and then she turned back to Evan. "Do you think he'd know you if he saw you? Mackley, I mean."

At this Evan laughed. "Oh, he'd know me all right. He was the one who held the power saw that took off my arm. This"—he waggled his right arm—"might surprise him, but he'd recognize me. No fear."

"Then he'd fight when he saw you? He'd want to finish the job?"

He cupped her chin in his hand. "Look, Thea, Mackley isn't going to get us. I've got away from him before, and even though he seems to be everywhere we go, he doesn't know I'm alive, let alone where I am. He doesn't know a thing about you. I tell you, we're safe."

"Let's get the sled packed."

"Okay. But don't worry about Mackley. He's the last thing to bother you. We'll avoid him. That's all."

They made sure the guns and ammunition were loaded carefully and lashed down before they started away from the service station. Evan looked back as they left. "You know, that's the sort of thing Mackley does, tearing up the floor of service stations. He thinks he can change the world back to the way it used to be. There's nothing anyone can say that will change his mind, either.

He knows that service stations will be back in business one day, and so he makes sure he keeps them in use. He won't listen to any contradiction about it. I know. I tried."

*   *   *

They spent that night at Fallen Leaf Lake, keeping well back from the shore and the nests of water spiders. The venom-filled mandibles killed quickly but far from painlessly. Of all the creatures which had adapted themselves to the new and deadly world, these were the most feared, the most dangerous.

The morning was gray, volcanic soot mixing with the clouds, obscuring the sun and coloring the world with a ruddy wash. Evan hurried their breakfast while Thea checked out the runners of the sled. The climb would be steep and would wind its way through the brushy remnants of the Tahoe National Forest. Dead trees and dying ones would fill their paths, and she knew that the sled could not stand much of that kind of beating without new braces and runners to take the impact.

She found two lengths of wood which a long time ago had been skis. These she lashed to the runners, securing them with heavy-test leader she had found in the sporting goods shop in Squaw Valley. As she tied the knots, she thought about the valley, the days there, and the nights. She wondered if the Pirates had found it yet, if they had used her house, or burned it. She could see it again, that practical brave octagon resisting cold and neglect. It would be terrible, she decided, if the Pirates used it. She hoped they would burn it. She tied the last of the knots and stepped back.

"Thea." This time Evan's voice was sharp enough to break through her reverie.

"What?" She pulled her mind back to the present and gave him and their breakfast her attention.

"I think we can get to Cathedral Lake by nightfall if we keep the climb steady and stick to the trails," she said as they finished eating.

"Good," Evan nodded.

"What's the matter?" she asked, seeing that he was not pleased.

"I was trying to figure out what month this is. It should be June. It's almost summer, and look at it. It's like April or October. That isn't very promising."

"No. Unless you think bad weather is promising." She stood

up, brushed her trousers, and tried to help Evan clean off the plates with handfuls of dried grass.

* * *

The lookout station on the south edge of Cathedral Lake facing the bulk of Cathedral Rock had been built fairly recently. "It must have been one of the last projects before they closed off the lake to the general public," Evan said as they walked around its thirty-foot legs. The ladder to the platform and station door zig-zagged through the center of the structure like laces up a shoe. "We're going to have a job getting the sled up there," he said, mentally calculating the number of steps.

"We can rig a sling," Thea reminded him, and rummaged in the sled for the two wide leather straps she had made for carrying the sled over water. "All we need is enough rope to haul it up. It'll be easy."

"Yes. You're right." He looked up the stairs. "Well, you or me?"

"You take the rope up and I'll get this thing ready for lifting. Then I'll come up and give you a hand. You'll need some help. This sled's heavy."

"Don't hold your breath until I get there," he called as he started up the stairs. He listened to the sound of his steps, hypnotic as the ticking of a clock. Then several minutes later the rope dangled over the edge of the railing and Thea knotted it firmly on the leather straps. She swung her full weight on the knot, and then called up to Evan on the platform high above her. "I think it'll hold."

"It better." His words floated down to her, remote as the call of birds.

There was an uncertain moment while she steadied the sled, helping Evan to lift it into the air, taking the load on her shoulders. Then, when it hung overhead, she reached up for one last helpful shove. Sure that it was on its way, she sprinted up the steps and made the long climb as fast as she could. The sled inched its way upward as she raced.

"Here," Evan said, nodding to the rope. "Grab hold here."

"All right." She braced her feet against the low rail that surrounded the platform and added her strength to his.

When they had the sled over the railing at last, they secured it, making sure that it could not fall or be blown from its high perch. Thea nodded to the station. "I hope this place has its own water. I saw water spiders on the lake and that's a bad sign. The water's probably contaminated. We shouldn't drink it."

"There's a cistern on top, and it's full. Not that what's coming down is much better. Between the volcano and all the other junk up here . . ." He gestured fatalistically at the sky. "It's too late to change it."

"Are you sure?" But the question had no meaning. She wanted only to banish the despair she suddenly read in his face.

*   *   *

They got into the station after prying two locks off the door. The room they entered was militarily neat, clean, and dull as a barracks. There were two stoves in the central room, and a third in the kitchen, and all were sternly functional. The kitchen stove had a water heater hooked onto it, a more advanced design than the one they had had in Squaw Valley. If there was water at all, it would be heated.

In the main room, three utilitarian sofas turned into equally utilitarian beds, all smelling faintly of mildew, a smell that Evan's newly kindled fire routed.

The fire created its own question. "How much wood have we got?" Evan asked as he finished rigging one of the beds. Above it on the pea-green wall a once-colorful poster displayed the attractions of Australia, kangaroos bounding in front of three aborigines, a sailboat, the Sydney opera house, and a cowboy. Evan remembered being there, many years before, and he was suddenly aware that he never learned what happened to Australia.

"Maybe three or four days' worth. I don't know how hard this place is to heat, yet. Up in the air like this, with wind all around, it might be very hard to keep warm." Thea knew he was not really listening, but she said it anyway.

He broke away from his thoughts. "You're right. The wind is a problem." He began peering into cupboards and found, to his surprise, five kerosene lamps with asbestos wicks.

"What is it?" Thea asked, hearing him call to her.

"Lamps. We can have light now, anyway." He searched further and found a few ten-gallon drums of fuel. "And these ought to keep them going for a long time." He felt a twinge of optimism.

"We can last quite a while up here, and with the traps out, we might do fine."

"If there's anything to trap," Thea said quietly.

"There will be. There's got to be game in the mountains somewhere."

* * *

It was four nights later that the dogs showed up. The ragged descendants of the pets kept by the summer residents of the lake, they had long since run wild, hunting whatever they could find, craftily avoiding traps and men in groups.

Thea scrambled out of bed at the first howl and stood at the observation window, squinting in an effort to see what had caused the sound. It was still dark, but the sky was beginning to pale in the east. The morning wind freshened and made weird singing in the struts that held the lookout station.

"What's happening?" Evan asked, muzzy with sleep, willing himself awake by main force. He reached out for an extra blanket and got unsteadily out of bed.

"It's dogs," she said without any preamble. "Maybe a couple of dozen, maybe less. One or two of them are climbing the stairs." If she felt fear, it did not color her voice. "I think a shotgun would do it," she said judiciously, after giving the problem her consideration.

Evan made no argument, but went to the cupboard which he had transformed into a gunrack. Carefully he loaded the shotgun and brought it to her. "Here. It's ready. Unless you'd like me to do it."

"Well, one of us has to. Would you like to do the hunting for a change?" She raised her brows, thinking of the three rabbits she had shot the day before. Evan had walked the trap line since he put it in, but there had not been any game to bring back.

"Fine. I'll take care of it. Do you think we can use the meat?"

"You're the cook. You decide." She touched his hand affectionately.

"I'll have a look at them. Open the door for me, Thea, will you?" He braced the stock and waited while she pulled back the bolt securing the door.

There was a scrabbling of claws on the lower steps, an anxious whine, mixed with pantings as the dogs worked their way upward.

Below them, on the ground, other dogs ran round the pylon legs, keening.

The early morning air was cold, and Evan felt his skin tighten as he stepped out onto the platform. Looking down the stairs he could barely make out the shapes of the dogs climbing upward. He gave his eyes a moment to adjust, then, bracing himself, he fired.

The shot echoed through the mountains and was followed by a high yelp. The pack on the ground stopped their noise, waiting. The first dog on the steps snapped once or twice, then fell back, his body hitting those that climbed behind him. Now distressed sounds came from the pack, and after milling about the pylons, they withdrew, leaving their leader where he had fallen.

"I guess this is the end of your trap line," Thea said when Evan had stepped back into the warmth of the observation station.

"I won't be able to keep up with a pack that size, certainly," he conceded. "We could try to trap the dogs, but I doubt we'll get much usable meat. They're hungry, these dogs." He cracked the gun and began cleaning it, handing the spent cartridge to Thea.

"What's this for?" she asked, turning the cartridge over in her hand.

"For luck. We need it."

*   *   *

The next day Evan checked the trap line and found that his scant haul had been wiped out by the dogs. In one of the traps a dog had been caught and had become food for his fellows. Evan cursed softly, then took what was left of the carcass down to the lake and flung it in for the water spiders. As long as meat was about, as long as there had been a fresh kill, the smell would attract the dogs again.

Thea came in late that day with a small hump-shouldered deer. She had gutted it when she killed it and promptly set to skinning it when she had lugged it up the stairs. There was a grimness about her as she worked the deer over the sink, and at last Evan asked her the reason.

"Those damned dogs," she said in subdued fury. "There just isn't enough food to go around. And look at this"—she pointed her knife to the pitiful carcass hanging over the drainboard—"this thing is full grown. It isn't a fawn. There's nothing out there much over this size. I haven't seen a bear or bear tracks anywhere. The one raccoon I've found was no bigger than a house cat. I don't know what's causing it, but it isn't good." Savagely she cut away the hindquarters. "Can you do something with that? I don't even know if there's enough meat to make it worth while."

Evan took up a position alongside her, trimming the meat, cutting it into collops and dropping them into one of his cooking pots. We'll have to scrub the kitchen later, he thought as he worked. Otherwise the dogs may smell the blood and come back. He didn't want to have to begin each day fighting the dogs.

*   *   *

Except for an occasional trap raid, the dogs did not come back. They did not have a chance to. A week later Mackley and his division of Pirates returned for vengeance to Lake Tahoe.

From their lookout on the mountain, Thea and Evan could watch the battles for the casinos. The fights were long and fierce, and no quarter was given by either side. It was obvious from the start that the Pirates had the advantage in mobility and training, but the defenders had a few skills and they held their own for far longer than Evan expected. One of the casinos, as the defenses broke down, went up in a rumbling explosion that rivaled the boom of the distant volcano. Slowly at first, then with gathering speed, the walls crumbled to the ground, burying the defenders and a large number of the Pirates in the rubble.

"I didn't think they'd have the guts," Evan said as the smoke drifted over the wastes of Lake Tahoe.

Thea watched in stunned silence, her face blank and eyes wide. "Evan, I . . ." she began, then put her arms around him, pressing her face against his shoulder.

"What is it, Thea?" he asked her, surprised at the intensity of her grief. He turned his attention from the battle on the lake to her, raising her face with one hand while his other arm held her tightly against him. "Your hair wants trimming, you know."

She ignored the last. "Is it always going to be like this?" she asked, a hurt in her face that was deeper than tears. "Look what's happening here, everywhere." She shook her head, her eyes showing a fatigue that rest could not relieve. "We try and we try and it just gets worse and worse."

His arm tightened, but he said nothing as he watched the sky beyond her where the smoke from the exploding casino had risen to join the volcanic cloud that covered the sky. "Yes," he whispered. "Come away, Thea. There's nothing out there for us."

She was about to object, but her shoulders slumped and her body stopped resisting. Inside the station she fell onto their bed and looked up at him, desperation in every line of her body. "Love me, Evan. Love me or I die."

* * *

The next morning the Pirates found the lookout station.

Evan had spotted them at first light, moving cautiously up the mountain. They were no longer in their vans and the smoke from the ruined casinos had hidden them until they had come much closer than Evan thought they were. Quickly he woke Thea and set about the business of readying their guns. Boxes of ammunition were placed next to each weapon and the stoves were stocked with extra wood, since they might not have the chance to set the fire once the fight got under way—and Evan knew for certain that there would be a fight, a decisive one.

"Keep changing—don't use the rifle all the time, or the shotgun. We have to keep them guessing. And keep these with you . . ." He handed her some torn strips of blanket and a quart of kerosene. "If you get the chance, wad this up, soak it in kerosene, light it, and fire it with your crossbow. There's enough here for about ten flaming quarrels."

"The brush will burn, Evan," she said, for although there had been no real summer, the scrub on the mountain was brittle and dry.

"It might," he agreed. "But we have to worry about us first. If there's a fire, we can't let it concern us. We've got to think about our lives now."

"If the brush goes, and we're trapped up here . . ."

He rounded on her, his face set and his eyes sad. "Now listen to me. That's Mackley's gang out there. Do I have to tell you what they'd do to you—or to me, for that matter—if they caught us? Do you really want to know what choice we have? Do you?"

The violence of his outburst stopped her. She thought again of the impaled bodies, imagining one of them with the ooze on his face where the eyes had been, and the grotesque, froglike posture forced by the upward thrust of the stake, to be Evan. Her whole body shook, and then she mastered herself. She would not allow it to happen, and if the whole world burned because of it, she did not care.

"I know Mackley." Evan's voice cut into her ruthlessly. "I know what he's capable of. Believe me, we can't negotiate with him." He stopped suddenly, put down his rifle and came across the room to her. "Oh, Thea, I could not bear it, the things they would do to you."

She nodded, a fragment of her vision still with her; then she turned and went back to her preparation for the fight.

They did not have long to wait. The first rattle of guns started shortly after they had hacked away the stairs to their platform, Evan thanking heaven that the pylons that supported the station were concrete-wrapped steel and hard to climb, and harder to burn.

"Are they coming?"

"They're coming," Evan said grimly. "They're coming."

Evan ordered her to wait until the Pirates were close enough to be hurt by their guns before opening fire. Saying that she understood, Thea put her attention on the guns and the dozen or so men coming up the mountains. She studied them, noting their precision, that they were well trained and well armed.

"There," Evan said as he watched the men approach. "That one in the orange crash helmet—that's Mackley. He's the one we have to kill. It won't be easy. He wears that helmet and he's got one of those old bulletproof vests. God only knows where he found it. He's not invulnerable, but he's damn hard to hit." He checked their defenses again, frowning at the sights on the Savage 300. He hefted it critically and handed it to Thea. "This has a longer range than the Winchester. If you can get him straight on with this, you can probably kill him. Try for the face."

"Do you want the Winchester?"

He gave the rifle an affectionate pat. "I've used a .30-.30 since I was a kid. My father used to go game hunting when he was in Asia. Mainly on private preserves kept for that sort of thing. It was an honor to be asked to kill there. He always accepted. I went with him."

He was interrupted by a second burst of fire, and Evan took up his place on the opposite side of the room. "Remember, the one we have to get is Mackley. Kill him and we'll rout the others. As long as he's standing, as long as he can give orders, we're in trouble."

And then they were silent, watching their enemies come toward them. At last they were close enough, those organized men, and Thea opened fire.

The smoky half-light made her work difficult. She pulled her window farther open and leaned out for a better sight line. This time it paid off and her next bullet took one of the attackers in the leg. That brought an answering volley from the Pirates and she retreated into the room, leaving herself just enough space by the window for good aim. She knew she had to be careful, that she could not afford to waste any shots. She forced herself to be calm, then took up her ammunition once more.

"Those bastards!" Evan started loading the 10-gauge shotgun. "They're going to stay underneath us." He had seen Mackley give a signal for this and he was determined to stop it. Taking the shotgun, he climbed out onto the balcony, ignoring Thea's protesting cry. He braced himself at the empty place where the stairs had been and fired directly down. The explosion sounded even louder than it was, and it sent the Pirates scattering. Quickly Evan reloaded and fired again for good measure.

An answering bullet grazed his thigh where he had braced it. He swore, then steadied himself, shouting, "Mackley! Mackley! It's Montague!" Then, wiping a trickle of blood from his leg, he waited.

The firing from the ground straggled to a halt. Then Mackley shouted up to him, "Montague's dead!"

"No! You and your saw didn't finish the job before Chico. You and Cox botched it. You only got my arm then, and it grew back." As he shouted he motioned to Thea to get a line on Mackley. "Those are my men you're leading, Mackley. They follow me."

"Not any more," Mackley taunted. "They're mine. They left Cox and Spaulding to come with me. Cox was as weak as you are."

"Left Cox? *Left?* Don't you mean murdered him?" Out of the corner of his eye, Evan could see that Thea was in the window above him. He wondered if Mackley were in her sights. He raised his voice again. "Murder, that's your way, Mackley. You don't allow a fair fight."

"I see him," Thea said softly.

Evan nodded, and continued his mocking. "Murder is the coward's way out."

"It's my fight now, Montague. Cox has nothing to do with this!"

Defiance stung his words and he pushed his fist into the air. The men around him who had been quiet for this exchange now let out a shout in response to their leader's signal.

Evan had started crawling backward, edging his way toward the door. He knew that Mackley had sent out a sniper to get him, and he could feel those stalking eyes watch him from the mountainside as he climbed.

"Do you hear me, Montague?"

"I hear you." His hand was on the door now, and his knees banged against the sill. Thea's hand touched his shoulder as he eased back into the lookout station. A bullet followed him, leaving a furrowed path along the floor. *"Now!"* Evan shouted, and she fired.

A howl of outrage went up from outside and the shots rang once more.

"Did you hit him?" Evan asked breathlessly as he loaded the Winchester. He had found a new vantage point that used one of the cupboards for cover.

"I think so," she said. "Not in the head: I couldn't be sure about that. He kept moving around, but I think I might have got him in the leg or the side." She jumped as two more windows shattered. "This noise is giving me a headache," she said without rancor. "I wish they'd all just shut up."

The fight continued and Evan's leg stiffened where the bullet had scraped it. Thea moved back and forth between her two guns, firing the 10-gauge and returning again to the Savage. She seemed impervious to fright or fatigue, but Evan had seen this calm efficiency before, and was not fooled by it. They would have to decide this fight soon, one way or the other. Neither he nor Thea could keep up this pace for long.

Once more there was a heavy thud as the Pirates' 375 ripped into the walls, leaving a swath of ruin behind it. "Where'd they get a big game gun now?" Evan asked aloud as the sound came again. He'd only used that heavy new Winchester once in his life, and he knew what it could do.

Judging from the sounds below they knew they had hit a few of the Pirates, but not enough, and not critically. They had not stopped the attack, they had not sent Mackley and his men back toward the leaden water of Lake Tahoe. When little more than an hour had gone by, Thea turned to Evan. "I'm almost out of shells for the Savage," she said as she moved back to her post at the window.

Evan nodded as he fired and had the satisfaction of hearing a shout that told him his bullet had gone home. By his estimation they were now up against five or six armed, whole men. That was too many.

There was a spurt of light on the other side of the room, and Thea, holding her crossbow, fired the flaming wad of cloth toward the center of the Pirates' assault group. There were more shouts then, followed by a muffled explosion and in a moment a small, black cloud rolled upward.

"You got something," Evan said proudly, hoping that it was ammunition. He knew that they had to balance the odds somehow. "See if you can drive them out into the lake. Let the water spiders take their minds off us." There was a feral light in his face now, almost a pleasure that fed his determination.

Thea muttered her response, then sent a ball of fire toward three men who stood together near the edge of the lake. One of them was wounded, the other two supported him. They could not move fast enough to escape the flaming quarrel, and fell screaming as their clothes burned.

There was another explosion, and this one rocked its way up one pylon, jiggling the lookout station like a puppet on a stick. Both Thea and Evan were thrown to the floor, and when the motion stopped, the whole station canted at a strange angle.

"They've blown up one of the legs," Evan said as he surveyed the damage, making his way over the tilted floor with care. "They're going to try to bring us down leg by leg."

"What do we do?" she asked, watching him as she hung onto the window and fired once more, letting the shot go wide.

"We have to discourage them before they try it again." Saying this, he wrenched open the door and climbed out on the deck at the side of the station. From here he could see the men below him working on their next charge. Taking careful aim with the powerful Winchester, he wounded two of the men before they could run from his fire. Once away from the pylon, they began shooting back.

"I've slowed them down a little," Evan announced as he lumbered back into the room, the crazy angle of the floor making it hard for him to walk.

"Slowed for how long?"

"Not very," he admitted. "But there's two less of them now, and it'll take them a lot longer to get the next charge ready."

"What about this?" She held up her crossbow and mimed the release of the trigger. "It hasn't got much range, but I think they'd pay attention to it. And it's quiet."

"They might not expect it now. It's taking an awful risk," he conceded, stroking his beard. "They're working with high explosives down there. Anything landing on a charge would mean hell to pay." He checked his dwindling supply of ammunition and went on, a harsh smile on his face. "Whatever we do, we have to do it fast. They're not going to wait forever to blow us up. They've got too much at stake now."

Her eyes resolutely fixed on some point far away, she said, "We can start a fire, can't we? Near the pylons, but not that near? Half a dozen of these things should do it, don't you think?" She held out the wadded strips of blanket, wet with their marinade of kerosene. Her eyes pleaded with Evan, begging him to tell her that they still had a chance. Across the wreckage of the station, she saw his eyes fill with despair. Turning, she readied the wads, saying quietly, "This is their world, Evan, not ours, and they make the rules in it. So we'll play by them, too, no matter what."

"If you'll wait a minute, I'll help you."

The first two flaming quarrels did not drive the men away, but the third was close enough to get results. The scrub began to burn in a steady, almost languid way.

"That's got it going," Evan said as he saw the fire grab hold of the scrub. "They're going to be busy with that for a while." He looked around from his position, his eyes hidden in blackened wrinkles. "Where's Mackley? It's him we want."

"I think he's with the wounded, in the bend of the lake, there." Although Cathedral Lake was almost circular, there was one end, away from Cathedral Rock, that was rather steep, where the curve was the greatest, giving it a teardrop shape. "It wouldn't take a lot to drive them into the water, if the aim was good," she said as if in a trance. She put down her crossbow and picked up the Savage. "I've got just eleven shells left and then I'm out."

Evan studied his Winchester. "All right," he said as the smoke from the burning brush reached them. "We can put all we've got left into the wounded and the bank above them. As fast as we can.

Hit anyone you're able to. But make sure you drive them back into the water."

"And then, if it doesn't work?"

"It has to work," he said.

At his count they began to fire, watching the wounded scramble, if they could scramble, and driving those that could be driven down the slope inexorably, toward the lake. Shouts for help went up after the first man hit the water and was attacked by the voracious arachnids, their venom doing swift, agony-filled work. The few men left unwounded rushed to the others, trying to break their falls. When it was over, there were three men left standing.

These men turned on the lookout station with fury, using the 375 to gouge holes in the floor and walls. The barrage was long and thorough and before it was over, Thea's right arm hung useless at her side, blood flowing from a deep flesh wound in her shoulder. Evan dropped what he was doing to wrap a pressure bandage around it, frowning as the blood quickly soaked through the wrappings. She turned a pale, shocky face to him, attempting to allay his fright. "I wish I were left-handed, like you," she whispered unsteadily.

"Never mind," Evan said, the vertical grooves between his brows drawn darkly now. He picked up his shotgun and began to fire again.

Some smoke from the burning scrub came roiling through the station, making it hard to breathe and hiding the ground and the men there. The bullets continued to pepper them, but randomly. Shortly there was a lull, and then a voice called up from beneath them.

"Montague! Montague, do you hear me? It's Mackley." From the way he tore his hoarse voice, Thea guessed that she had hit him earlier, because he was badly hurt. "You're still too frigging good, Montague! You killed a lot of my men," he went on, with emphasis on the "my." "You can't last up there much longer. You need food and water, Montague. Tonight, tomorrow, a couple of days, we're coming back to finish the job. There's more of us at Tahoe, Montague. You're a dead man."

"You come back, Mackley, and we'll give you more of the same." He paused. "If I'm a dead man, Mackley, so are you," he said softly, in terrible earnest.

"You've got to come out of there sometime, Montague!" The shouts were rasping his throat now, and every word cracked.

"Don't hold your breath!" The answer was nothing but bravado, and both men knew it. But it saved Mackley's face in retreat, which Evan knew this was, and it gave Evan a few crucial moments to think.

"What is it?" Thea asked when there had been silence for a few minutes. Only the crackling of the burning scrub came up to them now, and her ears were roaring from the silence. "Are they leaving?"

"For the time being. Mackley's hurt and he has to reorganize, go back for replacement troops." He put down his shotgun and went to Thea, half-carrying her across the slanted floor to the sofa that was their bed. Gently he set her down, leaning over her anxiously, his face now gray with exhaustion. "Thea? How badly are you hurt? Really?"

"Pretty badly," she admitted. "There's no broken bones, but something is pretty messed up. I'm not much good for anything." She made an effort to focus on his face. "Why?"

"We're leaving here tonight. As soon as those vermin are gone, we're packing up and getting out of here. I'm going to rig a bed for you in the sled . . ."

Fright came back into her eyes. "We can't go to the lake, Evan . . ."

"No. We aren't going to the lake. We're going around over the crest again. With the fire to confuse them, they won't be able to follow us, not for some time. But it's going to be very rough, Thea. You'll have to take a lot of hurting. We can stay here if you're too badly wounded to move, but"—he turned away before finishing—"if we stay here, we haven't got a chance in the world."

She knew this was the truth, and hearing it gave her strength again. "If you pack this thing with gauze," she said, gesturing to the bandages that enveloped her shoulder, "really pack it tight, I think I can walk a way. Not very far, but away from here."

"All right. I'll pack the wound. We should be out of here in a couple of hours."

*   *   *

When he finally lowered the sled, Thea, and himself to the ground with the station's bo'sun's chair, his whole body felt watery with fatigue. The ground was still charred and smoking, and the bodies of the Pirates who had not escaped lay where they had fallen. The night was very dark, as if the sky were wrapped in a vast muffler. On the lake there floated two shapes covered now with a mass of sticky filaments as the water spiders marched over their webs, mandibles clicking.

It would have been so easy to stop there, to sleep, trusting to the sun to wake them before the Pirates came back. Evan took a moment to ready himself for the hike ahead: he had rigged a kind of harness with the leather straps to draw the sled, but found it was harder to do than he had thought. With a little help from Thea the harness was adjusted, the runners balanced, and the sled moved off into the night, Evan bending under the weight, Thea walking unsteadily beside it.

CHAPTER 11

Morning was near when Thea realized that they were being followed. She had stayed on her feet, moving mechanically, making no sound to betray the intensity of the pain that shot through her with every shifting of her weight. Occasionally she would look back, as an automatic precaution. Concentration blended with hurt on her face, and this expression deepened as they went. Finally she said, "There's something back there."

"Mackley's men?" Evan asked, panting. The wound in his leg had opened an hour before and was bleeding with a slow persistence that sapped his energy and reduced his speed to almost nothing.

"No: dogs." As if to confirm this there rose a low wail, a soft cry from far down the slope, rising as the mountains rose.

"Shit!" Evan stopped, sagging against the straps. They had passed the fire line over an hour ago, and pulling the sled through the tangled scrub was more than he had bargained for.

"There aren't any trees," she said, looking around. "And I don't think we can outrun the pack. Not out here, with the sled."

"Not bloody likely," he agreed, putting his hands into the straps to ease their cutting pressure on his shoulders. "Where's the fire? Still behind us?"

"To the north. Still burning some. Not a lot. The smoke's been thinning out." She frowned. "I guess the stuff they sprayed the forest with keeps it from burning."

The sound of the dogs was louder now, and there was an urgency in their cry.

"Evan . . ."

"What?" he snapped. His leg hurt, his head hurt, and his throat felt scoured. He knew defeat was near, and the taste of it was gall-bitter in his mouth.

"Could we turn the sled over? We can fit under it, can't we?

And we can pile the supplies around the outside. . . . They couldn't get us then, could they? There wouldn't any way . . ."

He was about to give her a sharp answer, but some of her logic penetrated his resentment. "You're right," he allowed. "It would protect us. It will work." He struggled out of the harness and began to unload the breakables, setting them in a heap around the sled. At last he had them all prepared, and though the sounds of the dogs were now much nearer, he was ready to turn the sled over on its side and climb under it. "Sit down," he told Thea, pointing to the center of the bundles, and when she did, he centered the sled above her. "We're going to have a tight fit," he remarked as he squatted down next to her.

"But we'll be safe," she said, knowing that was all that mattered.

So while the dogs snapped and howled outside, pushing their noses against the slatted sides, Thea and Evan lay wrapped tightly together, asleep.

* * *

When they awoke the dogs were gone and it was raining. The ground under them had turned mushy and it was late in the morning. In the cramped space, Thea tried to stretch and found that she couldn't. Her shoulder hurt, but in a distant, selfless way, as if it belonged to someone else. She had difficulty thinking and her vision wobbled.

"Is that rain?" Evan asked, trying to clear his head. His body throbbed like a drum and his regenerated arm was stiff, more like an oar than an arm. When he tried to move his leg he felt it protest, and there was an acidic burn where the bullet had left its mark.

"It's rain," she confirmed, twisting unsuccessfully, and stifling a cry as she rolled onto her right arm. "I must have needed the rest more than I thought. It's such a relief . . ." A gasp ended this as pain flared again.

He reached across her inexpertly, his hand brushing her face as he stretched to touch the edge of the sled. "God, Thea. You're burning up."

"You don't have to look like that," she said testily. "I'm fine. It's just that I'm a little sore."

"You have a fever, Thea, and that shoulder of yours needs looking at." He started to lift the sled but she stopped him.

"Are you sure the dogs are gone?" She was frightened now, and could not control the trembling that seized her.

"They're gone," he promised and raised the sled.

The rain hit them then, coming down in sooty drops from a tattered gray sky. The wind blew along the ridge, ruffling the scrub and chilling the air. Evan reached for the tarpaulin, working with frightful slowness to rig a lean-to with the sled.

"What are you doing?" Thea asked, trying to crawl out from under the tarpaulin.

"Setting us up a camp," he answered, wrestling with a knot in the cord at one corner of the tarp.

"But why? I can go on. You don't have to do this. We can go miles by sundown."

Rather than argue with her, or let her see his worry, he said, "Maybe you can, but I can't. That sled is heavy and my leg is sore." There, he had it tied down. The next thing to do was to weight the other side. He looked about for usable rocks and found a few medium-sized ones which he lugged to the tarpaulin for its corner weights. Then he moved back to take stock of his work. It wasn't much, he knew, but it was the best he could manage. Carefully he hunkered down and crawled back inside.

"Is it raining hard?" Thea watched him with overly bright eyes, eyes that shone with the glaze of fever. Her face was flushed and dry.

"Not very. It doesn't seem like much of a storm," he said, touching her face again. "Let me have a look at your shoulder. You'll want the dressings changed, at least," he recommended gently, pushing her back into the mound of their goods.

"Oh, I think it's all right. You don't have to bother," she said dreamily.

"Humor me, Thea." He was less gentle now, and the steely cast had come back into his eyes. She sighed and resigned herself to his ministrations. She made no protest when he began to unwrap her bandages, but as he lifted the packing away, her face grew drawn, her breath hissed through her clenched teeth, and her brittle assurances vanished.

Evan clenched his teeth when he saw her wound. The flesh around it was inflamed and the exposed tissues were a deep angry purple. Frantically Evan ran through the extent of their first aid supplies, then made a rapid search for the kit, finding it at last under a box of food. One of the foil-sealed packets informed him, *Lacerations: for topical applications to a clean wound. In case of infection or fever, consult a physician.* Evan held back a bitter laugh and tore the packet open, sprinkling the powder over the wound and into it. He hoped that the medicine was still potent enough to stop the spreading infection. Then, carefully, he repacked the wound with the last of their fresh gauze and bandaged it again.

"Now let me see your leg," Thea demanded when he was through. "I let you check me." Evan sensed that behind her banter there was fear, and a realization that her wound was dangerous. He stripped off his pants and let her see the long red furrow down his thigh.

"It's only on the surface," he said. "Hurts like hell, but not very serious. I'll put some medication on it, if you like. To be on the safe side." He had every intention of doing so anyway.

"It isn't bleeding any more," she announced after peering at it for a moment, getting his wound into focus. "It looks pretty clean, too." Her hot, dry fingers touching his skin made him wish for a thermometer, but they had none. They had found only one in the time they had traveled together, and that one had been broken.

"There's some medicine here," he said, handing her a tube. "Will you put it on for me?" He waited while she worked the cap, then inexpertly squeezed the white paste over the wound.

"I'm sorry," she said as she worked. "I don't seem to be doing this very well." When she was through she fell back once more, breathing in irregular gulps. The little effort she had made had tired her out. Her eyes were distant and glazed and she did not truly see him when she looked at him. At last she brought him back into her thoughts, a frown of concentration showing between her brows as she stared at him. "Evan," she said, enunciating with painful precision, "I think I'm really hurt. Really."

* * *

That night she was fairly quiet, her sleep never deep, her dreams anxious. But she did not waken or cry out and by morning her fever seemed to have dropped. Evan rigged a bed for her in the sled and then started south, the rain beating on them from the west and slowing their progress through the rocky high country. Now the high lakes had taken on the slate color of Tahoe as the clouds returned their contaminants to the earth.

Toward the third evening as they neared Echo Summit, the rain let up, showing a sunset of spectacular colors, the sun shining an improbable green through its golden halo. The volcano to the north of them had been busy while the rain fell. Around them, in the burned-over desolation, Evan could see the crenelations of the crest of the Sierra Nevada, the vertebrae of granite that marked the highest ridge of the range. He knew that there had to be shelter for them somewhere on this imposing face. He thought desperately, trying to remember what he had seen on the maps at Squaw Valley. Surely he could recall the maps; he had studied them so carefully. As he set up the lean-to again for the night, he forced his mind back, seeking for details that had seemed so unimportant when the maps were in front of him.

"Evan," Thea spoke in a cracked voice as he settled her in the lean-to. "I'm thirsty, Evan. I'm hot. Something's wrong."

He looked down at her ravaged face and wiped the short hair off her forehead. "I know, Thea." He wanted to hold her, to make her well by wishing, but instead he began the horrible, necessary job of cleaning her wound.

This time, he thought with relief, the infection was no worse. It was also no better. The color was still bad and Thea moaned when the air touched it. As gently as he could, Evan probed it, fearing that the infection might be getting deeper. Thea cried out at this, trying feebly to pull away from him, from the nauseating pain he was giving her.

"No, Thea, no. Let me finish. Let me clean it. You'll be better then, I promise."

She quieted somewhat, leaning against the crook of his arm, but flinching whenever she moved, and wailing thinly as he tied on clean bandages. He hoped the healing would start soon. There was no more gauze and now he was almost out of torn shirts.

*   *   *

Her fever rose that night, and the next day he did not try to move her, keeping her warmly wrapped in the lean-to while he bathed her face with their dwindling supply of water.

"What's that?" she screamed, when, in the morning, the ground

began to shake. Evan was awake and on his knees in a moment, looking wildly about as the earth tremor continued. With a sense of foreboding he crawled around the lean-to and looked north. There, rolling against the sky, was another, greater cloud, dark and bright at once.

Thea was weeping, her jaw set and her hands moving nervously when Evan came back to her. She beat her left hand against the ground, as if trying to make the shaking stop. When she saw him, she tried to beat him off, fighting against the blankets and sleeping bag that engulfed her. She struck out at his face, but the blows were weak, hardly more than pats.

Tenderly he took her hand, speaking in a low, calm voice. "Thea. Thea. It's me. It's Evan. It's Evan, Thea. Evan."

Slowly her thrashing abated and some degree of recognition returned to her face. "Oh. Evan," she said. "What was that? Did I dream it? The ground was moving. It moved. It moved . . ."

"No." He sought for words, chafing the hand that lay in his. "One of the volcanoes has gone off," he explained with difficulty. "Perhaps all the way off."

She tried to keep her attention on what he was saying, watching his lips with a muzzy intensity that hurt him more than the welt on his leg. "That's bad . . . I think you said . . . it was bad."

"Yes, it's bad." He bent to kiss the palm of her hand, and felt the dry heat on his lips. "I'm sorry, Thea. I know it isn't wise, but we have to move on. It isn't going to be safe up here, not for a while."

She made an effort to rise. "I'll help you pack," she began, then gasped and fell back. "I can't . . . I can't . . . why . . . ?"

Carefully he hushed her, then set about preparing the sled to travel once again. Now he was worried about rock slides, and the deeper fear that the cold would be on them again sooner than he thought.

* * *

When they climbed over the rubble of Echo Summit, Thea was delirious.

And it was quite by accident that two days later, Evan found the road to Lake Kirkwood. It was almost dark, and the faint afterglow shone blue and green in the west. The road, which he had found earlier that day, had been in poor repair for nearly two decades and now had cracked into uneven chunks, destroyed by the earth tremor. Evan hated it and only took it because not even the sturdiest of the Pirates' vans could drive on it. The weight of the sled had become intolerable to him, and he moved drunkenly as he hauled this burden over the ruined road. Lack of sleep and food had taken a fearsome toll of him. He did not think clearly, his eyes sometimes played tricks on him, and his muscles felt as if they were trying to unhook themselves from his tendons and bones.

Then there was another road, just off the side on the right, a badly tarred strip leading down the side of the mountain into a pocket tucked away in the granite front of the Sierra. He stopped walking and looked at it stupidly, his mind hardly working. He knew they had to find protection. Through the cotton batting of exhaustion, he drove that thought home. They had to find protection. There was another road. At last he decided that the worst that would happen would be that they would be trapped in the place at the bottom of the road. This no longer worried him. With a lurch he dragged the sled off the crumbling highway, onto the old side road.

* * *

The lake was small and L-shaped, having a few vacation cabins on part of it, the wreckage of a campground and boathouse near a collapsed store. In the blue moonlight, Evan could see that there were a few buildings standing on the far side of the lake, and amazingly, three or four fruit trees with stunted apples still hanging on spindly limbs.

"I want to go home. I want to go *home,*" Thea kept insisting, her voice like a child's. "Who cares about spooly old Mr. Thompson's survival practice anyway? I want to go home."

Evan turned back to her, feeling helpless, feeling worn out, feeling angry. "All right, Thea," he croaked, his voice nearly gone from fatigue. "We're home."

She looked dazedly around. "Not here. Not here, home. Home. Camminsky Creek. Don't you know where that is? Mister?" Her face lost expression and there were tears on her cheeks. "I don't know where it is, either. I lost it. . . . Help me, mister. . . . I'm lost. . . ." Her words trailed off into sobs.

Irritated, Evan took the first cabin he came to that still had a roof. It was a small A-frame with a sagging floor, and the smell told him several animals had used it before now. But anything was better than standing up, being harnessed to the sled, listening to Thea, soaking from the rain. Leaving the sled outside he made a quick, sleepy survey of the place, and finding it passably sound, he looked for some light.

In the kitchen he found a few candles and set them up in the three lower rooms for the little light they could give. Chipmunks and other small rodents had destroyed most of the furniture but the stove, though a little rusty, was still sound, and its chimney was intact. He decided the house would do for the night.

Making a last effort, he pulled the sled inside, then jammed the door closed behind it. He reached for a can and a pot, then stumbled into the kitchen to start a fire. He had to eat. He needed to get something hot into him. Then, once he was dry, he would take care of Thea.

*   *   *

He woke the next morning still seated at the kitchen table, his head by his plate of half-eaten supper. For a moment he thought he was back at Squaw Valley, that the rest had been an unpleasant dream. Then he touched his leg and found the sore place where the bullet had creased it.

"Thea." He said it aloud, getting to his feet and shaking his head to clear the sleep from it. He went to the sink but the taps didn't work, and no water rushed out. Swearing now, he turned and stumbled into the living room, fear like ice in his vitals. "Thea . . ."

There was the sled, where he had left it, and Thea lay in it. Her face was very pale and quiet, framed by the still-damp tendrils of her dark hair touched with white. There was no sign of the pain that had racked her for the last several days. A curious half-smile lit her cracked lips, as if she had a secret all her own. One hand dangled listlessly over the edge of the sled.

"Dear God; dear f——ing God," Evan whispered. Not noticing the tears that filled his eyes, he flung himself across the room to her side, grasping the pathetic little hand in his, holding it against his wet face, his mouth pressed against it to stop the sounds he made.

The hand was cool against his skin, and it was not for some

minutes that he realized it wasn't stiff. Then the slender fingers curled weakly around his beard and her faint voice said, "Evan . . . Let me . . . stay . . ."

Jumbled words of relief choked him. He pulled her to him, his head pressed against her body. He felt the life in her. He did not care when he cried.

Looking up at her he saw for the first time the glory of her smile. Softly she touched his hair, his eyes, with her cool hand. "I do love you, Evan," she said. As his arms tightened around her, she closed her eyes and slept.

* * *

The day after they found a larger, more secure house at the far end of the lake. The plumbing there had been destroyed by the earth tremor, but the building was more sound and better insulated than the A-frame was. It was the best place to live at Kirkwood Lake.

Over her protests, Evan carried Thea down to the new house, saying that she was not fully recovered and he would take no chances with her. He had come too close to losing her and would not risk it again. He ceremoniously installed her in the largest bed she had ever seen and wrapped her in four layers of blankets while she laughed.

"But your leg was hurt," she reminded him when he was satisfied with the cocoon he had made her. "You were shot, weren't you? Didn't you have a wound in your thigh?"

"A scratch," he said, waving his hand to dismiss it. "You had me . . . so very frightened, Thea." His voice dropped as he spoke.

"But I made it. I'm still alive. Don't underestimate me, Evan." She pulled the covers back from her shoulder and watched him as he moved around the room. "And," he added when he had finished describing the closets and the chest of drawers, "there is an added bonus: three trunks with clothes. We're in luck."

"And what about food? Are we in luck there, too?" She knew that they had been on short rations for the whole time since her fever had broken, and the chill in the air told her that they would not have a chance to grow a crop of vegetables before winter.

"I've looked in the store, of course," he began evasively. "And there's a few things in the houses. Canned goods, mostly, and some dried fruits."

"But," she said, looking at him seriously.

He considered her for a moment, uncertain what to tell her, trying to judge how much she had recovered and what she could bear to know.

She saw this and said, "I am not a child, Evan. If there is trouble, I have a right to know."

He nodded. "All right: there's trouble. We've lost most of the stores we had. Don't ask me how. It happened, and that's all that matters. There are some things we can eat here, but not very much. Not enough to get us through the winter."

"I think the winter will be long," she said as she regarded him with her steady dark eyes.

"Probably," he admitted. "We can trap, and we still have our crossbows, so we can hunt. I've found a couple guns here, and we can make more crossbows, if we need to."

"You mean that we can hunt, but there might not be anything to kill?" She twisted in the bed to watch him more closely.

"Yes. That's what I mean. You wanted to know."

There was silence in the room, then she asked, "Do you think we can grow anything? Can we make a greenhouse or something? There's wood and glass, so maybe we can."

"We can try. If not now, in the spring." There was a false note to these words, and he looked out the window as he spoke, seeing the rocks and cold that made a lie of his assurances.

She nodded. "I see. Well, I'll do what I can." She did not speak of the anxiety that preyed on her, a worry that grew deeper each day as her wounded shoulder healed—healed without strength, without sensation returning to her right hand.

*   *   *

The first snow came early, scarcely a flurry on the October wind. It tapped at the mountains and clung to the hollows for a day and then was gone. But it left certainty and fear behind. In its wake would come winter, a winter colored by the fires of a volcano and the deadly rain that was steadily killing off the scrub that had grown where the first had burned away. Each day that it rained the brush shriveled, dried up, and the few animals living where the brush had died, died with it.

Evan had found some seeds, long past their season dates on their packages, but Thea had taken them with good spirit, sticking with winter crops of brussels sprouts, onions, and cauliflower. She had marked out the plots and with untutored hands set the seeds, surrounding the area with wide glass panes that would shelter and warm the seedlings. She tended this unpromising garden zealously and was rewarded with the most spindly of sprouts that poked unwillingly from the earth long enough to raise her hopes, then reddened, twisted, and wilted.

"Maybe they're too old," Evan said by way of consolation as he worked on stout wooden barricades at the entrance to the little valley. "They were dated for the nineties, and that's more than fifteen years ago."

"But they're all we have," she objected. "I think I'd better dig up the ground again, and see if I can make a better greenhouse."

"If that's what you want, there're other envelopes. Maybe you're right and some of the plants will grow." By tacit agreement he did not ask about her hand. He knew how wretched she felt about her continued weakness.

"I've got to try, Evan. I'll make a real greenhouse, and then we'll see."

"Fine." As he said it, he planned how to cut down their food once again.

* * *

When the next snow came, it stayed longer, frosting the mountains and chilling the lake. Now the nights were sharp with ice and packs of starving dogs howled in the dying forests. There were no sounds of engines on the roads, and no signs of tire tracks.

Although the fruit was bitter, Evan and Thea ate all the hard, tiny apples that grew on the trees, relishing them as rare and sweet until at last they were gone. After that their hunger was worse. Here there was no miner's lettuce, no watercress, no berries trailing their sharp vines through the underbrush, no wild currants, no grapes. If there had been fish in the lake, there were none now and the cold grew deeper every day.

One night, after the third snowfall, Thea turned to Evan as he lay beside her, half asleep. "Evan?"

"Um?"

"What will happen to us here? What if we go south? Can't we

get out of the mountains onto the desert? If it's this cold here, we might be able to get by on the desert. We could raise things if it were warmer. You said yourself that it's getting colder."

"We might go south," he agreed languidly, fingering her breast scar, which had recently turned a tawny color like his regenerated arm. He gave her a bemused smile. "It's catching, whatever it is."

"I know. My father thought the defective kids and the regeneration were all part of the same thing, all tied together somehow. He thought it might be a virus that changed." She returned to her first question. "Evan, why don't we go there? What's wrong with the desert?"

"We can't go, love, because if the rain falling here is poisoned, the rain falling there and everywhere else is poisoned too." He was staring up at the ceiling, thinking of the white, deadly snow that was falling, falling above them, around them.

She tugged at his beard, which was now almost entirely white. "What if there were just one of us, then, could you make it through the winter?"

"Stop talking nonsense," he said, folding his arms around her.

"No, Evan, I'm trying to figure something out."

He sighed. "All right. Could one of us last through the winter? I don't know. It doesn't matter. It's better here with you than out on the desert or anywhere else alone."

She moved impatiently. Turning close to him, she said, "Evan, promise me you'll think about the desert. Please. It might be better there."

"All right, I'll think about it." But the idea drifted from his mind as soon as he was asleep.

*   *   *

At first light he turned over, his arm stretched out to touch her, and he found nothing. Surprised but not alarmed he felt the covers, and was startled at how cool they were. He got out of bed into the cold morning: there had been many times when Thea had got up before him, going to check their eternally empty traps or to bring in kindling for the fire. But she had been gone much too long for that if the sheets were any indication. He dressed quickly and went into the living room, calling her name.

There was no response.

Puzzled, he tugged on his shoes and stepped out into the white morning. Snow clouds scudded over the sky and the smell of the air promised they would release their frozen burden by nightfall. Looking at the white ground he could see her tracks leading away from the house, toward the barricade and the highway beyond.

In sudden fear he went to check their storage closet. Her pack was gone. And he remembered then what she had said the night before, about one of them being able to make it through the winter alone. One, but not two. He closed his eyes convulsively and cursed himself. He had been blind, stupid and blind. He grabbed one of the crossbows from the closet and hurled it across the room, smiling as the window smashed.

*   *   *

An hour later he had packed his things and closed the house without regret. Then he set out, following her tracks through the crisp snow.

There were wisps of a storm in the wind when he finally caught sight of her that afternoon, on the trail south of Tragedy Spring. She was trudging steadily about half a mile ahead of him. She walked as if she were tired, as if her feet were reluctant to take her away.

"Thea!" he shouted, cupping his hands to his mouth and seeing his breath make a fog in the first white swirls that drifted out of the sky.

She hesitated but did not turn.

"Thea!"

This time she stopped, her back sagging at her name.

He increased his stride and came up to her several minutes later. Gripping her shoulder, he turned her to him. "Just what the ruddy hell do you think you are doing?" His hands tightened. "Well?"

She avoided his eyes. "Why did you follow me? Why didn't you stay there?" She faced him then. "I want you to live, Evan. Look at me. I'm barren as this world. I'm used up. My arm doesn't work right. There is nothing left for me."

"Nothing left? Damn it, *I'm* left." There was savagery in his voice and the Pirate light in his face. "Don't you ever say that again. Who wants children in this world anyway? Thea, I have what I want, and I don't ask anything more."

She touched his face lingeringly. "Go back. Please go back."

"Not without you."

Sadly she shook her head. "I won't."

"All right," he said, taking the hand that touched him. "Go where you want and I'll go with you."

She made a miserable attempt at smiling. "There might not be any place *to* go."

"There might not," he agreed. There was a moment of silence between them as the wind grew sharper. Then she turned southward again, and keeping his hand tightly in hers, she led the way into the dark mountains; and the snow that followed them covered their footprints as if they had never been.